THE NATURE OF RARE THINGS

THE NATURE OF RARE THINGS

Derek Wilson

CHIVERS
THORNDIKE

RYDE LIBRARY SERVICES

This Large Print book is published by BBC Audiobooks Ltd, Bath, England and by Thorndike Press®, Waterville, Maine, USA.

Published in 2005 in the U.K. by arrangement with Constable & Robinson Ltd.

Published in 2005 in the U.S. by arrangement with Carroll & Graf Publishers.

U.K. Hardcover   ISBN 1–4056–3344–1 (Chivers Large Print)
U.K. Softcover   ISBN 1–4056–3345–X (Camden Large Print)
U.S. Softcover   ISBN 0–7862–7581–2 (Buckinghams)

The text of this Large Print edition is unabridged.
Other aspects of the book may vary from the original edition.

Set in 16 pt. New Times Roman.

Printed in Great Britain on acid-free paper.

British Library Cataloguing in Publication Data available

Library of Congress Cataloging-in-Publication Data

Wilson, Derek A.
    The nature of rare things / by Derek Wilson.
        p.   cm.
    "Thorndike Press large print Buckinghams"—T.p. verso.
    ISBN 0–7862–7581–2 (lg. print : sc : alk. paper)
    1. Parapsychologists—Fiction. 2. Cambridge (England)—Fiction.
    3. British—Italy—Fiction. 4. Missing persons—Fiction.
    5. Murder victims—Fiction. 6. Spiritualism—Fiction.
    7. Seances—Fiction. I. Title.
PR6073.I463N38 2005
823'.914—dc22   2005002609

. . . all Bologna
Cried, and the world with it, 'Ours—the
  treasure!'
Suddenly, as rare things will, it vanished.

Robert Browning, 'One Word More'

An Open and Shut Case

...you talk ...
Of signs and wonders, the invisible world;
How wisdom scouts our vulgar unbelief
More than our vulgarest credulity ...
[All the quotations used for chapter openings are from Robert Browning's poem, 'Mr Sludge, the "Medium"'.]

Harriet Jermyn QC took her time. Deliberately. She allowed several seconds to elapse before she rose to her feet. Then she occupied more moments in sorting her papers on the desk before her. The eyes of everyone in the assize court were upon the diminutive figure who seemed totally absorbed in her notes. Not a large crowd, though some national press reporters were present. The case had aroused interest among the broadsheets. Odd, Ms Jermyn thought, that the vulgar sensation-mongering tabloids had not seen the potential of *Regina v. Gomer.* Stolen works of art might not be headline grabbers but when there was a whiff of the supernatural . . . She heard the judge tap a pencil on the light oak of his writing slope and glanced quickly up at him from beneath long lashes. She cleared her throat and took a sip of water. She would not look at the accused. Not

1

yet. She sensed his anxiety, his panic, and she would prolong it as long as possible. Only at the last moment before His Honour, Judge Deeping opened his mouth to enquire whether the prosecution was ready to begin cross-examination did she turn her attention to the witness stand.

'Mr Gomer.' She spoke slowly with a suggestion of boredom. 'I understand that you are a spiritualist. Is that so?'

Robert Gomer, a stocky figure in a well-pressed, grey-blue suit, radiantly white shirt and striped tie, shuffled from one foot to the other as he looked across the well of the court occupied by clerks and a recorder. He struggled to keep any wavering nervousness out of his voice. The nails of his clenched hands dug deep into flesh. 'Yes . . . er . . . but . . .'

'That means, I assume, that you believe strongly in the *beyond*.' Ms Jermyn raised her voice and rolled her eyes to make the word sound as absurd as possible and was rewarded by a light sniggering from the public gallery. 'A world invisible to mere mortals . . .' she elaborated, 'mere mortals like the members of the jury, but accessible to people with your special gifts.'

The accused shook his head. 'No . . . that's not . . . I mean, I've never claimed . . . Look, what's all this got to do—'

'I'll decide that, Mr Gomer.'

The judge laid aside his spectacles. 'The same question had occurred to me. Perhaps we could proceed to something more pertinent, Miss Jermyn?'

The barrister thought, It's *Ms* Jermyn, you shrivelled-up old coot. She said, 'Certainly, my lord.' Now she did stare long and hard at her quarry, taking in the upright, shoulders-back stance, the pale moon face atop the thick neck, the grey-black hair, cut 'short back and sides'. Everything about him shouted 'old school, military dinosaur'. She would have been hard put to it to say just why she found him so objectionable but now she relished the sight of the sweat beginning to form above his thick eyebrows. 'You see, Mr Gomer, it's just that I—and I'm sure the jury—are having great difficulty in understanding the sequence of the events in any way that squares with the laws of the physical universe with which we're familiar. If you have inside knowledge of the workings of some parallel world perhaps you could enlighten us.' She smiled at him across the court.

Bob Gomer stared back, mute and miserable.

'No? Well, let's just go over the events of that fateful evening last October, shall we? Perhaps we've missed some elemental point that will make everything crystal clear.' She referred to her notes. 'Now, according to what you told my learned friend who appears for the defence, your colleagues, Mr Hardwick and Mr Randall, collected you from your house in the security van because they'd been out on an earlier job and the three of you then drove, without stopping, to Heathrow, where you arrived at Terminal 1 around 4.30. You were directed to a security suite where you met Signor Brandini of Sicuro Pacioli and another member of his own staff who had arrived from Turin with the portrait expertly wrapped and crated in the box which has been identified to the court.' The barrister indicated a narrow wooden container some eighty centimetres square which lay on the table in front of the judge's bench. 'Also present were Dr Theophrast, of the Bath Millennium Gallery, and his assistant, Ms Miles. Have we got it right so far, Mr Gomer?'

The accused nodded. 'Yes . . . right,' he muttered.

'Good.' Ms Jermyn continued briskly. 'There then followed what must have been quite a solemn ceremony. Signor Brandini broke the seal that had been placed on the crate before it left Italy. The container was carefully opened and the painted panel still in its wrappings was removed. The protective inner case was opened and everyone's eyes were fixed on the fifteenth-century masterpiece that was revealed. Did you get a good look at it, Mr Gomer?'

'Good enough.'

'Good enough!' The prosecutor smiled round the courtroom. 'By that I assume you mean to suggest good enough for someone not remotely interested in rare Italian Renaissance works of genius.'

Gomer shrugged. 'I saw the picture. I'm not denying it.'

'And you want us to believe that you weren't curious about it, even though you knew it was worth a great deal of money—running into millions, as this court has been informed.'

'As far as I was concerned it was just another job.'

'Surely, you must have been anxious about having the responsibility for guarding this extremely valuable article.'

'The security arrangements were excellent, so I—'

'Excellent? Well, we wouldn't all be here if that was the case, would we? I'm sure Signor Brandini thought his employer's property was in good hands when he entrusted it to Dr Theophrast's gallery.' She glared across the courtroom. 'But then he couldn't know, could he, that you were anything other than an honest security guard—'

'So I was . . . am!' Gomer blurted.

Ms Jermyn ignored the outburst. 'Well, to continue. When Dr Theophrast had satisfied himself with the identity and condition of the painting it was parcelled up again and Dr Theophrast sealed it with his gallery's seal. He

5

gave Signor Brandini a receipt, then he handed the crate to you.'

'No.'

The barrister looked up sharply. 'No! But that's what you—'

'I wasn't given the crate straight away. Someone had brought champagne. The Ities and the gallery people stood about drinking for about twenty minutes before we left.'

She frowned. This was not in her script. 'Are you suggesting that someone could have tampered with the painting during those twenty minutes before it was given into your custody?'

'No, miss. The box stayed on the table all the time, in full view.'

'Those twenty minutes aren't really relevant then, are they?'

Gomer shrugged. 'Sorry, I thought you were trying to get at the truth. My mistake.'

A member of the jury giggled. Ms Jermyn hastened to retrieve the situation. 'Oh, we shall get at the truth, Mr Gomer. You need have no fear about that. So, after the others had enjoyed their celebratory drink, *then* the painting was handed to you and you took it out of the building to your van. Was that difficult?'

Gomer dabbed a folded handkerchief to his brow. 'I don't take your meaning.'

'What I mean is that you had to carry a bulky and valuable package carefully in both hands. There were doors and corridors to be negotiated. There were other people moving about in the building. It must have been a bit ... awkward.'

'Not really.'

'But perhaps that was what you were counting on. You had to find somewhere to make the switch. I suggest that you and your accomplice had planned the exact point at which you could do it. Going round a corner, passing a doorway, out of sight of your companions for a few seconds. That's all it would take.'

'Rubbish! Me and Charlie were together all the time. I couldn't have done anything with that box without him seeing.'

'Well, we'll leave that for the moment. You went into the back of your van with the painting. You fastened the box to the inside wall with special straps to prevent it moving about on the journey, then you sat down on a chair still in the back of the van, and the rear doors were securely locked.' She paused and glanced thoughtfully round the courtroom. 'Rather elaborate precautions, weren't they?'

After several seconds of silence Ms Jermyn switched her gaze sharply to the witness stand. 'Well, Mr Gomer, did you not hear the question? In your experience, have you ever had to sit inside a locked van with the object you were transporting?'

'Only once.'

'It does seem rather odd, doesn't it? After

7

all, no one could get into the vehicle during the journey, could they?'

'No, but sometimes we had a client who was very particular.'

'Right. So we have you locked in the van with the picture. That means, does it not, that the only person who could possibly have tampered with the crate during the two hours it took to convey it from the airport to the gallery was you.'

Gomer grabbed the front of the stand and leaned forward. 'I never touched . . .' He stared appealingly at the judge. 'My lord, I swear . . . !'

Judge Deeping scowled. 'You must confine yourself to answering counsel's questions.'

The prosecutor resumed. 'Now, we've already heard Dr Theophrast and Ms Miles state that they followed close behind the van all the way to Bath and that it was never out of their sight. At no point on the journey did the van stop, and the two vehicles arrived at the rear entrance of the Millennium Gallery at approximately 6.50. Tell us, in your own words, what happened next.'

Gomer cleared his throat and rubbed his moist forehead. 'Well, the doors were opened and Charlie helped me out with the crate. We was let in through the back door and—'

'You were carrying the crate?' The barrister was determined not to let the accused get into his stride. Her objective was to disorientate him with constant questions. 'By yourself?'

The accused looked back at her in pathetic bewilderment, suspecting some verbal trap but unable to locate it. 'Well . . . yes. It was quite—'

'And where were the other *dramatis personae* at that time?'

'The who?'

Ms Jermyn raised her eyes heavenward. 'Your colleagues, Messrs Hardwick and Randall, the gallery director and his assistant —where were they?'

'Charlie Randall was with me. Ted Hardwick took the van to a nearby petrol station to get it filled. Dr Theophrast and the young lady went on ahead to show us the way. We went up in the lift together. There was no chance for me to muck about with the picture.'

'Well, there was certainly no chance for anybody else to have done it. So, the four of you arrived in Dr Theophrast's office. What happened next . . . and, please, Mr Gomer, take us very precisely through the events of the next couple of minutes.'

The stocky ex-marine gripped the rail before him for support. He spoke slowly, dreamily, seeing yet again the scene he had played over in his mind a thousand times. 'Dr Theophrast opened the crate—'

'No, Mr Gomer! Before that. What did he have to do before he opened the crate?'

'He broke the gallery's seal.'

'Which up until that moment was still intact?'

'Yes.' The word was little more than a murmur.

'And when he opened the container what did he discover?'

Gomer's head drooped. His reply was scarcely audible. 'A blank wooden panel.'

'Precisely. A priceless work of art on loan from a private Italian collection had vanished without trace and in its place there was a square of cabinet maker's plywood. The last time the picture was seen was in the security suite at the airport. Thereafter, it was in the custody of one man and one man only. It follows that that man alone can explain to this court what really happened to Antonello da Messina's *Portrait of a Doge*. So, Mr Gomer, let us have no more subterfuge. Tell us in plain words how you spirited it away.' She fixed him with an accusing stare. 'Where is that painting?'

The reply was half wail, half sob. 'I don't know! I wish to God I did. But I don't—and that's the honest truth.'

10

The Other Side

What's a 'medium'? He's a means,
Good, bad, indifferent, still the only means
Spirits can speak by; he may misconceive,
Stutter and stammer . . .

Stansted Airport was thronged with getaway Easter holidaymakers when Nathaniel Gye, lecturer in paranormal psychology at the University of Cambridge, and his wife Kathryn arrived on a morning which was doing its level best to live up to April's reputation. Kathryn shook and closed her umbrella while her husband manoeuvred her holdall through the crowds towards the check-in desk.

She frowned as they took their place in the queue. 'You'd think the organizers would have more sense than to fix Good Friday for the start of the symposium.'

Nathaniel smiled down at her from his six-foot-two vantage point. 'It probably never occurred to them. Today isn't a public holiday in Italy.' He looked over the heads of the dozen people ahead of them to where a distracted mother with three small children was engaged in an argument with the airline representative. The atmosphere was tense with the excitement and anxiety of passengers wanting to get away and bothered about

11

tickets, passports, baggage and flight information. Perhaps, he told himself, his own misgivings were simply the result of catching the general contagion.

'That's odd, isn't it?'

'What's odd?' Nat asked distractedly.

'Catholic countries not celebrating Good Friday. When you're travelling through you see all those wayside crucifixes but the very day . . .' She stopped abruptly and stared at him with frank, jade eyes. 'Oh, for goodness sake stop fidgeting and go!'

'I'm not fidgeting,' Nat protested. 'I'm standing here perfectly calmly.'

'You're fidgeting inside; you know you are. Something's still bugging you about this trip.'

'I'll just stay and see you into the departure lounge.'

'You'll do no such thing!' Kathryn's New England drawl softened the command. 'I'm not exactly new to foreign travel, you know.'

She certainly was not. As London editor of *Panache*, a top-flight international lifestyle magazine, the number of air miles she had clocked up, laid end to end, would have stretched several times round the globe. 'I wish you'd tell me what's bothering you. You could have signed up with me to the Browning Symposium when I asked you weeks ago. I thought you'd have been interested in Robert and Elizabeth if only for the spiritualist angle—all that business with Daniel Home

12

and Sophie Eckley. But you said it wasn't your cup of tea. Then, when it was too late, you suddenly decided that you'd like nothing better than five days of lectures and visits about the Brownings in Italy. Ever since then you've been twitchy on the subject.'

Nat forced a smile and lied. 'Darling, that's pure imagination.'

Kathryn wasn't listening. 'This is really all about Errol Kaminsky, isn't it? The leader of this seminar is an old flame and that's woken the little green god.'

Nat laughed and this time the reaction was genuine. 'Kaminsky! Good Lord, I've scarcely given him a thought since he got smashed at our engagement party and took a swing at me. Now that he's fourteen years older and a highly respectable professor of Eng. Lit. at one of America's most prestigious universities, I'm sure the last thing he wants is to rake up old, embarrassing amours.'

They shuffled forward a few paces before Nat went on. 'As to Robert Browning, I suppose I've never really recovered from a surfeit of him at school. All those narrative poems we had to learn by heart—"The Pied Piper", "How They Brought the Good News from Ghent to Aix".'

'There's much more to him that that.'

'I'm sure . . .'

'His two intense love affairs—with Elizabeth and with Italy. It's all there in the poems. I left a copy on your desk. You ought to browse through it; get reacquainted.'

'I might just do that.' Nat picked up his wife's holdall as the queue moved again. He glanced up at the indicator board. 'Well, at least your flight seems to be on schedule. That's something of an achievement these days. There's usually an air controllers' strike somewhere in Europe to foul up the entire system at peak holiday times.'

Kathryn's dark brows lowered in a frown. 'My, aren't we a bundle of fun today? Nat, for goodness sake, *go home*! I don't need my hand held and I don't need your lugubrious observations about holes in the air traffic network. I'm going to have a great romantic wallow in Victorian poetry and belles lettres and I'll be back Wednesday evening. So, forget whatever it is that's bothering you and go and keep the home fires burning.' She reached up and gave him a swift kiss. It was a dismissal.

As he drove back up the M11, having extracted from his wife a promise that she would phone the moment she reached her hotel, Nat confronted his disquiet about her trip. Every rational impulse surging along the neural pathways of his brain told him he was being foolish to imagine that Kathryn was in any more danger on her brief tour of Florence, Rome and Siena than she had been on any of her numerous foreign visits. He certainly knew better than to take seriously supposed warnings from 'the other side'. And yet . . . No, the more reason and intuition sparred for mastery inside Nat's head the more bothered he became.

The unease was still there when he turned off the motorway and headed the last six cross-country miles towards Great Maddisham. He was almost home when he had a sudden change of mind. Just as the car rounded the bend coming out of Medley Wood, where the squat tower of All Saints, Maddisham came into view as a bump on the flat landscape, Nat turned abruptly down a narrow lane which, as the signpost advised strangers to the area, led to 'Frettlingham Village Only—No Through Road'. He would have a pub lunch at the Lamb. Little point in going back to the empty house to cut himself a sandwich. The boys—twelve-year-old Edmund and Jeremy who was nine—were already at Wanchester to spend Easter with their grand-father, Canon Gye, but Nat was not due to join them till the next day.

At the bottom of what passes in the fenland for a hill he turned the old Mercedes on to the gravelled car park beside the rambling brick inn, pleased to see that there were only two other vehicles already standing there. Frettlingham was an unobtrusively beautiful place that shared the secret of its charm with a small clientele who would not have dreamed of betraying that confidence to 'outsiders'. The Lamb's jumble of tiled roofs glistened in the sunshine that had followed the morning's showers. The little Frett gurgled past its garden wall and the hedges fronting the lane were spattered with new greenery. Nat unfolded himself from the driving seat and appreciatively breathed the rain-washed air. He could already feel the tension evaporating through his pores.

Twenty minutes later, having chatted briefly with Terry Hawke, the landlord, and a couple of regulars, he was cosily ensconced at a window table with one of Wendy Hawke's excellent steak and kidney pies and a pint of Greene King in front of him.

'Nat my boy, I didn't realize that you were a member of the select fellowship of the Lamb. May I join you or does your meditation demand solitude?'

Nat looked up and found himself gazing at the thin, patrician visage topped with luxuriant white hair of Barnaby Cox, sometime lecturer in law at the university, and emeritus fellow of Beaufort College.

'Of course, Barny. Glad of the company.'

The old man fastidiously brushed the chair seat with an immaculate handkerchief before settling himself on the other side of the table. He took an appreciative draught of ale. 'Should you not be deep in the bosom of your family at this Pascal season?'

Nat explained about Kathryn's seminar.

'Aha, then that doubtless explains your

16

doleful expression.'

Nat laughed. 'I wasn't aware that I was looking doleful. As a matter of fact I'm going up to Wanchester. The boys and I will do a bit of sailing. It'll be fun.'

'Really?' Barny looked at him shrewdly over the top of his glasses. 'In that case, "Why so pale and wan, fond lover? Prithee, why so pale?"'

'I don't think . . .'

'My dear fellow, years at the bar teach one a good deal about human nature, including how to read what people today call "body language". You resemble perfectly a defendant with something to hide. Now, if you choose to confide, I am, as the saying goes, all ears. If not, we can change the subject.'

'There's also an old adage about curiosity and the cat. I can almost see your feline whiskers twitching.'

The old man shrugged. 'What do you make of this nasty business in South Africa?' he asked with an innocent smile.

Nat grinned. 'Oh very well, Barny, you win. There *is* something on my mind—well, a couple of things, actually—and you're one of the few people I can trust not to tell me I'm being thoroughly stupid.'

Barny sipped his ale and carefully set down the tankard. 'Thank you for the compliment, Nathaniel. When you reach my advanced years the range of your experience becomes so restricted that other people's lives take on an intense fascination. So, say on.'

Nat was prevented from offering an immediate reply by the arrival of Wendy bearing a huge platter of cheese, crusty bread and salad which she set before Barny with a cheery 'Afternoon, Judge. Nice to see you again. You'll enjoy the Stilton—fresh in this morning.'

As she returned behind the bar, Barny raised an eyebrow. 'Well?'

'It's all to do with Bob Gomer,' Nat began.

'Ah, yes, poor fellow.' The older man scowled. 'You realize, of course, that his trial was a positive disgrace.'

'Because it was a public humiliation that drove him to suicide?'

'That, of course, plus the fact that the CPS should never have brought it to court *and* that when it was brought to court Gomer's defence counsel bungled the job miserably.'

'I didn't realize you had followed it that closely.'

'Gomer was one of our own, an ex-college servant. Naturally, I was interested.'

'The case against him was pretty black, wasn't it? I mean, it would surely have taken a brilliant defence to get him off.'

'It had its complexities, I grant you, but Gomer's barrister handed him over to the prosecution on a plate.' Barny began his attack on the Stilton.

'What do you mean?'

'A defendant like Bob Gomer is his own worst enemy. Too honest, too open, too lacking in guile. He should never have been put on the witness stand. If the prosecution really hoped for a conviction they should have been made to work for it.'

'But surely it's up to the accused to decide whether or not he'll take the stand?'

'Theoretically, but if I'd been defending Gomer I'd have said to him, "If you insist on testifying, get yourself another counsel."' He took a reflective sip of ale. 'A holy innocent is the worst kind of client. Give me a dyed-in-the-wool felon any day. Someone who knows the ropes. Someone who isn't under the illusion that all he has to do is stand up and tell the truth and the jury will believe him. Now, in the Gomer case the defence had very little to go on—but, by the same token, so had the prosecution. Someone, somehow, absconded with a valuable painting. The police were baffled. They brought no evidence whatsoever to explain how the crime was conceived and carried out. It was the prosecution's job to prove that Gomer did it; not the defence's job to prove that he didn't.'

'Yes, I see that. But in Bob's case no one else *could* have done it.'

'That's not the point. The prosecution had to convince the jury that Gomer *did* do it. Now the painting wasn't found in his possession. It wasn't in the security truck. No one had seen him pass it out of the truck to an accomplice during the journey. It had simply vanished.'

'But that's impossible.'

Barny smiled across the rim of his tankard. 'An assize court exists to uphold the criminal law, not the laws of physics. I have no idea what happened to that wretched painting, and nor had the prosecution. They were left floundering for an explanation and their only hope was to discredit the accused. All the character witnesses testified to Gomer's complete honesty. The police had looked into his financial affairs and could produce no evidence that someone had paid him to steal the picture. It was Gomer himself who threw his adversaries a lifeline. As we all know, the poor man was obsessed with things paranormal. A "nerd"—isn't that the modern terminology? The moment he stepped on to the witness stand he laid himself open to all the tricks of the trade—innuendo, bullying, ridicule. Poor Gomer was a sitting target. All that occult mumbo-jumbo! He was exposed to the jury as a weirdo, an oddball, someone who might be capable of any strange conduct.'

'Do you think he'd have been found guilty?'

'It wasn't a foregone conclusion, by any means. Who knows what would have happened if the poor fellow hadn't shut himself in a garage filled with carbon monoxide . . .' Barny shrugged. 'But this is all history. How does it transpire that you've taken a sudden interest?'

'Well, to start at the beginning.'

'Always the best plan.'

'I was in my rooms one wet February morning. I'd just finished a supervision with some of my psychology students when the phone rang.' Nat remembered the moment vividly. He saw himself holding the receiver clamped between chin and shoulder while his hands were occupied gathering some papers together.

'Bramley here, Dr Gye.' The head porter's tone was, as ever, emotionally neutral. It never varied, whether he was announcing the arrival of a distinguished visitor or the death of a senior member of Beaufort College.

'Morning, George.' Nat had turned to stare through the window at the massive, dripping cedar in the middle of the fellows' garden.

'I've got someone here at the lodge who was wondering if you could spare her a few minutes.'

'Not really, George. I'm lunching in Downing in half an hour. Who is it?'

'It's Pearl Gomer, Dr Gye.'

Nat's heart sank. 'Good Lord!'

'Just so, sir.'

'Do you know what she wants? I really think the college has done everything we can for her.'

'All she says is that she needs to speak to

you personally and urgently. She's come in specially. Arranged for a friend with a van to bring her. That can't have been easy. She's a lot worse than when I last saw her.' Nat caught the respectful innuendo: Bramley was telling him that he had some sort of obligation to see Bob Gomer's widow. 'Can I tell her you'll come down, Dr Gye?'

'Well, you can't very well ask her to come up, can you?' Nat felt trapped and irritated. He slammed down the phone. He strode down the staircase and out into Simeon Court. Avoiding the wet grass, he circled round to the passageway leading to Great Court, then along the paving beside the hall and chapel and so to the arched entrance of Beaufort College's gate tower.

She was waiting just inside the massive, half-closed door which fronted Trumpington Street. Bramley was chatting with her, leaning forward over the wheelchair. The contents (Nat could think of no better description) were all but completely covered in a bright green, glistening, plastic cape. Pearl Gomer's face seemed to be propped on top of the wet bundle. It smiled up at him, the eyes remarkably dark between the deep furrows scoured by pain. Nat immediately felt guilty about his irritation.

'Oh, Dr Gye, this is good of you. I should've made an appointment but it's difficult what with the phone and my sister.'

Nat did not try to unravel the invalid's explanation. 'That's all right, Mrs Gomer. How are you coping?' Even as he asked Nat knew the question was stupidly inadequate.

The face managed a slight smile. 'Some days better than others. Can you spare me a few minutes, Doctor? I know it's an imposition, you being such a busy—'

'Of course I can, Mrs Gomer. Perhaps we could take a turn round the fellows' garden. The rain seems to have eased off.'

'That *would* be nice. It's years since . . . Bob was always very fond of the gardens here. He never really wanted to leave his job as underporter at Beaufort but when I got ill we needed a bit more money . . . much good it did us as things turned out.'

'We missed Bob. A dozen years is a long stint in these days when it's so difficult to get college staff to stay for any length of time.' Nat fell into step beside the wheelchair as it buzzed electrically along the flagstones. They passed through the screens passage and out into the tree-walled gardens.

'He loved it here and the college was very good to him . . . and to me since . . .'

'It must have been terribly hard for you.' Nat groped for words that did not sound patronizing.

They moved slowly along the path between the grass and the rose beds flanking the seventeenth-century rear wall of the hall.

'Bob was always admiring of you, Dr Gye. Said you had some interesting long chats.'

Nat remembered those conversations with rather less warmth. Bob Gomer had already been on the porter staff at Beaufort before Nat had been offered his fellowship but it had taken him very little time to latch on to someone he thought of as sharing his own enthusiasm for the occult. As a lecturer, writer and occasional broadcaster on parapsychology Nat had long grown used to being button-holed by people who wanted to tell him about their 'odd' experiences. He sometimes felt like a doctor or priest, so keen were complete strangers to share with him anecdotes and beliefs which they hesitated to reveal to their nearest and dearest. The ex-marine sergeant had quizzed him over the years about everything from UFOs to Satanic rituals and from poltergeists to ESP.

'He was certainly very knowledgeable about his hobbies,' Nat responded cautiously.

'I'm sure he must have rabbited on something awful, Dr Gye, but he always knew that you'd listen and not laugh at him. That's why he wants to talk to you now.'

Nat did a mental double take. 'Sorry, what was that? I didn't quite catch . . .'

There was no mistaking the reply. 'Bob says would you please come because there's something he's got to tell you.'

Nat was glad that Mrs Gomer could not

turn her head to look at him. She would have read the pity in his eyes. She would have realized that he was working out how best to humour her. After all that this poor woman had been through, he thought, it was not really surprising that her mind was losing its grip on reality. Bob Gomer had been dead for all of six months. While on bail during his trial for robbery he had been found in his own locked garage on the day before the jury were due to deliver their verdict.

They turned the corner and moved slowly along the narrow edge of the lawn without speaking. They had reached the point farthest from the buildings where an eighteenth-century stone arbour sheltered a pair of benches before Pearl Gomer spoke again. 'You do know he didn't do it, don't you, Dr Gye? You do believe that? He couldn't. Not my Bob.'

'Everyone here couldn't imagine . . .' Nat felt the first few drops of a fresh shower. 'Shall we stop here a moment?'

He helped Mrs Gomer manoeuvre into the covered area and sat facing her on one of the stone seats. 'I'd have said that your husband was one of the most honest men I've ever met.'

'And you'd have been right. Straight as a die he was. Everyone respected him for it—in the service, here at the college and at Samson's, the security firm. They wouldn't have taken him on else. So, what they said about him in that courtroom was downright cruel. I couldn't go, of course, and Bob would never tell me but I had it from Ted, my brother-in-law. I made him tell me. Well, how could I help Bob if I didn't know what they were accusing him of? That bitch of a woman barrister!' Mrs Gomer sniffed and blinked away a tear. 'She tried to make out that Bob was lumbered with a wife who'd got MS and that he desperately needed more money to look after her. She said he'd been paid handsomely to steal that wretched picture. She was wicked! Wicked!'

Nat looked away from the woman's ravaged features. Lights gleamed behind the stained glass of the hall window where the meal was now being served. He thought of his own missed lunch appointment. He said, 'Please try not to distress yourself with these memories.'

'Quite right, Dr Gye, I mustn't waste your time with my prattle.' Again the wistful effort at a smile.

'I didn't mean . . .'

'That's all right. I know I go on a bit. I suppose it's because I don't get to see many people nowadays. I'd better explain properly why I'm here and then leave you to get on.' She began wrestling with the fastenings of her enveloping rain cape. 'I've got Bob's file under here. If I can just . . .'

Nat jumped up and helped her fold back the wet plastic. He winced at the sight of the shrunken, wasted body under the covering.

Even though it was draped in several layers of woollen garments it took up so little space. The image flashed into his mind of an Egyptian mummy, held together by its strips of age-browned cloth. Pearl Gomer's trembling hands found a buff folder where it lay on her lap and she held it out to him.

'Bob wrote down everything he could think of about the disappearance of that picture. He went over all the details again and again. He couldn't understand how it happened. He was sure he must have missed something— something he could have brought out at the trial. He knew the jury would never believe his story else, any more than the police did. I suppose you can't really blame them. I mean, old paintings that vanish into thin air with someone watching all the time! Then, right at the end, he thought he was on to something. He told me he was going to talk with his barrister about "fresh evidence". He suddenly seemed to see a glimmer of light. That's why it came as a real shock when he . . . did what he did.'

Nat glanced at the sheaf of neat, computer-typed sheets. Out in the street beyond Beaufort's high wall an ambulance wailed its way to an emergency. 'And you'd like me to go over these notes and see if I can discover that same glimmer of light?'

'It's not me, Dr Gye. It's Bob. I suppose it sounds wicked and selfish of me to say it but I really don't care any more. I've got enough to do getting through each day. But it's important to Bob. Very distressed he is. Things ain't what they seem and he won't be able to rest till you've found out the truth. He says would you be kind enough to read his file and then come out to Endfield Road because he's got something important to tell you.'

Nat stared into the dark eyes, iridescent sparks of life in a face that was a paper mask crumpled by pain. He knew what she was suggesting but took refuge in pretended incomprehension. 'Mrs Gomer, I don't quite . . .'

Her head drooped in disappointment. 'Bob said you'd understand. He said you were the only person I could turn to because you know the truth of these things. Other people thought he was a crank but not you. He always felt he could talk to you. "Go and see Dr Gye," he said. "He's the only person who can put the record straight."'

Nat sighed. 'I know your husband was a devout believer in spiritualism. We did, indeed, discuss spirit communication sometimes.' He racked his brain to find a way to explain to this distraught woman that his own interest in such claimed phenomena was objective, academic, analytical. In fifteen years as a lecturer and writer on parapsychology he had found himself fighting a war on two fronts. On the one hand there were sceptics who behaved quite unprofessionally in dismissing

28

as 'unscientific nonsense' and without open-minded investigation any propositions that did not fit into their purely materialistic theories. On the other there were honest cranks who believed steadfastly in the paranormal without subjecting their convictions to the discipline of rigid objective investigation. Bob Gomer had belonged to the latter category. He had certainly read widely, if not deeply, on a range of paranormal subjects, his motto being that there were more things in heaven and earth than were dreamt of in the philosophy of clever university dons.

'Bob and I didn't always see eye to eye on such matters,' Nat concluded rather lamely.

'Oh, I realize that,' the widow conceded readily. 'Sometimes he used to come home and say, "I had a right dingdong with Dr Gye today!"' She gave a little cracked bell of a laugh. 'But what he says now is that you and he were always discussing ideas, theories, things that couldn't be proved one way or the other. But now that he's passed over he *knows* and that's what he wants to tell you. Please, Dr Gye, it means a lot to him . . . and, well, if not for his sake then mine . . . It'll only take half an hour and I promise I won't bother you again.'

'You're not bothering me, Mrs Gomer.' Nat squirmed inwardly. 'You mustn't think that for one moment. All of us here at Beaufort want to be as much help as we can. It's just that . . .'

She reached out a thin hand to touch his

29

sleeve. 'Please, Dr Gye. Please.'

Here Nat paused in his narrative and Barny Cox, who had been listening intently, said, 'How awkward for you, dear boy. I take it Mrs Gomer wanted you to attend some sort of a seance or reading or whatever it is these things are called nowadays. And, being the good-hearted fellow you are, I assume you agreed.'

'Yes, I went out to her little semi in Endfield Road, near the railway, a few days later. It was, as you can imagine, a pretty dismal experience.' Nat recalled hearing a London-bound train rattle under the nearby bridge as he rang the doorbell of number 34.

The woman who stood before him a moment later, looking him up and down with aggressive curiosity, was in her forties, heavily and inexpertly made up, and had magenta highlights in her blonde hair. 'You must be the university bloke. I've seen you on the telly,' she announced, showing no signs of admitting him to the house.

Nat inclined his head. 'I'm Dr Gye, here to see Mrs Gomer. And you are?'

'Hardwick, Rosie Hardwick, Pearl's sister. I hope you've come to talk her out of this stupid mumbo-jumbo.'

'You don't approve of spiritualism?'

'Communing with the dead!' She snorted. 'No, I do not! And Pearl's old enough to know better. It was bad enough when Bob was alive—him and his weird ideas! But if anything she's got worse since.'

'How is Pearl . . . physically?' Nat asked. But his attempt to steer the truculent Rosie into more sympathetic waters only pointed her at another target for her wrath.

'She ought to be in a home or at least looked after by professional carers. Me and Ted do what we can but it's not right that we should be expected to shoulder all the responsibility. Pearl needs twenty-four/seven care but the NHS just don't want to know, not as long as there's relatives around to do the job for free. We had plans—big plans—and now we're stuck here . . .'

'It must be very worrying for all concerned. May I . . .?' Nat nodded towards the hallway.

'Be my guest. I'm off anyway. Someone has to do the shopping and the chores.' Mrs Hardwick stood aside. 'First on the left,' she muttered as she stepped across the threshold and pulled the door to behind her.

There were three people in the small lounge which Nat now entered. Beside a steadily hissing gas fire Mrs Gomer was in a large armchair, propped up by cushions, her knees covered with a plaid rug. Beside her, stiffly upright on a dining-room chair, sat a fiftyish, grey-haired, bespectacled woman in a black suit. In the matching armchair opposite Pearl Gomer there was a younger man with florid features who jumped to his feet as the new arrival came in and looked at him sheepishly, almost apologetically, from beneath lowered lids.

The hostess smiled at Nat. 'Thank you so much for coming, Dr Gye.' She made the introductions. 'This is Athalie George and her son, Kevin. Athalie is the medium Bob uses to come through to us.' She motioned Nat to a chair next to Mrs George.

'It's a privilege to have you with us, Dr Gye. You are no stranger to the seance room. I've often watched your investigative programmes on the television. Kevin, tea for our distinguished visitor.' The medium left no room for doubt about who was in charge. Her son obediently crossed to the bay window where a teapot, cups and a plate of biscuits were already laid out. 'I don't imagine we shall see eye to eye but it is very important that you are here. Mr Gomer has been most insistent that he speak to you.'

'I shall listen with great interest to what he has to say.' Nat maintained a carefully formal stance.

Mrs George proffered a tight-lipped, regal nod which effectively sealed off this line of conversation. Having acknowledged the academic's expertise, she was not going to allow it to impinge on the afternoon's activities. To have done so might have suggested that she was in some sense on trial. As inconsequential chatter drifted back and forth Nat took in his surroundings. He was struck with the very ordinariness of things. The lounge where they sat was decorated in warm tones of orange and gold—wallpaper, carpet, curtains and furnishings blending together harmoniously. The room might have been replicated in a million British homes. Its occupants were drinking tea from what was obviously Mrs Gomer's best china. No one walking in would have discovered anything odd. There was no 'special' atmosphere, no frisson of expectancy, no subdued lighting, no ouija board or other occult paraphernalia, no central table waiting to be moved by unseen hands. He wondered whether they would, in fact, transfer to another room for the seance itself. But when, at a signal from mama, Kevin collected all the cups on a tray, it was clear that the business of the afternoon was about to begin.

Mrs George folded her thin hands in her lap and looked round expressionlessly. 'For your information, Dr Gye, I will explain that I am a traditional trance medium. You will, of course, understand that that means I can take no responsibility for the messages that may come through to us from the other side. My control is the only intermediary.'

'You have a spirit guide?'

Athalie George nodded.

Nat thought, how quaint. Most modern mediums had long since dispensed with such intermediaries. 'And the name of this guide?'

he asked.

For the first time the medium betrayed slight discomfort. 'His name is Sammy Tuck. He is an uneducated Victorian chimney boy who passed over at the age of eleven. I'm afraid he can sometimes be a little . . . mischievous, even disruptive.'

Pearl Gomer laughed. 'He's quite a character, Dr Gye. You should hear some of the things he comes out with.'

Mrs George scowled. 'Not now, Pearl. I am about to commence the sitting.'

'I assume Sammy will have no objection if I record his revelations, mischievous or not.' Nat took a small cassette recorder from his briefcase.

The medium's only response was a slight fluttering of her bony fingers. 'If you are all relaxed we'll begin.'

She closed her eyes and allowed her head to slump forward. Her breathing became deep and regular. After about a minute she sat up abruptly, head on one side, eyes open. 'Afternoon, ladies and gents. Who've we got 'ere then?' The transformation, even to Nat, who had witnessed such manifestations before, came as a shock. The person sitting in the chair was still Mrs George. The voice speaking was Mrs George's. Yet, the prim, elderly woman had disappeared beneath the surface of another character who now dominated the room. The gestures and speech mannerisms

34

were those of an attention-seeking, precocious child. If this was an act, Nat thought, it was remarkably effective. 'Well, come on then. What's up with you; cat got your tongues?'

Mrs George's son was the first to respond. 'Hello, Sammy. I'm Kevin. We've met before.'

'And I'm Pearl Gomer,' Pearl added breathlessly. 'Have you got my husband with you, Sammy?'

'All in good time, lady. All in good time. There's someone else 'ere. Who's that?'

'I'm Nathaniel Gye, Sammy.'

'And just who might Nathaniel Gye be when 'e's at 'ome?'

'I'm a teacher, Sammy.'

'Ooooh, teacher, eh! I ain't never 'ad a teacher; leastways, not till I come 'ere. There's an old buffer 'ere, name of 'Ardy, been trying to teach me poetry. I've got a poem of me own. Want to 'ear it?' Without waiting for a reply, the boy raised his voice and, with the strident delivery of a street crier, intoned,

'Sammy Tuck
'as rotten luck,
Just learned to fuck
But only eleven
They sent 'im to 'eaven.'

He went into giggles of laughter.

'Now, that's quite enough of that, Sammy!' It was Kevin who surprised Nat by taking a

35

firm line. 'Dr Gye has come here to have a few words with Mr Gomer. Is he here?'

The child spirit, if such it was, became petulant. 'You ain't no fun, you ain't. I'm orf.'

Mrs Gomer was alarmed. 'Now, Sammy,' she pleaded, 'you can't do that.'

'Who says I can't? I don't have to waste my time with stuffed shirts like you.'

Again Kevin played schoolmaster. 'Come on, Sammy, act your age. Dr Gye's come specially to meet Mr Gomer and we know Mr Gomer has something important to say to him.'

There was a long silence, broken, at last, by a long, low moan from the medium. Pearl Gomer opened her mouth in alarm but Kevin motioned her to silence and after a few more moments his mother spoke again. This time the timbre of her voice was very different. The delivery was slow as though every word was being weighed before being uttered.

'Pearl, Pearl, are you there?'

'Oh yes, Bob, is that you? Yes, I'm here.' Mrs Gomer's eyes were glistening with tears. 'Bob, dear, how are you?'

'Something I've got to tell Dr Gye. He's the only one who can clear my name.'

'Dr Gye is here, dear.'

'Good. Listen, I haven't got much time before that bloody kid comes back. Doctor, you and I understand each other, don't we?'

'I hope so, Bob.'

36

'My good name's the only thing left on your side. I want you to do two things to clear it.'

'If I can.'

'Find out about the picture and about my death. I wasn't responsible for either.'

'But how . . . ?'

'You must go to Ferrara, in Italy. Find the man who knows about the picture.'

'What man is that?' Nat asked.

'Don't know the name.'

'Then, how can I—'

'But not Mrs Gye. She mustn't go to Italy.' The words were almost shouted.

'What do you mean?'

'I see great danger for Mrs Gye in Italy. Terrible! Terrible . . . Terrible . . .' Mrs George screamed and collapsed in her chair.

*   *   *

Nat paused to drain his glass.

The old lawyer stared across the table. 'How highly dramatic. I must say, Nathaniel, your life is far from dull. What game do you suppose this Mrs George was playing?'

'Game?'

'Well, one obviously can't take such people seriously. They are usually in it for the money, are they not? Or perhaps she has some sort of power complex; a need to hold something over her neighbours.'

'I wouldn't put her down as a deliberate

37

fraud. I've seen several mediums and they vary enormously in the techniques they use. Some employ very sophisticated trickery and pull in large, fee-paying audiences. Others charge through the nose for individual sittings. Then, there are some who are almost like family doctors or priests offering what they genuinely believe are professional services to people in need. I'd put Mrs George in the last category.'

'But what she had to say was hardly a help or a comfort to Mrs Gomer. I mean, suggesting that her husband had been murdered . . .'

Nat shrugged. 'For what it's worth, I think Mrs George and her disciples all believe in what they're doing.'

Barny was dubious. 'Possibly, dear boy. I bow to your superior knowledge. But what was it Thomas Huxley said about spiritualists? Something to do with crossing sweepers . . .'

' "Better live as a crossing sweeper than die and be made to talk twaddle by a medium hired at a guinea a seance." '

'Exactly so. If there's an afterlife, which I doubt, I shall certainly not take kindly to being summoned back to utter melodramatic warnings. Tell me, what does the charming Kathryn make of this prophecy about something nasty waiting for her in Italy?'

'Ah, now, there's the rub.' Nat gazed out of the window and noticed that the rain had begun again. 'I didn't mention it to her.'

'You mean to say you failed to recount this extraordinary incident?' Barny raised his eyebrows in mock astonishment. 'I've always been given to understand that shared experience is of the essence of happy married life.'

'Oh, I told her about Mrs George's sitting. I just didn't get round to mentioning anything about her and Italy.'

'Now I begin to see the first glimmers of your problem.' The old lawyer, who had consumed his meal with prodigious speed while listening to Nat's story, pushed his plate to one side, folded his arms and stared inquisitorially across the table. 'You haven't passed on to your wife what our sensationalist press might call "The Dead Man's Warning" for fear of being ridiculed.'

'There didn't seem much point. Kathryn would certainly have laughed it off.'

'And yet you can't laugh it off—even though you are rightly sceptical about Mrs George's performance? This sounds rather like a case of "physician heal thyself".'

'I certainly feel pretty foolish about the whole business. And yet . . .'

'And yet you can't help worrying about even the remotest possibility that Kathryn might be in some kind of unspecified danger.'

'Neatly summed up—Judge.'

'Oh, please!' Barny's nose wrinkled in disdain. 'Our ample hostess seems to find that soubriquet amusing and I'm prepared to indulge her but I should hate it to become common currency among our friends. Now, would you like an old lawyer's analysis of your situation?'

'A fresh mind on the problem would be valuable. But first let me get you a drink. Another beer or a coffee?' Barny glanced up at the window, now being pelted by flurries of rain. 'A coffee, I think—and perhaps something to ward off the chill of these riverain airs.'

Nat carried the empty plates to the bar and returned minutes later with two coffees and a large brandy for his companion.

He discovered his old friend, eyes closed, hands clasped beneath his chin, apparently deep in thought. Nat realized he was glad to have bumped into Barnaby Cox. To those who knew no better the aged lawyer seemed to be just one of the quaint anachronisms with which Cambridge was well stocked. His dress and mannerisms were those correct in university circles half a century ago. By contrast close friends had come to realize two important facts about Barny: he was lonely and greatly missed the stimulation of law practice and teaching, and his mind was not a whit less keen for the passing of the years. Nat set down his tray on the table.

'You won't join me?' Barny asked, cupping long fingers round the glass.

'No thanks, I want to keep a clear head. Some papers I need to tidy up before I drive to Norfolk tomorrow. As a matter of fact Bob Gomer's file is among them. I must make some effort to read it carefully before I give it back.'

Barny frowned. 'Are you saying that you've no intention of trying to untangle this twisted skein of mysteries?'

'There's not much I *can* do.' Nat found himself, uncomfortably, on the defensive. 'I've really had no time to study Gomer's dossier. As you know I'm on the sub-committee for the new Comstock Library. We've been up to our eyes in architect's plans and builders' estimates for weeks.'

'Bullshit!' Barny scowled ferociously at his companion. 'Forgive that descent into the vernacular, dear boy, but really you are talking nonsense.'

'I don't know what—'

'Look, Nathaniel, you would not be as worried as you clearly are about what passed at a dreary little back-street seance, if you were not already emotionally and intellectually caught up in the Gomers' plight. You are a scholar—one of our brightest stars in the fellowship at Beaufort—and as a scholar you can't bear to leave puzzles unsolved. Now you are faced with a whole raft of such puzzles: do the dead speak to the living; was Bob Gomer innocent of the crime of which he was accused;

41

was his death anything other than suicide; whether he was involved or not, how on earth was the vanishing trick with the picture managed; finally, and perhaps fundamentally, are there dark forces at work here which really could suck into an evil maelstrom people on its very outermost rim like Kathryn? You have a remarkable instinct for detecting when things are not as they seem and that instinct has been well and truly aroused by the Gomer tragedy.'

Nat opened his mouth to respond but Barny continued. 'And all this is lifted out of the realm of pure ivory tower speculation by the plight of Pearl Gomer. If there was skulduggery then it is quite monstrous that that poor woman should be the victim of it. You are outraged by that—and rightly so. Now,' he sat back with the air of a barrister who had just delivered a masterly summation to a jury, 'put your hand on your heart and tell me that what I have said is not true.'

*   *   *

Nat was fuming as he drove the last couple of miles home. How dare Barnaby Cox play the psychiatrist-cum-father confessor! It was all very well for a retired academic like him to say that the Gomer case needed following up. He had all the time in the world to pursue his own interests. Nat let himself into the empty house at Great Maddisham and trudged up the stairs

42

to his study. There, on his desk, stood the thick pile of proofs for his latest book, a TV tie-in linked to a forthcoming series, *Fear, Fantasies and Frauds—Exploring the Supernatural.* They had to be checked and marked up within the week—and that was on top of his heavy workload of college and faculty business. Underneath the wad of typescript lay the buff Gomer file.

With a deep sigh Nat pulled it out, opened it and began to read.

Crisis

What may be the mode of intercourse
Between us men here, and those once-men
  there?

The script was ploddingly meticulous, unremitting in its attention to detail. Clearly the writer had been determined to omit no fact that might have any bearing whatsoever on the disappearance of Antonello's *Portrait of a Doge.*

I commenced work at Samson's on 8th September 1997. The hours were erratic and quite a lot of travel was involved but the pay was good and often I had several days off between jobs so I could do most of the work round the house for Pearl. She was not too bad at the beginning and the doctors told us there was no way of knowing how quickly she would deteriorate. It was obvious she would need me more and more so I put in for as much overtime as I could get, so as to have a nest egg we could draw on later.

Nat pictured the stocky, conscientious Gomer torn between wanting to be at home to look after his wife and wanting to be away as much as possible to provide for her inexorably increasing needs. The ex-college porter had been stolid and dependable because nothing ever seemed to faze him. Whatever emotions he had he kept securely locked inside. Here he was, faced with the appalling prospect of his wife literally wasting away over months or years with a fatal and incurable disease, and calmly calculating the best way to help her. What did he really feel? What pressure had he been under? Nat wondered how he would cope under such circumstances. He tried to picture the energetic human dynamo that was Kathryn shrunken to a pathetically dependent invalid in a wheelchair, hating above all else being a burden to her loved ones. Would he be able to handle it? 'In sickness and in health' sounded fine at the altar but what did the reality do to relationships? Could it turn honest, dependable citizens into resentful sociopaths, who could justify to themselves any crime that might make life fractionally easier? Thinking of Kathryn brought back his irrational anxiety. By now she would be in the air somewhere over France or Switzerland. No reason whatsoever to suppose that her flight would encounter any problems. Another hour should see her safely landed at Milan, where most of the symposium participants were congregating before being bussed the three hundred kilometres to Florence. He thought of Italian drivers and envisaged the coach rushing at breakneck speed along the crowded autostrada. Damn Mrs George and her spirit prognostications! He turned his attention back to the file.

The work was cushy. Samson's is an upmarket security firm. They don't do much in the way of shop and bank deliveries. More confidential work for multinationals and private clients, celebrities and the like. That includes transporting items of value for museums, rich collectors and the like. We never had no trouble, not in all the time I was there.

Nat turned over a couple of pages in which Gomer described in detail the working procedures at Samson's. The guards, he explained, operated in teams, two or three to a van depending on the type of job. In the early days he had gone out as third man whenever an extra was needed for what were known as 'specials' but he had soon been paired up with Ted Hardwick, his brother-in-law, and the man who had got him into Samson's. Ted was always the driver and Bob travelled in the passenger seat. If a job called for a third man they usually took a larger vehicle with sufficient room for three up front, although it was not entirely unheard of for the extra guard to travel in the back of the van. When a third man was needed they usually tried to arrange for Charlie Randall to be assigned to them. He was, in Gomer's words, 'a good laugh', an ex-policeman with a fund of stories that always helped to pass the journeys agreeably. The three men, it seemed, got on really well together. The others sometimes teased Bob about his belief in 'spooks' and 'things that go bump in the night' but it was, apparently, all good-natured 'joshing' and he certainly never took offence at it. Nat mentally scribbled a question mark in the margin. He pictured himself cooped up with Bob Gomer for several hours with no chance of escape. Not an enviable prospect.

Nat flicked hurriedly through more paragraphs of inconsequential detail and arrived, at last, at Gomer's account of his final, ill-fated job for Samson's. Bob had carefully attached photocopies of relevant documents where appropriate.

First of all there was a consignment note from Sicuro Pacioli of Turin, Genoa and Rome, the company handling transport arrangements at the Italian end. It authorized Samson's to take delivery of *'Antonello da Messina (c.1430–1479), ritratto di Doge Pietro Mocenigo'.* Nat's grasp of Italian was good enough to cope with the description of the painting as an oil on panel 53.3 cm x 43.1 cm, the property of Signore Alberto Talenti of Ferrara. That presumably cleared up the identity of the man enigmatically referred to at the seance. It did not, Nat reflected, prove the authenticity of Mrs George's spirit voice. Doubtless Signore Talenti's name had appeared in newspaper accounts of the Gomer trial, from which the medium could have picked it up consciously or unconsciously. There was a creased reproduction of the painting clipped to the document. It showed the florid features of a man of middle years wearing the traditional embroidered pointed cap of a ruler of the Venetian Republic. Even from the poor-quality reproduction Nat could see something of what made the work of this Quattrocento master so special. The eyes of the old merchant-politician surveyed the beholder with sardonic humour while the firm set of the thick lips suggested a dealer who was seldom bested on the Rialto. It was a face one found it difficult to tear one's gaze away from.

47

Nat returned his attention to the narrative.

I was not down for the Heathrow job but the day before the depot manager decided it was a 'special' and he wanted a man in the back with the goods. That struck me as a bit odd at the time, Barry Cheeseman not being the sort to throw money about. I asked him if he had heard a rumour about someone wanting to snatch the picture but he said, 'No. The client is paying good money so we must give him our best service.'

On 18th October, Ted and Charlie picked me up from home at about 1 p.m. We agreed that Charlie would ride in the back as far as the airport, then he and I would swap over for the run from Heathrow to Bath.

When we got to the airport Charlie checked that the Turin flight was on time, which it was. The Italian guards had priority clearance to unload the picture and we was instructed to meet them in Security Suite One, which we did. Charlie and me, that is. Ted stayed outside with the van. The people from the gallery—Dr Theophrast the curator and his assistant Heather Miles—was there already and looked excited and nervous. Only natural, I suppose, what with the responsibility they was taking on. They opened the crate and checked the contents with Mr Brandini, the little Italian who had brought it from Ferrara. Everyone seemed happy, although most of the time the three of them spoke in Italian so I didn't pick up much of what they were saying. Dr Theophrast had the crate shut up again and he fixed a metal seal to it. Then they all had a drink together. It was about 5.15 p.m. when we was given the all-clear to take the picture out to the van. I carried it. Charlie and me strapped it up tight, with Miss Miles watching us like a hawk. When the doors were locked Charlie signed the delivery note to say that Samson's had taken responsibility for the consignment. Ted was in a hurry to get started so I got into the back straight away and we set off.

Nat took off his glasses, stretched and rolled his chair away from the desk. He looked at his watch. 4.28. Kathryn must be at Milan by now. He would have asked her to give him a call from the airport but that really would have aroused her suspicions. Still, she would phone when she reached Florence and settled into her room and that would not be for another couple of hours at least. Nat went downstairs and made himself a coffee.

Gazing out of the window towards the row of limes that marked the end of the back garden, he saw that the earlier clouds had rolled away. He surveyed the straggling edges of the lawn and the general signs of past-winter untidiness and decided to spend an hour or so with the mower, doing the duties of a conscientious householder. Later he showered and returned to his study. He dealt with a couple of routine emails. He looked at his watch. 6.12. He imagined a mini-coach full of eager Browning lovers hurtling southward along the autostrada towards Florence.

He turned his attention to the computer screen, typed in a password and brought up his Journal. This was where he kept notes of all interesting, potentially useful information which he came across or which was reported to him. He typed in a new heading.

BOB GOMER AND A VANISHING PAINTING

Robert Gomer: mid-fifties, ex-Royal Marines sergeant, under-porter at Beaufort College 1984-1996. Thereafter employed as a security guard with Samson's Security.

Character: strong, self-confident, straightforward, reliable.

Hobbies: interested to the point of obsession in all occult matters. Member of a small spiritualist church.

Married: no children.

Caring for his terminally ill wife put

pressure on him which he kept bottled up. Stress became worse when he was accused and tried for complicity to steal a valuable old master painting. Committed suicide during trial.

Pearl Gomer: early fifties. Housewife. Character: quiet, non-assertive. Easily dominated by husband and younger sister, Rosie Hardwick. Obviously possessed of inner strength because coping stoically with MS which she has had for three years. Also a believer in spiritualism, but perhaps more so since Bob's death. Amazingly seems to harbour no resentment at him for taking his own life. Now looked after (unwillingly) by sister Rosie.

Nat paused to check through what he had so far typed, then added a brief account of Mrs George's seance. He noted:

The medium's performance probably motivated by genuine self-delusion rather than fraud, power complex or desire to manipulate. No evidence of knowledge that she cannot have come by in normal ways.

Question: Who wants Bob Gomer exonerated? Why? Perhaps the initiative of Pearl's spiritualist friends to comfort her or give her something to think about other than her own sufferings. But, in reality, the suggestion that her husband might have been murdered has only added to Pearl's woes.

Action? Debunk the medium; show Pearl that Bob would not want to place this extra burden on her? No—probably ineffective; certainly cruel.

Find some evidence to prove Bob's innocence? Surely impossible. The police found nothing. Yes, but if Bob is innocent then someone has used him to carry out a crime of great complexity.

Next Nat made outline notes from the material in Bob Gomer's file. He dealt in a few lines with the collection of the painting from Heathrow, then described the ensuing events:

- Gomer settled in van with the crated picture.
- The van equipped with a semi-reclining passenger seat fixed to the front.
- Gomer had the crate in view all the time.
- Intercom connection with the cab meant that he could talk with his colleagues whenever he wanted.
- Uneventful journey. Gomer passed the time reading the latest issue of *UFOs Today*, eating his sandwiches and drinking a flask of tea.
- Journey passed 'surprisingly quickly'. Did

he doze off? He doesn't say so.
- In Bath the loading process went into reverse.
- Theophrast and Miles, who had followed the van in their car, watched Gomer and Randall unload the crate and carry it into the gallery by the rear door and place it in the director's office.
- Gomer and Randall stayed to watch the unveiling.
- Shock-horror as wrappings removed to reveal a panel of thick plywood.
- Pandemonium for several seconds. Theophrast screaming at Gomer 'What have you done with it?' and demanding a search of the van.
- Everyone rushed outside. No van. However it was immediately discovered at a service station almost opposite the back entrance to the museum where Hardwick was filling up with petrol for the return journey.
- Everyone having hysterics. Van searched minutely. Police sent for. CID impounded the van and even sealed off the service station for forensic tests. They took statements from everyone involved.
- It was gone midnight before the Samson's team was released. They found a hotel to stay the night and returned to Cambridge by train the following day.
- Gomer was shattered to realize that

everyone, including his colleagues, assumed that he was the guilty party.

Thankfully, Nat reached the last couple of sentences of Gomer's narrative:

I have set down here every detail I can think of in the hope of finding some clue about the disappearance of that picture, but I am still none the wiser.

Then, right at the end, Gomer had added a note which must have been written during his trial.

In his evidence to the court Inspector Hawkins of Bath CID said his men found the van empty. I've just been to check this with Barry Cheeseman. So where was my thermos? I've asked my lawyer to check this out.

Nat remembered Pearl Gomer saying something about Bob having made an important discovery. Was this it? A missing vacuum flask? The poor man had obviously been clutching at straws.

*   *   *

With a yawn of relief Nat closed the file. He looked at his watch. 7.34. Kathryn would be calling shortly. He went downstairs, ground and brewed some fresh coffee and constructed a sandwich. He carried them through to the sitting room, where he put a disc of Beethoven piano trios on to play before spreading himself on the sofa with his makeshift supper and his mobile phone beside him on a low table. He sank back on the cushions to enjoy the rippling playfulness of Beethoven's Op. 70, No. 1 but it failed to raise his spirits and when the opening allegro vivace of the 'Ghost' trio gave way to its wistful largo Nat switched the music off. It was almost eight when he found Kathryn's itinerary and contact numbers and called her hotel.

The desk clerk spoke precise, textbook English. Yes the Browning Symposium party had arrived.

'Please, may I speak to Mrs Gye?'

If the Signore would bear with him a moment, he would try to locate la Signora Gye.

The official was away from the telephone for a very long 'moment' during which Nat could just hear a staccato conversation in rapid Italian. Then there followed a succession of clicks and the voice was back.

It appeared that la Signora Gye had not yet booked in. 'But I thought you said the symposium group had arrived.'

That was quite correct, but it now transpired that the group was not quite complete. La Signora Gye was not with them.

'May I speak with Professor Kaminsky, the party leader?' Nat was aware that his throat had tightened and the pitch of his voice had risen.

Unluckily, it was regretted that this was not possible. The group had left for a meeting at the Browning Institute in the Piazza San Felice.

'And you've really no idea why Mrs Gye is not with them?'

It was indeed a bizarre circumstance. The Signora had certainly not cancelled her reservation or indicated that her arrival would be delayed. If the Signore would care to call again later—perhaps in a couple of hours—he would be able to speak to the Professor, who would doubtless have more information . . .

Nat switched off the mobile. He had no intention of spending another two hours in anxious inactivity. He went to his computer and checked the availability of flights to Florence.

Lost and Found

How many lies did it require to make
The portly truth you here present us with?

As the plane levelled out over the Channel Nat stretched his legs and rubbed a hand wearily over his eyes. It was a relief to be in someone else's hands. He had spent the last few hours in nervous hyperactivity: scanning the internet to find the first available flight; phoning his father with an explanation— suitably shorn of alarming detail—for the sudden change of plan; making the nocturnal drive to Heathrow and trying to keep his mind on the road; attempting to check with Kathryn's hotel en route, only to discover that he had left his mobile at home; sleeplessly worrying away what remained of the night in an airport hotel; making an early call to Florence and discovering that there was still no news of his wife's whereabouts; going impatiently through the embarkation procedures. Now he was released from all that. There was nothing he could do but let the Boeing's crew convey him to Italy and if that did not take away the panic that was gripping him, at least it gave him time to impose some kind of order on his churning thoughts and emotions.

Scores of times he had gone over all the possible reasons for Kathryn's failure to reach her hotel. The airline had confirmed that she had taken her seat on the plane and that the flight had arrived on time. According to the hotel all the other members of the symposium had arrived. Nat's attempts to check what Kaminsky knew had been frustrated. The Professor had, it seemed, been out until very late and when Nat had asked, in the small hours, to be put through to his room an officious under-manager had declined to disturb him. Nat had ranted that he was calling on a matter of great urgency, only to have the man at the other end of the line retreat behind a barrier of feigned linguistic incomprehension. Nat told himself that there were a hundred reasons why Kathryn might have failed to make contact with other members of her group; why the other Browning addicts might eventually have been obliged to go on without her. He tried to convince himself that it was illogically morbid to assume a sinister explanation.

'Breakfast, sir?' The appearance of the club class stewardess with a menu and a plastic smile brought him out of his mental malaise. Nat suddenly realized that he was hungry. He ordered smoked salmon and scrambled egg. It was good. So was the coffee. It was amazing, he reflected, how food could revive the most jaded spirits.

After the meal Nat steeled himself to train his mind on a subject far removed from his current problem. He had picked up the volume of Robert Browning's poems that Kathryn had left him. He turned to the only one that he had read since leaving school, the one in which he might be said to have a professional interest, 'Mr Sludge, the "Medium"'. In this extended monologue by an exposed charlatan Browning had poured out all his loathing of the spiritualist craze which swept smart society in the 1850s. Nat smiled as he read again the attempts of Mr Sludge to escape the wrath of his one-time patron, by turns pleading, wheedling, flattering and threatening; now confessing his trickery, now insisting that the spirits really did speak through him. The fraudster's acrobatic mind leaped from one plausible excuse to the next, letting go of each trapeze just as its absurdity began to show, in order to grasp the next which might offer a more secure support.

Whatever put such folly in my head,
I know 'twas wicked of me. There's a thick
Dusk, undeveloped spirit (I've observed)
Owes me a grudge—a negro's, I should say,
Or else an Irish emigrant's; yourself
Explained the case so well last Sunday, sir,
When we had summoned Franklin to clear up
A point about those shares in the telegraph:

Ay, and he swore . . . or might it be Tom
　　Paine? . . .
Thumping the table close by where I
　　crouched,
He'd do me soon a mischief: that's come
　　true!

The greasy, odious Sludge was Browning's
version of the most celebrated medium of the
mid-Victorian age, Daniel Dunglas Home, and
the poet was particularly incensed by him
because the spiritualist had come between him
and his wife. Nat set the book aside and closed
his eyes to search his memory for details of the
old story. Robert Browning had clandestinely
married his beloved Elizabeth Barrett and
they had settled among the small, introverted
Anglo-American arty set in Florence. Despite
Elizabeth's delicate health, there was little to
disturb their happiness. They drew inspiration
for their poetry from the monuments of
ancient culture around them—or from their
romanticized notions of that culture—and
from the aspirations of the 'heroic' Italian
people struggling for unity and freedom from
the yoke of Austrian domination. Then the
new craze burst upon their little Bohemian
world and Mrs Browning became caught up in
it.

The beginnings of the spiritualist movement
were well known, though none the less
remarkable for that. Two teenage girls in

upstate New York, Margaret and Kate Fox, gained instant celebrity by claiming to receive messages from the spirit of someone who had died in the cottage where they lived. Years later, one of the sisters confessed that the 'rappings' had been faked and that, having become instant celebrities, she and her sibling had been afraid to admit their trickery. Even had they done so it would probably have been too late to stop the waves of excitement and near hysteria that were rapidly rippling out from Hydesville, N.Y. Hundreds of people were discovering that they, too, had mediumistic powers. The most remarkable was Daniel Dunglas Home, a nervy, adolescent Scot, who had spent a disturbed childhood in Connecticut. Home's 'manifestations' included some phenomena, such as rappings and table lifting, which were to become the stock-in-trade of mediums but others, such as levitation and musical instruments which played tunes while floating in mid-air, were unique, baffled contemporary sceptics and were never to be explained away by later critics.

Home's fame spread far and wide and Elizabeth was agog to meet him and attend his seances. Her chance came during a visit home the Brownings made in the mid-1850s. Spiritualism was wildly in vogue. Members of the *haut monde* were falling over themselves to 'adopt' their own mediums. Seances became the favourite after-dinner entertainment.

Some London friends of the Brownings had managed to 'bag' Home and they invited Robert and Elizabeth to come and be amazed by their protégé. The medium really went overboard in his attempt to impress these prestigious guests. There were spirit voices and table movements. Ghostly hands mysteriously appeared and at the climax of the performance a wreath of flowers was placed on Elizabeth's head. She was thrilled. Robert was not. He was convinced that Home was a charlatan and when, months later, the medium arrived in Florence Browning mortified his wife by refusing to receive him.

Remarkable medium or first-class conjurer? The question had never been settled. The important issue for the Brownings was that Home stayed in their lives, an unseen presence, an invisible vibration in their marriage and one that shattered their romantic idyll. Fraud. Gullibility. Scepticism. What was it that had the power to undermine love? Perhaps the love had always been too intense to last. Whoever . . . suggested that *amor . . . vincit om . . .* The book slipped from Nat's fingers. The next thing he was aware of was the stewardess shaking his shoulder and asking him to fasten his seat belt.

An hour later he was being hurtled along the Pisa-Firenze autostrada, regretting having told the taxi driver that his mission was *'urgente'*. Once in the city the vehicle barged and hooted its way through the mid-morning traffic, finally jarring to a halt halfway along the Via Maggio outside the Della Robbia Hotel. 'Here we are,' the driver announced, flashing his passenger a triumphant grin, though whether he was applauding himself for his command of tourist English or his death-defying performance was not altogether clear.

Nat strode up the steps and across the foyer. The first thing he became aware of was raised voices. In the middle of the space a black-jacketed official—presumably the manager—was trying to placate a middle-aged German couple who were operating on the principle that the language barrier could best be overcome by shouting and arm waving. Nat side-stepped the hubbub and addressed himself to the receptionist, a young woman who was much more interested in the altercation in progress than in attending to routine enquiries. Smirking at her superior's discomfort, she lent only half an ear to Nat's enquiry for Signora Gye and shook her head. He tried another tack. *'Il gruppo di Professore Kaminsky,'* he demanded. *'Il seminario Browning.'*

'Ah, si.' Comprehension briefly illuminated the features on the other side of the desk. The girl waved an arm in the direction of the lift. *'Primo piano. Sala Giotto.'*

Nat took the lift to the first floor and emerged on to a wide landing off which three function rooms led, labelled *'Sala Leonardo'*, *'Sala Raphaelo'* and *'Sala Giotto'*. Gently he pushed open the door of the last of these and as he did so he encountered a wave of polite applause. He slipped into an empty seat in the back row of chairs. Behind a table at the front he recognized the figure of Kaminsky, fatter than when they had last met but quite unmistakable with his thick mass of swept-back black hair. It was apparent that he had just proposed the vote of thanks to the speaker seated beside him. 'I'm sure Jim will be delighted to take questions.' The Professor beamed around at his little flock.

Nat also surveyed the group of thirty or so people, well spread out over the six rows of seats. Somewhere in the middle of the audience a hand shot up. Nat looked in the direction of the eager student. Suddenly he caught his breath. Sitting next to the questioner was Kathryn. He jumped to his feet and, trying not to attract attention, slid round the back of the room until he could slip into a chair behind his wife.

When he tapped her on the shoulder she turned with a frown of astonishment. 'Nat, what on earth . . . What's wrong? Is it Ed or Jerry?'

'The boys are fine.' Nat dropped his voice to a whisper as people around began to glare at him. 'I've been worried about you. Where have you been?'

Kathryn flashed her annoyance. 'Oh, for heaven's sake! Have you come rushing out here just because . . .' A heavily built lady sitting in front of her turned with a shushing sound. 'We'd better talk outside.'

With muttered apologies they stumbled their way from the room. Out on the landing, Kathryn faced her husband, arms belligerently folded. 'Nat, this I do not need. I've had a hell of a time since I got here and just when I thought things were getting back to normal . . .'

Nat scowled. 'Nice to see you, too.'

'Oh . . .' Kathryn's expression softened. 'I didn't mean to be beastly.' She gave him a quick hug. 'It's just that your behaviour at the airport was so strange and then, as soon as we landed at Milan, everything went pear-shaped and I've hardly had a wink of sleep and now you turn up out of the blue. Hardly the relaxing break I planned.'

'I've had a pretty rough time, too. What went wrong at the airport? Why didn't you phone me?'

Kathryn linked her arm through his. 'I need some fresh air. Let's take a walk.'

'What about the seminar?'

'We're about to break for coffee. No one will mind if I take some time out.'

They strolled arm-in-arm down the Via Maggio and paused, leaning against the parapet of the Ponte Santa Trinita to watch the sunlight sparkling on the Arno and gaze at the arches and shuttered windows of the Ponte Vecchio mirrored in its surface.

'Some bastard at the airport snatched my purse,' Kathryn explained. 'It was while I was waiting for my bag in the luggage hall. There was quite a crowd and a lot of jostling. Then I felt a hand in my back and as I fell forward someone grabbed the strap from my shoulder.'

'Poor you. How dreadful. What about the people round you? They must have seen the thief. Didn't anyone do anything?'

Kathryn pursed her lips. 'You know what folk are like when they're forced to witness a crime. Basically they don't want to know. They'd all got people to meet, places to go. By the time I'd recovered and looked around there was no sign of the bastard and all anyone had seen was a slight young man in jeans and leather jacket who'd run off through a doorway. The luggage had started to arrive and people were busy finding their things. No one wanted to waste time to give a detailed description.'

'Charming!'

Kathryn shrugged. 'In all fairness the thief was slick and quick. The airport security people said he'd worked the trick before. The police reckon he's part of a gang that target tourists and make a packet on currency, passports, credit cards and traveller's cheques.'

'But how could he get in and out of the airport buildings?'

'Yeah, I asked the same question. Sounds to me like an inside job but, of course, no one wanted to admit that.'

'So, what happened after that?'

'Huh! What didn't! They took me to a room and gave me a cup of tea for my "shock". Hell, I wasn't shocked—just bloody angry. Then the police came and I had to give a statement. Then there were forms to fill in so that I could get permission to enter Italy without a passport. Then I had to call the credit card hotline to have my cards cancelled, arrange some emergency cash and organize a visitor's visa. You wouldn't believe how long all this took. Of course, I totally missed linking up with the other symposium guys.'

'What time did you get away from the airport?'

'It was gone ten. By then all I wanted to do was book into a hotel and get my head down. I called you as soon as I got to my room but there was no reply either at home or on your mobile.'

Nat grinned sheepishly. 'I'd already gone by then and I left the mobile at home.'

'But why the rush? It was sweet of you to be worried but I don't see why you were in such a hurry to believe the worst.'

'Let's adjust the caffeine intake and I'll try and explain.' They continued across the bridge. 'I seem to recall that there's a café on the Piazza Santa Trinita that doesn't get swamped with tourists paying through the nose for latte and cappuccino.'

A few minutes later they were seated at a window table gazing out at the ancient Column of Justice, transferred to Florence from Rome by a favour-currying sixteenth-century pope. Nat stirred his coffee. 'You remember that business with Pearl Gomer? Well, I didn't tell you quite everything that happened at the seance.' Hesitantly Nat explained the warning issued by Mrs George's spirit voice.

Kathryn was obviously unimpressed. 'But I thought you'd dismissed Mrs George and Co. as a bunch of self-deluding old biddies.'

Nat nodded. 'I know, but the devil of it is that it's easy to be all objective and coolly critical about other people's beliefs and superstitions. When your own nearest and dearest are involved the perspective changes.'

'Surely, that's when your own intellectual faculties are most put to the test. Once you conceded, however unwillingly, that there just *might* be something in the medium's warning about me, then everything else that Mrs George's voices supposedly revealed also comes within the realm of possibility.'

'Don't imagine that I haven't told myself that over and over again. Fortunately, Bob Gomer's shade got it wrong. I'm sorry you had your handbag pinched yesterday. That was a rotten experience but you certainly weren't in any danger.'

Kathryn looked thoughtful. 'The Ides of March are come but not gone.'

'Meaning?'

'Meaning that I'm here in Italy for a few more days. Who's to say that there isn't an assassin lurking round the next corner?'

'You don't believe that.'

'No, I don't. What I do believe is that there's part of you that won't really rest easy till I'm home safe and sound.'

'Not at all! I'm perfectly happy . . .'

'Bullshit!'

Nat frowned. 'You're the second person who's said that to me in as many days.'

'Who was that other?'

'Barny Cox.'

'He's a pretty wise old bird.'

'Yes, but I'm getting a bit tired of people telling me they know what I think better than I do.'

'Well, perhaps we do. Look, darling,' she took hold of his hand across the table, 'you may not want to accept it, but it's perfectly clear that this Gomer business has really got under your skin. That poor man's widow has a hell of a life and she's come to you for help and now you're emotionally involved and you can't walk away. You don't believe Bob Gomer had anything to do with the theft of that

69

picture, do you?'

'Absolutely not. He was a straight up and down man of the old school. Even if he was somehow involved he could never have carried on the deception month after month, lied under oath in court and refused to vary his story under interrogation. And what clinches the matter is that Gomer got nothing out of the crime.'

'What do you mean?'

'It's obvious, isn't it? God knows the poor man had temptation enough. He desperately needed money to make his wife's life as tolerable as possible.'

'So?'

'Well, look, supposing you and I are complete strangers and I come up to you and say, "I'll pay you a hundred thousand pounds to help me steal a priceless old master." And suppose you think it over and decide that it just might be worth the risk. What's the first thing you want to be absolutely certain about?'

Kathryn sipped her coffee thoughtfully. 'I'd want to be sure I could trust you to pay up.'

'Exactly! And being the smart girl you are, you'd insist on a good chunk of cash up front. Gomer would have done the same. It would be his only way of making sure that Pearl was provided for if anything went wrong.'

'Yes, I see that.'

'Well, she isn't—provided for, I mean. She's appallingly hard up and has to rely on the

70

grudging help of her sister. The district nurse comes in fairly often and I believe there's some occasional night care, which the long-suffering Rosie pays for. Apart from that—nothing. I didn't see any of the gadgets and apparatus in her house that are available to disabled people these days—or, at least, disabled people with money.'

'So, whichever angle you look from, Bob Gomer was innocent.'

'I believe so.'

'And that means that someone else set him up.'

'It's the only explanation I can see.'

'And if Gomer didn't commit a felony then he probably didn't commit suicide, either.'

Nat frowned. 'Now that's a different matter.'

'Is it?'

'Of course. We can deduce Gomer's innocence from the available facts and from what we know of the man. But we are dependent on what came out at the seance for any suggestion that he might not have taken his own life.'

'And we can't take that seriously?'

'No . . . I . . .'

'Which brings us back again to what made you come rushing hotfoot out to Florence.' Kathryn sat back with a smile of triumph. 'I rest my case.' She looked at her watch. 'I must be getting back. We're having an early lunch,

71

then going up to Siena.'

'Lucky you,' Nat said, as they emerged into the sunlit square. 'Where does Siena fit into the Browning story?'

'They went there in the high summer of 1859. Elizabeth was almost at death's door and had to be moved out of the heat. I suspect Robert also wanted to get her away from the dreadful Sophie Eckley.'

'Wasn't that the American woman who befriended Elizabeth and shared her interest in spiritualism?'

'"Smothered" would be a better word than "befriended". The Ecksleys were stinking rich East Coasters and Sophie was an aggressive do-gooder. She trailed her wretched husband round the world, always on the lookout for fresh victims to inflict her benevolence on. Elizabeth Browning fell into her clutches and was almost buried under an avalanche of gifts and letters dripping with effusive protestations of undying love.'

'The sort of person who needs affection and tries to buy it?'

'Yeah, and the sort who clings leech-like to any celebrities they come across. But what was worse from Robert's point of view was her obsession with spiritualism. She'd taken up the new craze with a vengeance and convinced herself that she was a gifted medium. For a couple of years Elizabeth was totally under her spell.'

'Not good for a marriage.'

'No sirree. Why don't you come along to our session at the hotel tomorrow evening? Kaminsky is doing a talk all about this relationship.'

'I might just do that. Are you sure I won't be in the way?'

'No, he will be delighted. And that will give you a good twenty-four hours to fit in your trip to Ferrara.'

'Ferrara?'

'Of course.' They had reached the hotel and Kathryn preceded her husband into the foyer. She turned and kissed him briefly. 'It's your only lead and I sure as hell don't want you prowling round here playing nursemaid. Eight o'clock tomorrow in the Sala Giotto.' She strode away towards the lift.

Qui Fecit Qui Fake It?

Don't let truth's lump rot stagnant for the lack Of a timely, helpful lie to leaven it!

Nat reached Ferrara in mid-afternoon not knowing what he would do now that he was there. He found a small hotel with a frontage on the Via Trente e Trieste hard by the cathedral and a rear courtyard where he was able to park his hired car. This gave him easy access to the centre of the old city from which all motorized vehicles were banned.

He felt the lightheartedness of someone stealing an unexpected holiday in a place he loved. No longer worried about Kathryn, he had enjoyed the drive through the vine-draped hills north of Florence and across the fertile plain of the Romagna and was delighted to renew acquaintance with the old capital of the Este dukes with its massive moated castle, Romanesque cathedral and the labyrinth of medieval streets and alleyways leading from the Via delle Volte. He had given little thought to the Gomer case during the journey because, as he told himself, the chances of learning anything pertinent to it during such a brief visit were remote. Despite what Kathryn and Barny might insist, he felt no inner compulsion to pursue to 'the last syllable of recorded time' the mystery of a vanished painting. He would make enough simple enquiries to placate his conscience and to be able to tell Pearl Gomer that he had given the problem his best shot. He would do a little gentle sightseeing, enjoy some of the local wine and gastronomic specialities, then return briefly to Florence, before heading home for his delayed sailing holiday with the boys.

So the response to his first request for information took him by surprise. Coming down from his room after a shower and a change of clothes, he went over to the reception desk and asked the custodian if, by the remotest chance, he knew someone by the name of Alberto Talenti. The man behind the counter was a thin nervous-looking individual with a floppy ginger moustache that gave him a perpetually mournful appearance. In response to Nat's question the receptionist's face seemed to freeze. The mouth below the moustache gaped open and the watery eyes stared back at Nat as though they were having difficulty focusing. It was some seconds before the features reassembled themselves into an obsequious smile. If the Signore would be good enough to wait a moment, the man said, he would make some enquiries.

Nat watched him retreat into an inner sanctum and, through its glazed door, he saw him engage in animated conversion with a thickset man, presumably the manager, seated at a paper-strewn desk. It was this man who hauled himself from his swivel chair and came out to meet his customer.

He donned a professional smile. 'Is everything satisfactory, sir? The room . . . it is OK. If it is not completely to your liking we can show you another . . .'

'The room's fine, thank you. Very comfortable. Perhaps your colleague misunderstood what I said. I am trying to locate—'

'Signore Talenti. Yes, yes, that is understood. You have not, then, heard?'

The man seemed reluctant to elaborate and Nat could only make a bewildered response. 'Heard? What?'

'Signore Talenti . . .' The man seemed to be searching for the right word. 'He . . . died.'

'Oh, I'm sorry. No. I did not know.'

'You are a business associate, perhaps?'

'No. In fact I never had the pleasure of actually meeting Signore Talenti.'

The manager seemed to be relieved. His shoulders relaxed. He nodded. 'A journalist, perhaps?'

'No, not that either. As a matter of fact I am interested in his art collection.'

That explanation had a further placatory effect. The man seemed much more comfortable now that he could fit his guest into the right pigeonhole. 'Ah, *si*, of course. I had heard that it was to be broken up.' He spread his hands. 'Unfortunate, eh?'

Nat gave a sympathetic nod. He said, 'Thank you for your help. It is unfortunate—'

The manager, still eager to be of service, interrupted him. 'You will need to speak with Signora Talenti. A moment. I will find her telephone number.'

Before Nat could stop him the manager went back into his office. Nat saw him rummage among his papers, find what he was looking for and scribble the information down on his notepad. He re-emerged and handed Nat the little square with the number in bold, clear figures. 'Please, sir, to use my telephone.'

Nat wanted to take stock of the situation before deciding what, if anything, he should do next. 'That's kind, but I don't want to impose . . .'

But the manager had already opened the little gate in the front desk and was ushering him through. 'No trouble at all, sir. It will be more private in here and you will want to talk with Signora Talenti as soon as possible. You have come a long way.'

Before he knew what was happening Nat found himself in the leather swivel chair while the manager stood beaming at him from the doorway. 'I will see that you are not disturbed, sir. Oh, and please tell the Signora that Arturo Bruni sends his salutations.' He closed the door quietly behind him.

Not for the first time in this business Nat felt that he was being propelled in a direction he was not completely sure that he wished to go. However, since there seemed no alternative, he picked up the receiver and punched in the number.

A woman's voice answered.

'Signora Talenti?' Nat enquired.

'No. Qui parle?'

'Signore Gye. Io arrivo d'Inghilterra.'

'Ah, si. Io dice la Signora. Momento, Signore Gye.'

The line fell silent while the maid or secretary went to find her mistress. It was apparently a long quest, for Nat waited fully a minute before the lady of the house came to the phone.

Now Nat had another surprise. 'Hello, Mr Gye from England. Have we met?' The voice had a pronounced Birmingham accent.

'No. I'm afraid this is a bit presumptuous of me, I'm just passing through Ferrara and thought I'd call very much on the off-chance.'

'How fascinating.' The voice was faintly mocking. 'I didn't realize I was that famous. What can I do for you?'

Nat improvised. 'Well, I teach at Cambridge University and naturally I've heard of your late husband's art collection and I just wondered whether there might be the remotest chance—'

'Oh, an art professor, eh?'

Nat did not disabuse her. 'It's a bit of a cheek but I'd greatly appreciate—'

'Well, why not? Sure. Come out here lunchtime tomorrow. I'll show you around and you can tell me everything that's going on in the old country. *Ciao!*'

'Oh, one more thing, Signora,' Nat added hurriedly. 'Arturo Bruni asked me to remember him to you.'

'Oily creep!' The words were spoken with real passion. 'You're not staying in his fleapit, are you?'

'Well, as a matter of fact—'

'Poor you! See you tomorrow.' The line went dead.

*   *   *

The Villa Talenti was to be found, according to Arturo Bruni, some ten kilometres outside Ferrara in the direction of Modena. The road was quiet in the middle of Sunday as Nat made his way through an open landscape speckled with patches of woodland and there was little to distract him from his thoughts. The woman he was going to meet had sounded formidable and shrewd. Nat could not help agreeing with her assessment of Bruni, harsh as it was, and he had little doubt that she would see through him equally quickly if he tried to keep up the pretence of being a visiting art expert. Better, he decided, to pose as an enthusiastic amateur with a particular passion for Renaissance portraiture and hope to steer the conversation in the direction of the missing Antonello. She just might have some ideas about anyone who could have had designs on it. He sensed that it might well be difficult to conceal from her the real reason for his own interest, though she was almost certain to enquire.

He knew that he had reached journey's end when he encountered a long wall beyond which stood a double row of poplars. Another kilometre brought him to a pair of wrought-iron gates. When he had announced himself on the intercom these parted to admit him to a long, straight drive leading to a solidly imposing castellated building of glowing pink brick. Nat reflected that the Talentis' country residence looked more like a fortress than *a villa in campagna.* Doubtless it was stuffed with ancient treasures which had to be protected.

The door was opened by a mid-thirties woman in a smart business suit who announced that the Signora was expecting him and led the way through an entrance salon whose proportions were immaculate and yet, somehow, chilling. A floor of mottled grey marble reflected walls of palest blue punctuated by alcoves containing classical statuary and above them ran a grisaille frieze of gods and goddesses who seemed to be enduring rather than enjoying the amenities of Olympus. The contrast presented by the next room could scarcely have been greater. Nat's eyes were assaulted by the glare of sunlight pouring in through a glazed roof and reflected from a wide expanse of water. He looked around and realized that what had once been an internal courtyard had been transformed into a swimming pool of almost vulgar proportions.

'*Il Professore Gye, Signora,*' his guide announced.

A figure sprawled on a recliner at the far side of the pool waved an arm languidly. 'Come on over, Professor,' Signora Talenti invited. 'Drink?' she enquired, as Nat perched on another lounger. 'Please help yourself.'

On a low table between them stood a tray with tall tumblers and a cut glass jug containing ice and slices of lemon and lime floating in an amber liquid. Nat poured himself a drink and sipped it. It was surprisingly potent but also refreshing and, already aware of the heat, he was grateful for it.

'I must put one thing straight, immediately, Mrs Talenti—'

'Sylvia,' his hostess announced. 'And you are?'

'Nathaniel—Nat to most of my friends.'

'Well, Nat, nice of you to call. I don't see many Brits here and you're the first professor.'

'That's what I wanted to explain. I'm not actually a professor. In fact—'

'Well, that's a relief. When you said you were from Cambridge University I pictured someone with glasses, a bald head and a stoop. That description doesn't fit you at all.'

Nat was aware that he was being minutely and unashamedly scrutinized. He had no compunction about staring back. That was a pleasurable enough experience, for Sylvia Talenti was an extremely attractive woman. He estimated that she was still the right side of thirty and blessed with a very slender figure, though that was difficult to judge because she was wrapped in a deep pink bathrobe. That garment enhanced her fresh

81

complexion. The face was a perfect oval and made up with such artistry and precision as to appear not made up at all. It was framed by long, lustrous hair that really did deserve the description 'golden'. The shrewd smile that curled her full lips told Nat that Sylvia Talenti knew she was being admired and took considerable pleasure from that knowledge.

'I am really from Cambridge,' he explained.

'Are all the teachers there as handsome as you?' she asked disarmingly.

Nat laughed. 'No, some have glasses, a bald head and a stoop.'

She joined in the laughter.

'I must confess that you are not exactly what I expected, either,' Nat continued.

'A beautiful young widow?'

'Something like that. I was sorry to hear of Signore Talenti's death.'

'Don't be.' A look of utter loathing momentarily disfigured her face. 'Dying was the only good thing the old sod ever did.'

Since there was nothing that could be said in response to that, Nat took refuge in his drink.

'I know what you're thinking,' his hostess went on after a pause. 'You think I'm a heartless gold digger, a beautiful model who exploited her sex appeal to ensnare a wealthy man and is now dancing on his grave. It's what everyone else thinks.'

Nat was embarrassed. Sylvia Talenti seemed

quite coherent but he wondered whether it was drink that was prompting her to unburden herself to a complete stranger. He tried to steer the conversation into a less emotional channel. 'What line of business was your husband in?'

That produced a raucous laugh. 'My God, you don't know? What a sheltered life you must live in Cambridge.' She drained her glass and held it out for a refill. 'What was Alberto's business? Well, do you want the upfront ones? There were newspapers, vineyards, food packaging—you name the pie, he had a finger in it. But you might find the other ones more interesting—prostitution, extortion, drugs. Many people will tell you that he was the most powerful man in Romagna and they're probably right. His arse-lickers—and he had plenty of those—called him the 'Duke' because he saw himself as a feudal lord, the reincarnation of the d'Este rulers of Ferrara. He was the great philanthropist, always in the headlines—building a new hospital wing, presenting big cheques to local charities, standing on the champions' podium to hand out prizes at sporting events. Everyone loved the Duke.' She sneered. 'Even many of those who knew where his money came from.'

Nat persevered in his attempt to divert the runaway diatribe on to a safer track. 'And some of that money went into building up his art collection?'

'Image building. Just another part of the act. Alberto Talenti, the man of culture, the great patron of the arts.'

'I guess there's nothing new in that. Think of all those old popes and aristocrats who patronized Michelangelo, Raphael, Titian and others. How many really cared about encouraging great talent as opposed to enhancing their own prestige?'

'No. I must give the bastard his due; he did know about art. He had a good eye for beauty. Paintings, sculptures, women. Oh yes, he was a clever collector. And passionate with it.'

'Do you plan to keep the collection together, perhaps extend it?'

Mrs Talenti suddenly sat up, flicking her long hair back over her shoulder as she did so. 'Let's go and have lunch. I've told them to serve it on the terrace. It's such a lovely day.'

She stood up and Nat followed her out through a doorway behind her, thankful to escape the humidity of the pool area.

A gentle breeze stroked the open landscape and ruffled the low shrub hedge which fronted the wide terrace at the back of the house. The conversational mood lifted with the change of location. Over a delicious lunch served by a white-gloved waiter they talked of life in Italy and England. Sylvia Talenti was fascinated to learn that Kathryn was the editor of *Panache.* It was a magazine she knew well, having been for some years a leading fashion model. She became animated as she recalled the world of catwalks and photographic shoots, of jetting to exotic locations and meeting members of the international social elite. That was how, at the age of twenty, she had encountered Alberto Talenti, a man twice her age, and been swept off her feet by his charm and his wealth.

'Of course, I thought it was love.' She gave a sardonic laugh. 'What the hell did I know about love? Alberto swore he couldn't live without me. What he meant was he had to have me for his trophy collection.'

'And now you are mistress of all this.' Nat waved a hand towards the villa. 'Most women would envy you.'

She nodded wistfully. 'I suppose so. They'd never understand that I'd cheerfully give it all up for the chance to go back to Solihull and start all over again.'

'So, why don't you? You are a free agent.'

'What's your interest in the art collection?' Once again the change of subject was abrupt.

'Pure self-indulgence. I've heard about it, of course, and since I was in the area I thought I might enquire whether there was any chance of seeing it for myself.' Nat decided not to abandon the disguise of the academic art expert he had inadvertently assumed.

'I'm surprised, Nat. It's a very private little collection. Alberto wasn't the kind of kid who shares his toys. He liked to gloat like a miser over his secret hoard. Who told you about his obsession?'

Nat was aware that his hostess was watching him very carefully and that his answer would be important. He shrugged. 'These things get around in specialist circles. Dealers, gallery directors, connoisseurs—everyone's intrigued by stories of masterpieces rumoured to be hidden away in old castles and aristocratic family vaults. Things like that are always more interesting than the great paintings and sculptures that can be readily admired in galleries or pass through the salerooms. There's a great deal of vanity in the art world. We all want to see things that no one else has seen.'

'So, if I show you what I have here you will be able to boast about it to your colleagues and rivals?'

'I wouldn't put it quite—'

'You see, I can only share my secrets with you if I can trust you to keep them. I acted on impulse when I agreed to let you come today. I'm an impulsive sort of woman. But now—'

'Oh, I quite understand.' Nat hastened to reassure her. 'Security is a major problem for all collectors. I can assure you that I would make no use of my knowledge without your express permission.'

Sylvia sat back with a long sigh. She gazed out over the plain. 'Men are very good at making promises.'

The waiter reappeared to clear the table and to set down on it a tray with a decanted wine and two glasses.

'Do you like Lachryma Christi, Nat?'

'I've only ever tried it once, but yes, it's a very distinctive wine.'

'They call it the Tears of Christ because the vines are grown in the bitter soil of Vesuvius with all its tragic history and yet the wine that comes from them is sweet.'

The waiter poured the deep red liquid.

'To the bitter sweetness of life,' Sylvia said, raising her glass and draining it at a gulp. She stood quickly. 'Will you excuse me while I go and change. Please relax and finish your wine. I won't be long.'

Nat was not surprised that this well-groomed woman took almost half an hour to assume what she considered a suitable persona for the afternoon. The result was a metamorphosis. Casualness was banished. Sylvia reappeared in a dress of apple green silk that flowed loosely around her yet also clung revealingly to her figure. Her hair was now caught up in a coil like an Anglo-Saxon torque on top of her head. The scent of jasmine wafted about her.

'Are you ready for the grand tour?' she asked as Nat stumbled to his feet. She linked her arm in his and led him back into the villa. Alarm bells sounded in his brain but they were muffled by alcohol and the nearness of this delectable creature.

They crossed the classical frigidity of the entrance hall and Sylvia opened a side door by pressing a number code on a key pad.

'Welcome to the play area,' she announced.

They were in a kind of internal cloister. To the left was a wall with doors leading to other rooms but on the right a series of arches gave access to a long gallery filled with beautiful things. There were no windows but pools of artificial light illumined the late Alberto Talenti's treasures. Small statues in bronze or marble stood on basalt pedestals and a score of paintings glowed from the walls.

Realizing that some comment was expected of him, Nat said, 'What a wonderful collection. Can you tell me about some of the items?'

Sylvia shrugged. 'They leave me cold. You're the expert.'

Nat advanced into the room, aware that his hostess was watching his reaction closely. With no informative gallery labels to help him he racked his brain to find points of reference that might enable him to say something intelligent and fervently wished that he had not drunk so much wine. His first impression of the pictures was that several of them vibrated with colour, gilding and exuberant voluptuousness. That suggested a Venetian rather than a Florentine orientation. He peered at what was probably a panel from an altarpiece. The ornate armour worn by two

Roman soldiers had an almost jewel-like quality. Mantegna? Surely not. 'This is very reminiscent of Mantegna,' he ventured.

Sylvia came and stood close beside him—very close. 'Could be. I wouldn't know. Alberto tried to educate me about his old bits and pieces but frankly they bore me. Well, most of them. This one I do like.' She pointed to a depiction of the Temptation of St Anthony. The old man was shown recoiling in horror on the left side of the painting but not, as in other versions Nat had seen, from assorted grotesque demons, but from two naked females whose charms and gestures left absolutely nothing to the imagination.

'Most unusual,' Nat suggested.

'It's by Giovanni Pallegrini. Alberto took me to see the exhibition of his work in London a couple of years ago. Even I enjoyed it. You must have seen it, too. Didn't you think it was very well done?'

Nat nodded gravely. 'Yes, remarkably well presented.' He was looking round for the Antonello da Messina portrait or, at least, a gap on the wall where it might have hung, and trying to work out how he might casually turn the conversation in the direction of the stolen portrait.

'I can see why your husband kept his collection so secret. It's breathtaking and obviously extremely valuable. Have you ever had any problem with attempted thefts?'

Sylvia laughed and Nat felt her body vibrating against his. 'This place is better guarded than Fort Knox. The security alarms are state of the art. There's a staff of twenty just looking after little old me and these bits and pieces, and the grounds are constantly patrolled by guard dogs. I wouldn't fancy the chances of anyone trying to break in here. Why do you ask? Have you come to case the joint?' She looked up at him with a sardonic smile. 'Are you planning a heist?'

Nat grinned. 'No, I confine my interest to studying art, not trying to acquire it. I just feel that it's a pity, the world being as it is, that more people don't get a chance to see such magnificent objects.'

That manoeuvre failed. His guide made no comment about lending objects from the collection for public exhibition. She steered him round the gallery and Nat had to concentrate on making what he hoped were suitably erudite comments on the works displayed.

They reached the end of the tour and were making their way back along the 'cloister' when they came to one of the doors that stood half open.

'This is my bedroom—my boudoir,' Sylvia said in a soft voice loaded with suggestiveness.

Nat was about to step hurriedly past when he stopped suddenly in his tracks. On the wall of the room facing the door was a small head-

and-shoulders portrait of a man. It was Antonello da Messina's *Portrait of a Doge*. Inadvertently he took a step towards it. His eyes fixed on the painting, Nat was only half aware that Sylvia had entered behind him, closed the door and was leaning against it. 'That's a fine piece,' he observed, nodding towards the painted panel.

'Oh, that,' she said dismissively. 'It's nothing.'

'Oh, I wouldn't say that.' Nat went forward and peered closely. He had never seen the original but, even to his untrained eye, the subtle flesh tones, the colours of Mocenigo's intricately embroidered cap and the subtle half-smile, half-sneer that played about the lips screamed quality.

Sylvia came up beside him and her arm encircled his waist. 'Alberto was paranoid about his pictures. Terrified at the thought of having them stolen. Every time he bought something he had it copied. That way, if a piece did go missing he would at least have something to remember it by and the duplicate might help him to recover it. That is the copy.'

'I see. So where is the original?'

Sylvia pouted at him. 'You haven't come into my room to talk about boring old masters, have you? There's something in here more interesting than that picture. You're not like St Anthony, are you? You don't want to resist.' She pushed him gently and he sat heavily on a velvet-covered stool.

A snake pit of emotions coiled and churned within him. Part of him was more than ready to submit but his better feelings warned him to keep the siren at bay. Then there was that other voice that said, 'Don't upset her—you're within an ace of finding out the truth about the picture.'

He tried to stand but Sylvia was in front of him now, her hands on his shoulders. 'Won't you satisfy my curiosity—first?'

A light frown drifted, cloud-like, across her face. 'OK, it was my fault. One of Alberto's old friends who now runs a gallery in England wanted something for an exhibition. Alberto was away in the States for several months. I thought he wouldn't mind, so I said this guy, Jonah Theophrast, could borrow it. God, with a name like that you'd have thought I'd have had more sense, wouldn't you? When Alberto found out he was furious. He told me to get it back but days later he got himself killed and I had other things to think about. The picture went to England and, of course, it was stolen. That'll teach me, won't it?'

With a quick movement, she hitched up the green dress around her thighs and straddled him. Her arms went round him and she bent forward to whisper in his ear. 'So now the copy stays in my room to remind me to be on the lookout for fakes. Fakes like you, my dear.'

Nat's hands had begun involuntarily to

feel the slippery silk. Suddenly alarmed, he stopped them. 'Whatever do you mean?'

Sylvia giggled. 'Giovanni Pallegrini! I made him up. He never existed so there couldn't have been an exhibition of his work in London. You fell for it hook, line and sinker.'

'I'm sorry.'

She ran her fingers through his hair. 'Does it look as though I'm angry?'

'I really should explain . . .'

'Later, Nat, or whatever your name is.' She writhed her body against his.

Somewhere from deep in Nat's fuddled brain a gleam of common sense appeared and pierced its way to the surface. He knew he had to regain control of the situation. The woman was holding him very tight and making low growling noises and his body was definitely responding. He took a deep breath. He cleared his throat.

'Mrs Talenti,' he said, in what he hoped was a firm, authoritative voice, 'will you please remove your breasts from my face?'

There was a long frozen moment. Then Sylvia jumped to her feet. 'How dare you!' she screeched, her visage distorted with humiliation and rage. It was as though an immobile mask of perfect beauty had been torn away to reveal a reality of appalling ugliness. 'You trick your way in here . . .!' The woman was almost incoherent. 'Bastard! Fucking bastard! What do you think . . .'

Nat stood up. For a moment he thought the termagant was going to fly at him with claws flailing. Instead, she turned her back.

'Look, I'm really sorry,' he said. 'It's just that—'

'Get out!' she shouted. 'Out! Out! Out!'

Without another word, Nat did just that.

Other Worlds

. . . wise men hold out in each hollowed palm
A handful of experience, sparkling fact
They can't explain . . .

'Whew! What randified you?' Kathryn lay back, her chestnut hair spread out over the pillow, and stared up at the ceiling of her hotel room.

Beside her Nat smiled. 'Can't a chap show how much he misses his wife without being accused of having some other stimulus?'

He had returned to Florence an hour ago and caught up with Kathryn just as she and her party returned from an excursion to Siena. They had retired to Kathryn's room in order to shower and change before dinner but had very quickly ended up in bed.

'Not when the wife knows him as well as I know you,' Kathryn replied. 'Just what have you been up to in Ferrara?'

Nat clasped his hands behind his head. 'I'm not sure. Finding loose wires that might or might not be connected.' He gave a résumé, slightly censored, of his meeting with Sylvia Talenti.

'So what did you make of her?'

'Lonely. Unhappy.'

'Beautiful bird in a gilded cage?'

'Something like that. She has an army of servants but, as far as I could tell, no friends, no companions.'

'No lovers?'

'It would seem not.'

'So, why doesn't she sell up and go back to mum?'

'I asked her that and she clammed up completely. I got the impression she isn't a free agent.'

'Do you think she's expected to stay on as lady of the manor, filling her husband's place?'

'I doubt whether Ferrarese society is that feudal. Anyway, Mrs Talenti is a foreigner.'

'What of her late and very unlamented husband?'

'Obviously a top drawer mafioso. I got the impression that his demise occurred in a fairly bloody and typical manner for someone in his line of business.'

'Which would explain your red carpet treatment at the hotel.'

'Yes, they're obviously terrified of the Talenti organization. What seems to have happened is that Don Alberto got his comeuppance in a violent takeover bid and now rival factions are squabbling over control of his empire. Anyone who has any dealings with them is worried about getting caught in the crossfire. That proved quite useful. The manager thought I was some kind of associate, so he treated me with kid gloves. When I called back at the hotel this afternoon I pumped him for more information and he was very co-operative.'

'So what about the painting?' Kathryn asked. 'Is it a copy or the genuine article which has mysteriously found its way back home?'

'Couldn't say. It looked pretty convincing but, then, so was Sylvia Talenti's story about it. I didn't get a really good look at it.'

'No.' Kathryn propped herself on one elbow and looked down at him, a wry smile on her lips. 'You were otherwise engaged, weren't you?'

Nat sighed deeply. 'That's for sure.'

She kissed him lightly. 'You sound as though you regret putting up a heroic resistance.' She stared hard at him. 'You're quite sure you *did* resist?'

'Oh, yes, but I'm not all that proud of myself. She was quite right about me. I was a shameless fraud. One little deception led to another and I ended up treating her pretty shabbily.'

'Oh, I wouldn't mind betting she had you

pretty well sussed from the beginning. She certainly didn't tell you anything useful.'

'Not altogether true. She made it very clear that her late husband was an Ivy League criminal *and* she let on that Theophrast, the gallery director, was an old friend of his.'

'So you reckon the two of them put their heads together to abduct the portrait—presumably as an insurance rip-off?'

'Well . . .' Nat paused thoughtfully. 'According to the golden-haired Signora, lending the picture was her idea and her husband was furious when he found out.'

'And, of course, we believe the poor grieving widow, don't we?' Kathryn suggested with a sardonic smile.

'Miaow!' Nat grinned. 'No, I'd say she was a pretty accomplished, spontaneous liar. She took me in completely with her story about the St Anthony painting.'

'Well, I don't see that you're any further forward and I certainly think you should distance yourself permanently from the clutches of the Talenti woman. Time to call it a day. You can report back to Pearl Gomer with a clear conscience. Tell her that you gave it your best shot.' Kathryn looked at her watch. 'Hey, come on, we can't laze here all day. We're going to be late for dinner.' She jumped out of bed and grabbed up clothes from the floor.

Nat remained beneath the sheets. 'I did get

97

one lead—from my eager-to-please hotelier. I asked him if by any chance he knew who did restoration work on the Talenti collection and immediately he took me into the office to show me the register. It seems that an expert from Rome paid frequent visits to the Talenti villa and sometimes stayed at the hotel. So I have a name and address to follow up.'

Kathryn was struggling with the zip of her dress and only half listening. 'Will you get out of that pit and make yourself decent? We should have been downstairs five minutes ago.'

With a groan Nat rolled himself out from beneath the covers.

*　　　*　　　*

'The "great authority" sat there completely po-faced and pronounced that Caroline Lamb was quite right to call Byron "mad, bad and dangerous to know". I looked at him hard and said, "Dr Coulter, wouldn't you say that was better than being null, dull and sanctimonious for show?" I tell you, you should have seen his face; it could have sunk a thousand ships.' Kaminsky threw back his head in a braying roar of laughter.

Kathryn said, 'Didn't I read somewhere that Coulter died a few months back?'

Kaminsky's reply snapped back immediately. 'Oh, he's been dead for years; folks have only just gotten around to noticing.' Again came the self-approving belly-laugh.

The term 'OTT' might have been invented for Errol Kaminsky. The American was enthusiastic and effusive in everything he did. He greeted Nat with a bear hug, told him how delighted he was that his 'old friend' had been able to join the party and insisted on having the Gyes at his dinner table, for 'what you English call a chinwag'. The resulting conversation turned out to be little more than a monologue. Kaminsky gave a detailed account of his rapid rise through the academic ranks, spiced with some wicked and occasionally funny anecdotes about prominent figures in the world of literary studies.

There were six people gathered round the table and Nat gained the distinct impression from their body language that they had heard several of the Professor's stories before and were tiring of both them and him. There was a sudden lull as Kaminsky energetically waved his napkin to attract the attention of a waiter. A thin, elderly lady sitting opposite Nat grabbed the opportunity to say, 'Dr Gye, Kathryn tells me that you are a lecturer in psychology.'

'Parapsychology,' Nat replied with a smile and was about to expand on what the subject covered when Kaminsky shouldered his way heavily back into the conversation.

'Nat, you couldn't possibly have joined us at a better moment. Right after dinner I'm delivering my lecture on the Brownings and the Eckleys. I guess you'll have some interesting thoughts on that.'

'I'm sure your expert opinion on spiritualism will be far more interesting than anything I might be able to contribute, Errol,' Nat replied, guessing correctly that the sarcasm would be lost on Kaminsky but not on the other diners.

When the group convened in the Sala Giotto after dinner they found that the chairs had been rearrranged in circles. Taking his place in the inner ring, Errol explained:

'I thought we'd be less formal this evening. As you know, we move on to Rome tomorrow for the climax of our seminar and I wanted to encourage a free flow of ideas about this relationship we've been exploring as we approach its sad, I might even say its tragic, conclusion.'

The cultural shepherd beamed around at his attentive flock. 'Friends, I've tried to find a word, an expression, which would sum up the life of Robert and Elizabeth in their last months together. The best I can come up with is "tumult". Armies were marching to and fro across Italy. The passion for unity had reached a new, an irresistible intensity. Elizabeth lived to witness the birth of the new nation, whose first parliament met in June 1860, and her heart came close to bursting with joy for her adopted country. The Brownings were caught up in the excitement of these events—the eager expectation of birth . . . and its pain.' The words tumbled from Kaminsky in an effervescent torrent, accompanied by ebullient hand gestures. 'But there was tumult also in their personal lives. Robert, whose patient devotion had liberated Elizabeth, not only from the claustrophobic, oppressive tyranny of her father's regime, but also from the depression and physical debility to which she was prone, found himself supplanted in her affections by another—by Sophie Eckley.'

Kaminsky described how the wealthy American couple, David and Sophie Eckley, had entered the Brownings' lives and immediately 'adopted' the poets, showering them with expensive gifts and paying for shared holidays. 'Sophie,' he asserted, 'was a monster, possessive and obsessive. Brought up as a rich New England brat, she was determined always to get her own way and to control those around her. David was her willing slave and, for a time, Elizabeth Barrett Browning was swept up into her admiring entourage. There were two hooks on her line, two weapons in her armoury, two spells in her book. One, of course, was her wealth. She used that to obligate people to her, to buy their gratitude and affection. The other was spiritualism. This was the current craze sweeping high society and Sophie wasn't slow to observe the power it gave to self-proclaimed mediums, who asserted their ability to link folk with their departed loved ones. Daniel Dunglas Home had just stunned the international *haut monde* by becoming engaged, in Rome, to a Russian countess. I believe this was, for Robert, the final straw that broke the back of his reticence on the subject of spiritualist charlatanism. He had tried arguing with Elizabeth but was quite unable to shake her faith in Home and other manipulative tricksters. So, he poured out his anger in the long poem, "Mr Sludge, the 'Medium'", which is nothing less than a vicious attack on Home and his whole tribe. Of course, he never showed it to Elizabeth and the poem wasn't published till after her death.

'But to return to Sophie Eckley. Realizing how susceptible Elizabeth was to all things of the spirit, Sophie "discovered" that she possessed the gift of mediumship. When the two couples spent much of 1859 and 1860 together in Rome Mrs Browning fell completely under Sophie's spell. She regarded the American woman as her "spiritual sister". They engaged in spiritual writing together— that is, they sat with pens poised waiting for ghostly hands to guide them—and they practised thought transference. And all poor Robert could do was look on and fume silently within. What made it worse for him was that his wife actually seemed to thrive on all this nonsense. We know this from Elizabeth's letters. This is what she wrote to her sister back in England: "Intercourse with the unseen makes me calm and happy—full of hope and understanding of the two worlds." And to her spiritual sister she wrote imploring her to initiate her further into the mysteries of that other world with which she was so familiar: "Tell me more, more, as you know it, for there is nothing to me of such grand and at the same time intimate significance." And Robert? Well, he could only watch in miserable impotence. He experienced the bitterness of having to acknowledge that his wife was being kept alive by two things—morphine and Sophie Eckley's supposed revelations.'

The audience was hanging on Kaminsky's every word and Nat acknowledged to himself that the American told a good story with panache. He listened with interest as the speaker came to the end of his narrative. In the summer of 1860 Elizabeth Browning had suffered a relapse and Robert had taken her to Siena. There her physical health had somewhat recovered and, away from Sophie's persistent influence, she had come to her senses and realized that her 'spiritual sister' was nothing but a manipulative fraud. She had written a long more-in-sorrow-than-in-anger letter and broken off their relationship. Inevitably, blind devotion had turned to virulent contempt. Elizabeth felt herself to have been deceived and betrayed but she was also disgusted with her own naivety, with her refusal to be guided by the one person who genuinely and selflessly adored her. The relationship between husband and wife had been sorely bruised and would never completely recover. In a final peroration Kaminsky rounded on Sophie Eckley and the 'cruel delusions' of spiritualism as contributory factors to the final deterioration of Elizabeth Barrett Browning and her death at dawn on 29th June 1861.

Kaminsky sat back in his chair. There was a long moment of silence, then the tension was broken with a burst of vigorous applause.

The Professor made a deprecatory gesture. 'Thank you. Thank you. Before we take questions and feedback I have an unexpected treat to announce. We have with us one of the world's foremost experts on the paranormal and I know we will all be fascinated to hear what he has to say about the influence of spiritualism in the lives of our two poets. Ladies and gentlemen, friends, it's my privilege to introduce to you Dr Nathaniel Gye of Cambridge University.'

Nat smiled, muttered, 'Thank you,' then, realizing that a more elaborate response was expected of him, he said, 'That was a fascinating exposition, Errol. I must confess to knowing much less than you about the Brownings' brush with spiritualism. Perhaps a few more general comments might be helpful?'

He paused to collect his thoughts as a murmur of welcoming approval rumbled through the audience. 'I suppose I'm always a bit worried by the use of words like "fraud" and "fake",' he began. 'Certainly there have always been charlatans around—conjurors, alchemists, pseudo-magicians, hucksters, sham mediums, people who prey on our fascination with and fear of the unknown. But it's equally true that there have always been people who believe they have some insight into whatever it is that lies beyond the material universe. If that weren't so there would be no religions and very little art or literature to speak of.'

Someone said, 'Hear, hear' in a high-pitched voice before Nat went on.

'Now, it seems to me that something very interesting was going on at the time the Brownings were living here in Florence. For centuries the vast majority of people had believed that there was a world beyond this one, a spirit world, and that it was more important than the world we can experience through our five senses. Then along came the physical scientists. They made stupendous advances in understanding the universe and that implied a challenge to anything that didn't fit in with their concept of reality. Some, but by no means all, claimed that there was no longer any need for a spiritual realm; everything could be explained in terms of scientific "laws". I think it's very difficult for us to understand just how profoundly disturbing all this was to men and women of traditional belief. It seemed to them that religion and morality were being undermined. They hit back fiercely and throughout the second half of the nineteenth century an intellectual war raged, which drew in most thinking men and women.'

Someone behind him asked, 'Do you mean the row between Darwin and church leaders over evolution?'

Nat nodded, getting now into his stride. 'The natural selection debate is, of course, the best known. Darwin provides us with a very pertinent case in point. His own family was deeply split on the spiritualist issue. His brother-in-law, Hensleigh Wedgwood, was a founder member of the Society for Psychical Research and they had fierce arguments.'

Beside him Kathryn coughed pointedly.

Nat looked round apologetically. 'Sorry. I'm getting long-winded. The point I'm trying rather clumsily to make is that Christians and deists of all kinds were ready to grab at any straws which seemed to *prove* that material existence is not all there is, that there's another world, a world which lies totally outside the competence of scientists to probe. I'm sure it's this that explains the sudden appearance of spiritualism and the explosion of interest in table rappings, spirit voices, objects flying through the air. They all seemed to provide evidence to confute the wilful, often arrogant disbelief of the scientists. I like your word "tumult", Errol. The quest for meaning in which the Brownings and the Eckleys were caught up was just that—tumultuous. So, was Sophie a deliberate fraudster or was she driven—were they both driven—by unconscious needs to reassure each other about the supernatural?'

The debate that followed was vigorous and as Nat and Kathryn sat in the hotel bar afterwards enjoying a nightcap, several people came up to thank Nat for his contribution.

'You made quite a hit,' Kathryn said as she sipped her G and T. 'Quite stole Errol's thunder.'

'I hope he didn't mind. He did invite my opinion.' Kathryn laughed. 'Oh, he loves an argument and you won't have shaken his conviction that Sophie Eckley was the very princess of darkness, throwing mud into the poetical fountain which fed both the Brownings.'

'Robert was certainly intensely bitter. I've been reading "Mr Sludge" again. Vitriolic stuff. I guess his experience with Sophie convinced him that all mediums are fakes.'

'Aren't they?'

'Not if they genuinely believe in the spirit world and are convinced they've had some experience of it.'

'But surely—'

'Look, suppose you meet someone who says he's seen an alien spaceship or the ghost of a lady in grey. Simply to dismiss his claim as unscientific nonsense would be in itself unscientific. You'd have to look for the truth in that person's psyche. Ask such questions as "Is this guy an attention seeker?", "Is he prone to hallucinations?", "Is his story supported by any other witnesses?" In my experience many scientists are incredibly bad at sticking to the first article of their creed—"Keep an open mind."'

'I think Robert Browning would have agreed with you on that. He got just as angry with what he regarded as scientific arrogance as with spiritualist naivety. What was it he said about the evolutionists?' She closed her eyes in an effort of memory.

'I climb, you soar.
Who soars soon loses breath
And sinks. Who climbs keeps one foot firm
    on fact
Ere hazarding the next step.'

Nat grinned. 'Good for Robert.'

Kathryn drained her glass, then yawned. 'I'm ready for bed. Early start for Rome tomorrow.'

They made their way to the lift, saw a crowd of people waiting for it and headed for the staircase.

Kathryn asked, 'Do I take it that you're coming along for the ride?'

'Now that I'm here . . . Anyway, I may as well try to find this picture copyist.'

Kathryn stopped halfway up the first flight. 'Are you crazy?'

'What do you mean?' Nat recognized the angry gleam in his wife's eyes.

'When you discover a hornets' nest it's not a very bright idea to stick your head in it.'

Nat stared back for several seconds, then continued the climb. 'Since I'm going to be in Rome anyway there's no harm in locating the artist who's supposed to have done a copy of the stolen painting.'

Kathryn marched up the stairs behind him. 'And what will you do when you find him? Blunder in and say, "Excuse me, aren't you the crook who used to fake old masters for that well-known mafioso, Don Alberto Talenti?"'

'Don't be silly!' Nat stood aside for a couple who were on their way down. They gave him a disapproving glance as they passed.

'*Me* be silly! A few days ago it was you who were having kittens because of some crackpot prophecy that I was going to be in danger. Now you want to go charging into a situation that really is dangerous.'

'You're exaggerating.'

They had reached the second floor and Nat held the fire door open for Kathryn. She stood in the corridor beyond, arms akimbo. 'My

God, Nat, you can't see it, can you? You're still thinking in terms of some piffling art theft in England and a guilt-ridden security guard who topped himself. Now it appears that Bob Gomer was on the outer edge of something bigger—a hell of a lot bigger. We're talking major gang crime. You know, professionals. Men for whom assassination and kneecapping are all in the day's work. If Talenti got himself gunned down by his own people they're not going to think twice about some foreigner who's making a nuisance of himself. For heaven's sake, just tell the police what you know and leave it at that.'

They had reached Kathryn's room. She jabbed the key card into the lock and went in.

'But, darling, that's all I intend to do,' Nat said as he followed her. 'I just need something concrete to give them, that's all. At the moment I don't have anything they'll pay any attention to. I've seen a picture that *might* be stolen or *might* be an honest copy. If I report that they'll pat me on the head and say, "Thank you, Signore. Very interesting," and do not a damned thing about it.'

'Well, that will be their problem, won't it? You'll have done all you can.' Kathryn strode into the bathroom and slammed the door.

'That's just it,' Nat shouted at the panelled woodwork. 'I won't have done all I can. Someone's responsible, directly or indirectly, for Gomer's death. If I went home knowing that I could have done something to bring that person to book and that I'd failed to do it . . .' There was the sound of the lavatory flushing and he did not bother to finish the sentence.

The following night was uncomfortable. Nat lay beside a figure as rigid as a stone statue and drifted in and out of sleep haunted by dreams in which he seemed to have entered into some old master painting. He saw himself cowering before a taunting troupe of naked Sylvia Talentis while an ethereal Bob Gomer, enthroned in cloud, urged them on.

The Price of Silence

I know I acted wrongly: still I've tried
What I could say in my excuse . . .
. . . And I've lost you, lost myself,
Lost all . . .

Nat's quest took him across the Tiber into Trastevere. He found the establishment he wanted in a back street close by the art gallery of the Palazzo Corsini. In this socially muddled region of Rome, Renaissance and Baroque mansions, long since appropriated for museums or government buildings, rub shoulders with boisterous taverns and what were originally artisan dwellings but have now become fashionable 'pads' for the arty subculture. Some streets overlook or back on to the Botanical Gardens but between them straggle narrow passageways which still mark out the lanes of the old village.

The day had not started well. The ice wall between him and Kathryn had scarcely thawed at all and the more she displayed her disapproval of his 'irresponsible, self-indulgent sleuthing', the more determined he had become to find out all he could about Antonello da Messina's *Portrait of a Doge*. They had both affected a relaxed, 'normal' pose in public and Nat had travelled from Florence in the coach which brought the seminar party to the capital. Having been adopted by the Browning aficionados, he checked into their hotel, sharing a room with his wife. Kaminsky had gathered his brood together to go off for lunch in the Caffe Greco, on the Piazza di Spagna, where the Brownings had mingled with the likes of Tennyson, Thackeray, Walter Savage Landor and other denizens of what was known in the nineteenth century as the 'English ghetto'. Nat had excused himself in order to pursue his own agenda. Now, in the warm mid-afternoon, he stood with his jacket over his arm gazing across the street at an establishment whose weathered signboard declared that these were the business premises of *'P. Bregnolini— Commerciante di Pitturi'*. The small window was tastefully arranged with two Venetian canal scenes on easels.

Nat's first impression was that this was an odd place to find what had every appearance of being an upmarket gallery. He looked up and down the quiet, almost deserted road. In one direction a group of children played close to a car that filled almost half the width of the street. In the other two elderly ladies in black sat on a low wall talking with their heads bent close together. There were no other signs of life. Several of the buildings, a mix of shops and private houses, presented frontages which were decidedly rather dingy. Did this mean that Signor Bregnolini could not afford more prestigious premises or, contrariwise, that he had such an assured reputation that, wherever he was located, his customers would beat a path to his door?

That door stood now intriguingly ajar, presumably, Nat guessed, to allow a cooling through draught. A strange indulgence, though, for any shopkeeper in these security-conscious days. Nat took a turn along the narrow pavement in order to check over in his mind the script he had devised for himself.

As he passed the parked car the driver's window slid down and a man called to him, *'Mi scusi, Signore.'*

Nat stopped and smiled. He thought to himself, why is one always asked for directions when one is no position to give them? The man fired off a salvo of rapid Italian, of which

Nat was able only to pick out a few words. He shrugged and explained in guidebook phrases that he was a stranger here himself and foreign, to boot.

The stranger muttered something to his companion, then, glancing back at Nat, he said, 'Sorry. Excuse me.' Nat thought that he was probably stretching his own English vocabulary to breaking point. The window was closed.

Nat resumed his slow walk. He assembled the sentences that he planned to try out on the art dealer. He was, he would explain, custodian of a small collection of inherited paintings faced with an enormous annual insurance bill. He was exploring the possibility of having copies made which he and his family could enjoy while the originals were locked away in a bank vault. Signora Talenti had recommended Signore Bregnolini on the basis of a facsimile he had made of a portrait by Antonello da Messina. Nat hoped that he would be able to gauge something from the dealer's reaction. He turned at the end of the street and retraced his steps. When he was once again opposite Bregnolini's gallery he stepped across the road's uneven surface, pushed the door open and went in.

The scene that met him was one that might have been described as expensive chaos. Here were not the manicured interior, the pastel-coloured walls and the focused spotlights such as one would find in an exclusive establishment in Bond Street, the Faubourg St Honore or, indeed, in Rome's own Via del Corso. There were some exquisite paintings on display but there were as many empty spaces and other pictures were stacked haphazardly against the walls along with empty gilded frames. A desk in one corner was unmanned but Nat could hear voices coming from the other side of a closed door which stood behind it. He pondered again on Bregnolini's casual attitude towards security. It would be easy, he thought, to scoop up an armful of valuable art and make off with it. But then, he reflected, perhaps this was not valuable art. What if all this casual profusion of artefacts represented only the proprietor's skill as a forger?

The muffled conversation between two male voices continued and Nat wondered whether he should tap on the door to announce his presence. As he raised his hand to the unvarnished oak he heard the sound of another door being slammed, followed by silence. He knocked on the unvarnished oak. There was no reply. He knocked again with the same result. This time he opened the door cautiously and peered round into the room beyond.

If the shop itself was something of a jumble, this was total confusion. Canvases, papers, brushes, cans of solvent, old jars containing nameless brown substances, two chairs (one broken), a large easel, piles of books and magazines, several empty wine bottles littered the area between where Nat stood and an outside door opposite. He steered his way through the obstacles to this back entrance, yanked it open and looked out.

He was confronted by a small, untidy, walled yard. To his left there was a passageway between the building and its neighbour and from this there came strange scuffling sounds. Nat looked round the corner and was just in time to see a group of three men at the street end of the alley. They were making heavy weather of it because two of them were half marching, half dragging the third, who was clearly reluctant to go.

Nat shouted something and took a couple of steps after them. One of the trio, whom he immediately recognized as the man in the car, raised an arm and pointed at him. There was a crack and a shower of brick fragments flew at him from a point inches above his head. Nat ducked and retreated round the corner. He returned to the back room, negotiated his way to the shop, cautiously crossed to the front door and peered along the street. He saw an unwilling passenger, presumably Bregnolini, being forced into the back seat of the car. One of his captors followed while the other, still brandishing a gun and looking behind him, jumped into the driver's seat. Seconds later the vehicle leaped forward and accelerated at a speed reckless of anyone who might have got in its path. It turned the corner and a surreal calm fell upon the street. The children played and the old women gossiped as if nothing had happened.

Nat realized that he was trembling. He went across to the desk and sat down in the swivel chair behind it. His thoughts were fluttering chaotically like birds in a dovecote. He was sweating. His pulse was racing. It was several minutes before he could consider what he should do. There was a telephone before him but he did not know how to make an emergency call in Rome. He would need to find help. Best get back to the hotel and locate someone there who could alert the police. As soon as he had recovered something of his composure, Nat locked up the premises as securely as he could, made his way to a main thoroughfare and hailed a taxi.

The first person he encountered in the hotel lobby was Errol Kaminsky. The large American came up to him, an anxious frown on his face.

'Nat, hi. You OK?'

'Sure. Why shouldn't I be?'

'Heard you were in a spot of bother.'

Nat thought, news travels fast but not that fast. 'What do you mean?' he asked.

'When we got back from the Spanish Steps about quarter of an hour ago this woman was waiting for Kathryn. She said you'd been involved in something unpleasant. Naturally Kathryn was worried. She went with her straight away. I was afraid you might be in hospital or something. It's a relief to see you safe and sound.'

Nat felt as though all the blood had been drained from his body. 'Woman? . . . What woman? . . . Who was she? . . . Did she leave a name?'

Kaminsky looked nonplussed. 'Not with me. She may have given a name or address to the receptionist. She was talking to someone at the desk when we came in. Then your wife was pointed out to her and she walked over to us. Seemed like a nice enough woman. Is there . . .'

But Nat was not listening. He strode across the foyer. The receptionist was dealing with an elderly woman who was flustered about something or other. 'Excuse me,' he said, butting in. 'My name is Gye. I gather my wife met someone here a few minutes ago.'

'*Si*, Signore, if you'll just wait a moment.'

'No, I can't wait. This is urgent. Do you know who my wife met?'

The girl's polite smile was set in aspic but her eyes warned that she was not to be browbeaten. 'No, Signore, I do not. Now—'

Nat tried to keep any note of hysteria out of his voice. 'I'm sorry to be persistent but I believe Mrs Gye is in danger. *Please,* if you know anything . . .'

The receptionist heaved a deep, theatrical

118

sigh. She rummaged beneath her desk and produced a white envelope. It had his name typed on it. 'The lady left this,' she announced. Then, very pointedly, she turned away from him.

Nat strode to a corner of the vestibule and sat in an armchair. He ripped open the envelope. The message was sparse and in English: 'Be on the first London plane out of Rome. Tell no one. Do as you are told and your wife will be returned unharmed.'

Nat slumped forward, head in hands. 'Oh, my God, what have I done?' he groaned.

'Hey, friend, what's the matter? Bad news?' Nat looked up to see Kaminsky's frowning face.

'Errol . . . hello . . . No . . . er . . .' Nat struggled to be coherent. 'It's just . . . something unexpected. Excuse me.' He hurried away to the seclusion of his room.

He sat on the edge of the bed and tried to force himself to think clearly. He read the note a dozen or more times. 'Your wife will be returned unharmed.' Could he believe that? Could he trust these people—whoever they were? He thought of the art dealer being bundled away by gun-toting thugs. What was it Kathryn had called them? 'Men for whom assassination and kneecapping are all in a day's work.' What had they done to Bregnolini? What would they do to Kathryn? He glared at himself in the bedroom mirror.

119

'You bloody fool! Why didn't you listen to her?' Then he told himself that breast-beating would do no good at all. What he needed— what Kathryn needed—was that he should keep a clear head.

Nat began to pace the room. He had two options. He could do as he was told or go to the police. He hated the idea of the criminals getting away with the abduction of innocent people but would the Carabinieri or the Guardia be able to do anything? Doubtless they had their files on these people but would they know where to look for them and their prisoners? Would they simply waste valuable hours in plodding bureaucracy—taking statements and interviewing suspects? Nat pictured himself being subjected to hours of pointless interrogation. What could he tell the police that would be of the slightest use to them? That he had inadvertently upset members of the late Alberto Talenti's organization? That Bregnolini was involved with them and that he, too, had been abducted? Every hour that passed would raise the likelihood of the criminals carrying out their implied threat. Their intelligence was obviously of a high order. It had only taken them a few hours to track down Kaminsky's party and locate Kathryn. They would be watching closely to make sure that he followed their instructions.

But why Kathryn? The question struck him

with sudden force. They could have captured Nat himself in Trastevere this afternoon. Why target his wife? What could they possibly want from her? Again Nat stared into the mirror. 'Think! Think! *Think*!' he ordered himself.

If they wanted to discover what he knew, why he was asking awkward questions, they ought to be interrogating him. So why snatch Kathryn? Presumably to kill two birds with one stone. They could quiz her about Nat's snooping into their affairs and they could frighten him into giving up his interference. If that was their game, they had certainly won hands down. The only thing Nat wanted was to get Kathryn back all in one piece and close the accursed Gomer file for good and all.

But, if he followed the kidnappers' terse instructions, would they keep their side of the bargain? It might prove easier to drop her in the Tiber or dispose of her in some nocturnally dug grave out in the country.

Nat went to the wardrobe, took out Kathryn's clothes. He started to pack and with every item that went into her familiar holdall he vowed what he would do to anyone who harmed her in any way.

Protesting Too Much

And if at whiles the bubble, blown too thin,
Seems nigh on bursting,—if you nearly see
The real world through the false,—what do
  you see?

When Kathryn was approached by the dumpy but well-dressed Italian woman with the pink highlights in her hair she knew instinctively that something was wrong.

'Mrs Gye, I am Maria Strossi, *polizia giudiziaria*—what you would call CID.' The woman flashed an identification card. 'Your husband—'

'My God, Nat!' Kathryn gasped. 'What's happened?'

The police officer smiled reassuringly. 'It is nothing serious but you should come.' Her English, though heavily accented, was fluent.

'Yes, yes, of course.' Kathryn looked around distractedly and saw Kaminsky just entering through the revolving doors. 'I'll just tell my friend.' She made her way across the foyer, through the gaggles of returning seminar members. 'Errol,' she gabbled, 'something's happened to Nat. I have to go. I'll call as soon as I can.'

The woman was waiting by the door. She ushered Kathryn out, down the broad flight of steps and into a large, black car which was waiting. Kathryn found herself sitting in the back beside a burly man in a grey suit who stared straight ahead and ignored her completely. The woman sat in the front beside the driver, equally darkly clad and silent.

'Is he injured? In hospital?' Kathryn asked anxiously.

'He is OK. You will see. Just routine,' the woman muttered, without turning. Then she, too, lapsed into muteness.

When no one had spoken for several minutes and her own questions were ignored, dark suspicion crept into Kathryn's mind. These people were not behaving like any police officers she had ever met. When the car passed the same cinema for a second time she knew something was wrong.

'Where are you taking me?' she demanded loudly. No response.

'Who are you? You're not police.'

She grabbed the door handle and tried to turn it. It was deadlocked.

'Let me out! Let me out!' She was shouting now. But all to no effect. Only when she grabbed the driver's shoulder and yelled, 'Stop the car! Do you hear? Stop this instant!' did she achieve any response. The man beside her fastened a vice-like grip on her wrist so tight that she squealed with sudden pain.

'Keep quiet and you'll come to no harm,' the woman announced dispassionately. 'If you are a nuisance my colleague will exert whatever force is necessary to restrain you.'

'OK, OK. But you're going to regret this.' Kathryn's arm was released and she shrank into the corner of the seat.

The journey lasted for over twenty minutes but Kathryn could see that they were taking a circuitous route and guessed that they had not, in fact, travelled very far. At last the car came to a halt at the back of a smart apartment building. Kathryn was bundled out and, flanked by the two men, hustled inside. A service lift took them to the top floor. They emerged into an empty corridor. The woman went on ahead, and opened a door and they all entered.

Kathryn found herself in an expensively furnished penthouse. The decor was minimalist, with white hide sofas and chairs and chrome light fittings. It was all very clinical, not lived in. She had little time to observe her luxurious surroundings. She was marched across the deep pile carpet and thrust through a doorway. The door was closed and locked behind her and she found herself alone.

She was in a large bedroom, immaculately decorated in shades of blue and pink and totally lacking in personality. She crossed immediately to the window and found herself staring into space. The building she was in was taller than its neighbours. As far as she could see there was nothing but a jumbled roofscape.

The window itself was firmly locked and resisted all Kathryn's attempts to move it. A door in the opposite corner led into a bathroom complete with shower and jacuzzi. A quick glance showed that it was an internal room. With a sinking feeling in the pit of her stomach Kathryn realized that she was hermetically sealed into her sumptuous prison.

Kathryn took off a shoe and banged on the outer door but there was no response and when she pressed her ear to the glossy woodwork she could hear no sound. Her captors, it seemed, had deposited her and gone away. She threw herself down on the wide bed and gave way to a jumble of emotions.

It was three and a half hours before her solitary confinement was relieved. She heard sounds from the sitting room and, minutes later, her door was opened. Her two male captors had returned and they beckoned her to a table where food had been set out. A single place had been laid at the long dining table and tempting aromas emerged from covered dishes. Kathryn stood her ground, demanding to know how long she was to be kept here against her will. The men staunchly kept up their Trappist act. Cautiously Kathryn moved to the table. She was certainly hungry.

Twenty minutes later, when she had dined off an excellent saltimbocca washed down with a more than passable Chianti, she was ushered back to the bedroom and once more locked in.

She heard her guards clear the table and leave the apartment. Once more silence fell.

An hour later they were back. This time both of them came into her room. They were accompanied by the woman who called herself Maria.

'Please put your hands together behind your back,' she ordered in a matter-of-fact voice.

'I'll do no such thing,' Kathryn shouted, retiring into a corner.

Moments later she had been dragged back to the centre of the room where her wrists were firmly tied together behind her. The woman stepped forward with a black silk bag rather like a cushion cover. She raised it to slip it over Kathryn's head.

Kathryn screamed. Visions of hooded prisoners being led out to firing squads rose before her. She struggled violently but the grip of her captors only tightened.

'Don't be frightened.' Maria donned a smile that was, presumably, intended to be reassuring. 'It's only a blindfold.'

When the bag had been forced over Kathryn's head she was, indeed, 'blind'. The men led her through the doorway and into the adjacent room. They helped her into one of the leather armchairs. She sensed the presence of another person before she heard him speak. The voice was rough-edged with what seemed to be a southern accent. She found it impossible to get the gist of the rapid Italian.

However, the woman interpreted for him.

'Mrs Gye, we regret this discourteous treatment but it is the activities of your husband that have made it necessary.'

'Where is he?' Kathryn shouted. 'What have you done to him?'

The emollient reply was relayed through the woman. 'Like yourself, Mr Gye is being detained in comfortable conditions. No harm will come to either of you—if you co-operate fully.' The hint of menace was unmistakable.

'This is all a ridiculous mistake.' Kathryn forced herself to be calm and reasonable. 'Whoever you are, we pose no threat to you. We're only here to attend a symp—'

She was cut short by a grunt of annoyance from the unseen Mr Big.

The interpreter was quick to interject. 'We will ask the questions. Confine yourself to answers. Who does your husband work for?'

'He is a lecturer at Cambridge University.'

'He lectures on art or art history?'

'No, he is in the Psychology faculty.'

There was a pause and a muttered conversation between the interrogators. Then, 'When he is not lecturing who does he work for?'

'He doesn't work *for* anybody else. He writes books and sometimes presents television programmes.'

'What is his connection with the police?'

Kathryn faltered. 'The police? He has no

127

connection with the police.'

'Or Interpol?'

'Certainly not. I told you, there's been a terrible mistake—'

'What is his interest in valuable works of art?'

Oh God, Kathryn thought. What has Nat told them? How can I make my story tally with his? She said, 'Purely an amateur interest. He enjoys visiting galleries and exhibitions. He collects—in a very small way.'

'He came to Italy to see the Talenti collection. Why?'

Again, Kathryn tried to think fast. Inside the opaque hood it was uncomfortably hot and stuffy. She felt sweat on her brow. 'He didn't tell me much about it. I think he knew there were some interesting items in it and he thought that, while he was in Italy, he would see if Mr Talenti would allow him to view them.'

'The collection is private. Very few people know of it. How did your husband come to hear of it?'

'I'm afraid I don't know.'

When her reply was relayed to Mr Big he became very voluble. Angry sentences poured from him in a torrent. Their translation was remarkably brief.

'We find it difficult to accept your explanation. Please do not try our patience or we will be forced to use other methods to get to the truth. Now, what was Mr Gye's interest in the Talenti collection?'

Kathryn's head swam. Her parched throat craved water. The suffocating heat was intolerable. Her mounting anxiety unbearable. She felt herself swaying. Being held upright by powerful hands. Then, mercifully, all sensation ceased.

*   *   *

When Kathryn came to she was lying on the bed in her prison room. There were no lights on and beyond the window the day was fast fading into night. She sat up and rubbed her chafed wrists, which still bore the marks of the cords. She tried the door, more in hope than expectation. It was, once again, locked and no sound came from beyond. Clearly, she was alone again.

She remained alone all the following night. Or rather, she spent the darkness hours in the company of a thousand fears. She lay between the sheets thinking of Nat and Jeremy and Edmund, of the blonde siren of Ferrara, of an ex-Beaufort College servant slipping into easy death in a fume-filled garage, of Elizabeth Browning dying, less easily, here, in Italy, of press headlines reporting mysterious disappearances. Then her thoughts returned to Nat. Was he somewhere in this city? Perhaps in this very building and only yards from where she lay, sweating and frightened between ruffled sheets.

*   *   *

Nat shared every one of his wife's anxieties and every second of her sleeplessness. But not in Rome. He was over twelve hundred miles away, sick with worry, guilt and frustration but obliged to go through the motions of ordinary life as casually as possible for the sake of the children. He called his father on Wednesday, the day after his return, and asked if the Canon would not mind driving the boys home. He excused himself the chore by lamely explaining that something had 'cropped up' to detain him in Cambridge. The truth was that he was waiting, hour after hour, for a call from Kathryn or her captors and did not dare to be away from the phone. He tried to work, as much to keep at bay the sick-making worry as to fulfil his numerous obligations. That proved almost impossible. It was vacation time—no lectures or supervisions to be given. The college was deathly quiet. Many of Nat's colleagues as well as the undergraduates were away.

There were, however, domestic matters that had to be attended to. One was stocking up the fridge before his sons' return. On Wednesday afternoon he made an excursion to the supermarket. It was while he and his half-

130

laden trolley were en route from Cakes and Biscuits to Frozen Desserts that he almost literally bumped into Rosie Hardwick. She was accompanied by—or, more accurately, she had in tow—a heavily built man in his forties with close-cropped hair and an ear stud.

Nat was about to pass with a smile and a nod when Rosie said, 'It's Dr Gye, isn't it?' Turning to her companion, she continued, without drawing breath, 'Ted, this is that university bloke Pearl called in, though why he should want to trouble himself with her and her crackpot friends I'm sure I don't know, I'd've thought he had better things to do with his time.'

'How is your sister?' Nat enquired politely.

'Worse by the day. I've arranged for her to go into St Luke's Hospice. They're equipped to deal with the likes of Pearl. I really can't cope any more. Anyway, me and Ted've got our own lives to lead, haven't we, Ted?' Without waiting for her husband's confirmation, she went on, 'We don't intend to stay in this dump for the rest of our natural.'

Nat smiled at the long-suffering Ted. 'You must be Mr Hardwick. I'm Nathaniel Gye.' He held out his hand and the other man somewhat diffidently shook it.

Before he could say anything his wife was again in full flood. 'Pearl isn't over the moon about going into the hospice but I know she'll appreciate it when she gets there. They're wonderfully caring people.'

Nat wondered whether Rosie Hardwick would recognize a caring person if she saw one.

'And it'll get her away from that godawful George woman.' Mrs Hardwick's nose wrinkled as though it had just been assailed by a particularly unpleasant smell. 'Ooh, what I'd like to do to her. She's an evil, dominating, manipulative woman. She lords it over all those poor souls at the spiritualist church, you know. Well, I suppose you *do* know, Dr Gye, you being an expert in all that communing with spirits rubbish. These so-called mediums make a packet out of poor souls who're grieving over the dead, don't they? I've tried reasoning with Pearl—heaven knows I have, time and again—but it's no use. Well and truly in Mrs George's clutches, she is. She tries to tell me the woman doesn't make money out of her sessions but I know better. You don't get to live in a big, smart house like hers without raking it in from somewhere.'

Nat took the opportunity of a rare pause in the discourse to ask Ted Hardwick, 'Do you still work for Samson's?'

'Yes, it's been, let me see, how many years . . .'

'How many?' Rosie spluttered a contemptuous laugh. 'Too bloody many, that's how many. Still, not much longer, eh, Ted?'

'Planning a change?' Nat asked, looking at Ted.

But it was Rosie who answered. 'A good friend of ours has moved to Spain and he keeps on phoning to tell us how good the life is there and how we ought to go and join him. So, it's off to the sunshine we are, away from all this godawful English weather. Going to lead a life of ease, we are. Villa overlooking the sea . . .'

Ted gave his trolley a shove. 'Must get on, dear. I don't suppose Dr Gye wants to stand here gossiping all day.' With that, he nodded to Nat, muttered something that might have been 'Nice to meet you' and set off purposefully in the direction of Cold Meats.

As Nat continued his own shopping he reflected that he could well understand why Ted Hardwick had a job that involved a great deal of travelling.

The boys returned the next day and Nat was relieved that he did not have to field a lot of questions about the whereabouts of their mother. Twelve-year-old Edmund and his younger brother, Jeremy, were quite used to Kathryn being away on business trips and were never curious about her movements. Not so their grandfather.

'I thought you and Kathryn were coming back together,' Canon Gye probed as they worked in the garden in the afternoon sunshine. The boys were kicking a ball about on the lawn and Nat's father, secateurs in hand, was prowling the borders, snipping here and giving horticultural advice there.

'The seminar doesn't finish till today,' Nat lied.

The elderly clergyman bent to pay close attention to a rose bush that was in danger of overgrowing itself. He plied his tool with savage efficiency. 'Things all right between you two?' he asked without looking up.

'Yes, of course.'

'Forgive the question. It's just that when a man rushes after his wife in a foreign country, then returns without her . . .'

'Well, I can set your mind at rest on that score. Kathryn wanted to stay for the whole seminar and I have a mountain of work that I daren't leave to get any higher.'

'So what's bothering you, then?'

'What makes you think . . .'

Canon Gye straightened up and stared Nat in the eye. They were of similar height and build, the older man's ascetic frame kept in trim by physical as well as spiritual exercise. 'Because I have a pastoral sixth sense. Because I know you would not have disappointed the boys over their sailing trip without good cause. And because you never have been able to pull the wool over my eyes. Something is troubling you and a trouble shared is a trouble halved.'

Nat lent on the spade he was using to trim the lawn edge. He sighed. 'It's a long story.'

His father smiled. 'So is Christianity but I'm trying to cope with it.'

Nat went over the events of the past weeks, while Canon Gye listened in silence, occasionally plying the secateurs. The sun was warm on their backs and the air around was alive with the sound of territorial birdsong and the children's laughter. The story of violent death and abduction seemed bizarrely out of place amidst this comfortable suburban normality.

'Now, with every hour that passes,' Nat concluded, 'I keep asking myself whether I did the right thing. Just walking away feels like deserting Kathryn, letting her captors do whatever unspeakable things they want to her.' He slumped on to a garden bench.

Canon Gye sat down beside him. 'It's no consolation, I know, but I would agree that, given the situation, you did the only thing you could do.'

'Yes, but trusting violent criminals to keep their word . . .'

'My intuitive impression is that it's not in their interests to harm Kathryn.'

Nat grasped at what he wanted to believe. 'Why do you say that?'

'Well, let us try to analyse logically your Italian adventure. Presumably it was your visit to the Widow Talenti that set the cat among the pigeons.'

'Yes,' Nat muttered miserably, 'I thought I was being so damned clever but she was obviously suspicious . . .'

'And angry at having her advances spurned. Hell hath no fury!'

Nat nodded. 'And that. I suppose she alerted her late husband's colleagues that some Englishman was snooping around. They certainly reacted very quickly.'

'Yes, but cautiously.'

'What do you mean?'

'Well, think about it. They check on the seminar party's movements—not difficult with their contacts—but they don't take any action apart from keeping a watch on the art dealer's establishment. It was only when you turned up there that they made a move. They wanted to be sure that you didn't meet Signore Whatsisname . . .'

'Bregnolini.'

'Yes. And it was only after that that they abducted Kathryn. So, it seems pretty obvious that they are not indulging in kneejerk or gratuitous violence. If they simply wanted to silence you they could easily have done so at Signore Whatsisname's shop, couldn't they?'

A vivid memory of ducking flying bullets flashed into Nat's mind. 'I suppose so.'

'And their reasons for taking Kathryn are, we may safely assume, twofold.'

'To find out what I know and to ensure my silence.'

'Both of which objectives they will have, by now, achieved. Kathryn, being a sensible girl, will have told them all they want to know—

namely that her husband is a well-meaning busybody who poses no threat to them.'

'Yes, but what worries me is the methods they've used to get the information out of her.'

Suddenly, a football landed in the Canon's lap. He leaped to his feet, deftly dribbled it down the lawn and eventually allowed Edmund to win it off him. He returned to the seat. 'Where were we? Ah, yes, how the captors are likely to treat Kathryn.' He gazed out across the line of limes that marked the end of the garden. 'A few of us in the close at Wanchester have a poker school, a fact which would, doubtless, alarm some of our congregation. Of course, we don't play for high stakes. In fact, the money isn't important at all. It's more an exercise in applied psychology. You can learn a surprising amount about people if you play poker with them. Canon Albright believes that his face gives nothing away but I can read his eyebrows. They flicker when he has a good hand. Our dean is the biggest stick-in-the-mud you can imagine in chapter meetings but at the green baize he takes the most outrageous risks.'

Nat scowled. 'What's this got to do with Kathryn?'

'Only that we should learn to observe patterns of behaviour. So far her captors have not overreacted. That leads me to suspect that they won't do so now—and for a good reason.'

'Well, it's one that escapes me.'

137

'Supposing they had gunned you down at the dealer's shop. Can't you imagine the tabloid headlines—"TV don killed in Mafia shoot-out". Similarly, if Kathryn went missing or was seriously harmed there would be a great deal of press interest. Stories of British victims of foreign crime always sell papers. That would mean vigorous police activity—perhaps even diplomatic activity—between London and Rome. And that is the last thing the criminals need. Whatever you've stumbled on is something they want kept very quiet.'

'I wish I knew what it was.'

The clergyman shook his head emphatically. 'It's as well that you don't. We must hope that Kathryn can convince them of your ignorance and that you are no danger to them. The point I'm making is that whatever their guilty secrets are, they don't want to attract undue attention to them. So, I'm sure they'll continue with their softly, softly approach.'

'You're just trying to cheer me up,' Nat said mournfully.

'Not at all. I'm sure we should not allow false optimism to colour our judgement but, by the same token, we must not assume the worst. I've always held you and your family in my prayers and I'd like to think they have had some influence. Your crusading attitude to other people's problems, which by and large I admire, has got you into several scrapes and this is undoubtedly the worst of them but somehow you always manage to come out on top.' He stood up to continue his gardening. 'All will be well, I know it. There's a special providence that watches over holy fools and perhaps you qualify as a member of their club.'

That night, as Nat tossed and turned in bed, his father's words kept echoing in his head. 'Holy fool! Holy fool! Holy fool!' I don't know about the 'holy' bit, he thought, but I've certainly been stupid. He reran his memory tape, going over the sequence of events that had led up to the present crisis. There was the medium's warning about Kathryn being in danger in Italy. Should he have taken it more seriously and talked her out of joining the seminar? Or had he, in fact, taken it too seriously by rushing out to Florence just because she had not phoned? Was it his fault that she was now in the hands of murderous thugs or, if things had fallen out differently, would she simply have met up with some other misfortune? Nat imagined his father, with his habit of quoting old proverbs and epigrams, insisting that there was 'a divinity that shapes our ends, rough hew them how we will'. What a lame excuse, Nat reflected bitterly. We make appalling cock-ups and blame them on unseen powers.

It was as first light edged the bedroom curtains that the phone rang.

139

Scared to Life

There's something in real truth (explain who
  can!)
One casts a wistful eye at, like the horse
Who mopes beneath stuffed hay-racks and
  won't munch
Because he spies a corn bag.

In his haste to grab the receiver from the
bedside table Nat dropped it on the floor,
spent panicking seconds fumbling for it, then
got it tangled in the loose sheets.

'Hello! Hello!' he almost bellowed as soon
as he had pressed the implement to his ear.

'Nat?'

With soaring relief he heard Kathryn's
voice. 'Darling, is that you? How are you?
Where are you? Are you OK?'

'Darling, I'm fine. Really.' She certainly
sounded it. 'Don't worry. I'm at the airport.
Pisa. My flight's due off in half an hour and I
have a burly escort here to make sure that I'm
on it. I'm due in at Heathrow at 8.25 your
time. Can you meet me?'

'Yes, of course.'

'Good. See you then.'

'Fine. Kathryn—'

'No time now. Tell you everything later.
Drive carefully. Love you.' The line went dead.

*　　　*　　　*

Nat did *not* drive carefully. On the M25 he hooted and weaved his way through more than three miles of tortoise-like, nose-to-tail vehicles, he had a close shave with a taxi on the airport slip-road and was still ten minutes late. By the time he had parked and rushed into the terminal building it was 8.45. He checked the arrivals board, saw that the Pisa flight was in and joined the small crowd of people waiting to meet friends and relatives. He scanned the trickle of travellers as they emerged, some flight-weary, others waving enthusiastically to those who had come to greet them. There was no sign of Kathryn. Surely she must be here. The phone call could not have been a cruel trick by the kidnappers . . . could it?

Suddenly arms encircled him from behind. He turned and she was there, smiling up at him.

'Did I startle you? I was first off. No luggage.'

Nat hugged her to him, wordless. At last he was able to murmur, 'I'm so sorry.'

She kissed him tenderly. 'No need. Everything's fine now. Can we go home, please?'

In the car, travelling more sedately northwards, Kathryn told her story.

141

'This woman turned up at the hotel. Very pleasant. She said you were in some sort of trouble. My first thought was, Oh God, he's got himself mixed up with some dodgy characters and they've done something horrible to him. I had visions of you dumped in a back street with blood all over you.'

'Darling, I'm sorry.'

She gave him a look which was half smile, half frown. 'If you say that again I'll clobber you!' Kathryn described her captivity in the penthouse apartment and her interrogation by her abductors. 'That was Tuesday. Wednesday was the same again, only more so. Solitary confinement; regular meals; punctuated by third degree questioning. Same questions over and over again.'

'That must have been terrible.'

'Strangely, it seemed to be worse for them than for me. Once I'd decided what I was going to tell them and not tell them all I had to do was play the same record over and over. But the boss man got progressively more angry. At one point I thought he might start knocking me about but he vented his spleen on the underlings. That was when he made his mistake. They all obviously assumed that I had no Italian at all, so, when he got really agitated, the boss man ranted and raved and let slip one or two interesting facts that I wasn't supposed to know. He told the woman that she was to "make out"—*fingere*—that you

142

were under lock and key and would be tortured if I refused to tell them what they wanted. He said that it had been stupid to let you go. I got the impression that there had been a cock-up somewhere in the organization. It was a great relief to know that you were safe. It meant I could ignore their threats and stick to my story. I think in the end they must have been convinced.'

'They didn't ill-treat you?'

'No. All day Thursday—yesterday—they left me alone. Then, at some horrendous hour this morning, they got me up and the terrible trio drove me to the airport. They gave me a first class ticket, stood over me while I called you and stayed there till I boarded the plane.'

'And that was it?'

'Yeah, apart from a little parting homily from Maria, or whatever her name is.'

'What did she say?'

'That any inconvenience I had suffered was all your fault. That you should keep your nose out of other people's business. That I must make sure you forgot whatever you thought you had discovered. That we shouldn't think we were safe in England. That they would know if we continued to take an interest in their affairs. And that, if we crossed their path again, we would not escape with our lives.'

'Whew!' Nat exhaled slowly. 'Well, they needn't have any worries on that score. There's no way I'd risk putting you through all that again. The Gomer file is definitely closed.'

'Like hell it is!' Katherine shouted the words.

Nat, concentrating on swinging into the outside lane to pass an overtaking lorry, was not able to respond immediately. As he steered back into the middle lane he said, 'What's that supposed to mean?'

'It means that whatever those bastards are up to, we're not going to let them get away with it.'

'But the other day you said—'

'That was before I had the dubious pleasure of making their acquaintance. After what they've put me through I want to see them all behind bars.'

'That's understandable, darling. There's part of me that agrees with you. But . . . no, you were right when you tore me off a strip back in Rome. I was stupid, headstrong, hubristic to think that I could act as a one-man army against international crime. These things are best left to the experts.'

'Huh!'

'Huh, what?'

'Do you really think that the *experts* are going to do anything?'

'Probably not, but—'

'Look, Nat, I've been doing a lot of thinking all the way over in the plane. Even made some notes. Why don't we get off this motorway and find somewhere quiet where we can discuss

144

things properly. Anyway, I could murder a beer, even at this hour.'

Twenty minutes later they were sitting at one of the outside tables of a small Essex pub. Kathryn took eager gulps of lager while Nat dutifully sipped a glass of Coke. 'OK,' he said, 'what's on your mind?'

Kathryn took out of her bag—a new one bought in Florence—an airline menu card scribbled all over with her own almost illegible scrawl. 'Well, the most obvious fact is that you've stumbled on something big enough to worry these Italian crooks. From the questions they kept on asking it's clear you saw something in Ferrara you weren't meant to see. Hopefully, I was able to convince them that you don't understand the significance of the missing portrait.'

'Great, let's leave it that way.'

Kathryn scowled. 'And let them get away with coming over here to murder poor Bob Gomer?'

'We don't know that they did.'

Kathryn swallowed her frustration. 'OK,' she said, 'square one. A fabulous painting went AWOL and miraculously turned up eighteen months later back in its owner's house, where it's hidden away from prying eyes. What does that suggest?'

'Insurance fraud.'

'Exactly. And when we find out that Dr Theophrast, who borrowed the painting for his

145

gallery, is an old buddy of the Talenti character, that clinches it.'

'Not "clinches" exactly. At best it gives us a working hypothesis.'

'Oh, for heaven's sake, Nat,' Kathryn spluttered, 'stop playing the prissy academic!'

'Can't help it.' Nat grinned. 'I am a prissy academic.'

Kathryn peered at her notes, ignoring the intervention. 'So, what happens next? You show an interest in the portrait in Madame's boudoir and she quickly responds, "Oh, it's only a copy." You, quite rightly, don't buy that and when you try to check the story the poor guy who's supposed to have done the work gets bundled into a car.' Kathryn mused, 'I wonder what happened to him.'

'I expect they just shook him up and let him go—like you.'

'Yeah, and that's the next point,' Kathryn rushed on eagerly. 'We got off pretty lightly. Why was that?'

'Because they wanted to scare us off without drawing attention to their activities. If you or I had gone missing in Rome the police and the press would have investigated our movements.'

Kathryn looked disappointed at having her deductive ace trumped. 'You have been doing some thinking about all this, then?'

'I've been running over the possibilities in my mind.' Nat said nothing of the conversation with his father. 'All this is very feasible but whoever has taken over the Talenti organization, with its octopus-like tentacles, wouldn't go to all that trouble just to cover up one example of fraud. Compared to the drug business it can only be a tiny part of his operation—almost a sideline.'

Kathryn nodded vigorously. 'Precisely! I'm way ahead of you, brother. What about all those other pictures in the oh-so-secret Talenti collection? Where did they come from? I'll bet IFAR would be interested in that little lot.'

'IFAR?'

'International Foundation for Art Research. Their main job is tracking down stolen works of art. We did a feature on them in the magazine a couple of years ago. I'll look it out when I get back to the office. What I do remember is that art theft has become a major feature of syndicated crime. The mobs use paintings, sculptures and so on as currency for buying drugs and arms. It's a way of getting round the money-laundering problem. I'll bet my bottom dollar that what you saw was a Mafia strong room.'

'That doesn't make sense. Why was I allowed to see it?'

'I asked myself the same question. Could it be that La Talenti was lusting after your body so badly that she threw caution to the winds? I dismissed that notion as ridiculous.'

'Thank you very much!'

'You're welcome. Then I tried to put myself

147

in her position. She gets into a loveless marriage with a top level crook, who runs her life for her and doesn't let her be her own person. That's bad enough but after he's killed life gets worse. She knows too much about the organization to be allowed to leave the country. You, yourself, said she seemed like a prisoner in that grand villa. Well, that's exactly what she is. Her late husband's associates watch her night and day. She can't go where she pleases, make her own friends, throw parties. She's trapped. What does she do? Well, I know what I'd do in her place. I'd rebel. Perhaps only in small ways but the choice would be between that and going mad. So when you turned up out of the blue she thought, What the heck; this is my house; I'll invite whoever I want.'

'Then, afterwards, she has to face the music from her minders.'

'And how! They'll know that she's taken you into the inner sanctum and they'll want to find out exactly what happened there. It doesn't take much guesswork to think what she would have told them: "That Englishman was a fake who wormed his way in here in order to snoop around in dear Alberto's collection." '

Nat stared out over a mill pond which reflected the vivid green of willows coming into full leaf, the advance guard of summer. Kathryn's recreation and analysis, he reflected, chimed very closely with what he had worked out. The difference lay in the conclusions they drew from these events.

'All this means that we'd better stay well clear of these people. They have international connections and I've no doubt what they said to you about watching us to make sure we behave ourselves was absolutely true. I blundered in once and, more by luck than judgement, got away with it. It would be crazy to go round asking more questions.'

'But, Nat, these people are scum. They destroy lives—big time. We've got a unique opportunity to expose their operation, to enable the police to seize some of their assets. You can't seriously be suggesting that we walk away from it and let the crooks go marching on their pernicious way.'

Nat frowned. 'I still can't get my head round this amazing U-turn of yours. It couldn't have anything to do with your journalist's nose sniffing out a good story, could it?'

The barb went home. Kathryn sat back and looked him straight in the eye. 'Don't knock it, darling. It is a hell of a good story and I'm right at the centre of it. If we can get the low-down on these people and put a giant spoke in their wheel we'll be performing a major public service and, yes, I will be able to sell the story—worldwide syndication, TV rights, the works. It'll be worth millions.'

Nat stared back. 'Fine, if we manage to stay alive to spend them. I'm sorry, but it's far too risky. They'd be on to us long before we had enough evidence to lay before the police. We can't go probing Theophrast, that's for sure, and I reckon they must have had someone on the inside at Samson's, the security firm. So we can't go asking awkward questions there.'

'Do you imagine I haven't thought about that? Theophrast isn't a problem. I can get one of my journalist friends to do an interview with him.'

'For *Panache*?'

Kathryn pursed her lips indignantly. 'Now, that would be *really* stupid, wouldn't it? I'll get some freelance to do a piece on the Bath gallery. There'll be no possible connection with my magazine. Meanwhile, you can find out how the picture vanished.'

'I'm flattered by your confidence. That's a puzzle that's defeated everyone who's looked into it.'

'Don't be so defeatist. Ask your conjuror friend—unless you suspect him of having links with the underworld.'

'If you mean Victor Zeeman, he prefers to be called an illusionist.'

'Whatever. If anyone can work out how the trick was done, he can.'

Nat stared moodily into his glass.

'Oh, come on,' Kathryn goaded. 'You're dying to solve this riddle; you know you are.'

' "Dying" might be the appropriate word.'

'And you're still angry about what these

people did to the Gomers. You'll never forgive yourself if you walk away from this opportunity.'

'I'll certainly never forgive myself if anything nasty happens to you—or to me, for that matter.' He stood up. 'Come on, we'd better be getting back.'

Kathryn stepped over and threw her arms around him in a bear hug. 'Darling you're the boss. If you say no, then no it is, but at least think about it seriously.'

He held her close. 'Subtlety, thy name is woman. If I go ahead—and it's still a very big if—you're not to be involved. I'm not going to risk losing you again.'

'Deal,' Kathryn responded immediately. Behind Nat's back her fingers were firmly crossed.

Unlocking

. . . those tricks
That can't be tricks, those feats by sleight of
    hand,
Clearly no common conjuror's . . .

Columns of scarlet smoke writhed upwards. Ethereal music from the Dolby sound system wafted over the rows of empty seats. In the middle of the stage a large, shimmering steel box was suspended from chrome chains. The synthesized wailing hit a crescendo and, with perfect co-ordination, the sides and bottom of the hanging cube flew open to reveal empty space. Four cloaked female assistants stood in statuesque poses, arms aloft, backs to the audience. They turned, throwing aside their coverings to appear as lightly clad, nubile bodies. Except one. This figure was revealed as a slender man in jeans and T-shirt, his hair drawn back into a long pigtail. He stepped to the front of the stage and made a deep, theatrical bow. Nat, three rows back in the stalls, applauded.

Victor Zeeman—'Big Zee' as his name appeared on the playbills—peered into the auditorium. 'Nat, is that you? Be right with you.' He turned upstage. 'OK, gather round, people. Where's Penny?'

As the illusionist's surprisingly large entourage formed a circle around him, a bulky, middle-aged woman appeared from the wings, clipboard in one hand, stop-watch in the other.

'How was that for time, Penny?' Victor asked.

'We could still do with shaving three seconds off the cube opening,' the woman replied.

Big Zee nodded. 'Fine. Did you get that, Tom? We'll go through it once more before lunch. Otherwise, I'm happy. Let's take five.'

As the crowd dispersed, the illusionist ran

lithely down the steps from the stage. He clasped Nat's hand warmly then slipped into the seat beside him. 'Good to see you, again, maestro. How's things?'

'OK, and you? I see you're still keeping yourself remarkably fit.'

The other man groaned. 'Don't mention it. That's the worst part of this job. The tricks are easy: the dieting is hell.'

After some more initial small talk Victor asked, 'So, Nat, what's on your mind? Need my help with another ghostbusting TV show?'

'No, Victor, I've got a real life puzzler I'm hoping you can help me with.'

'Sounds intriguing. Shoot.'

What Nat admired most about this professional entertainer was the absence of showbiz airs and graces. Victor Zeeman was a man of many thoughts and few words. He had actually done a stint in an American university as a professor of media psychology before branching out as a corporate consultant and stage magician. Now, the showman listened with eyes-closed concentration as Nat went over the story of the disappearing painting. When it was finished he asked several questions.

'So,' Nat asked after a pause, 'any ideas?'

'Not really, because you haven't told me everything.'

Nat frowned. 'I don't think I've left anything out.'

Victor chuckled, an attractive, low, bubbling sound. 'Now don't get me wrong, old friend. I'm sure you haven't consciously left out any detail you think significant. The thing is that your judgement is faulty. I know because my act is based entirely on getting people to make false judgements, making them believe they've seen something they haven't seen—and vice versa. I don't need to tell you how the brain works, constantly sifting the thousands of signals it receives every minute, selecting what it considers important and discarding the rest. Look, up there.' He pointed to the back of the stage where two of the theatre staff were working. 'Now, that chap with the sandy hair, what's he just done?'

'He's walked from stage right to stage left.'

'Uh-huh, and in the middle of the stage there's a Greek pillar, right?'

'Yes.'

'So, for a fraction of a second, as Ginger moved behind it, he was invisible.'

'Yes.'

'So, how do you know that the man who walked behind the pillar is the same man who emerged from behind the pillar? The answer is, you don't. Your brain doesn't have the necessary information, so it makes a deduction. My job is to make sure that my audience makes the wrong deduction and goes on making similar deductions all evening.'

'I see what you mean. So I need to question

every statement in Bob Gomer's account in order to distinguish what he thought was happening from what actually was happening.'

'That would be a good start but let me see if I can give you some leads. What we have here looks like a pretty neat trick. It involves a switch.'

'Well, that's obvious. Someone switched a valuable painting for a worthless slab of timber.'

Victor chuckled again. 'You see, there you go making deductions. How do you know it was the picture that was switched? It could have been the crate the picture was in or it could have been the van the crate was in.'

'But these were watched all the time.'

'Just like you watched Ginger walk behind the pillar?'

'I see.' Nat turned over in his mind some of the details of the case. At last, he said, 'There was something . . . but it can't possibly be relevant.'

'Observe first, deduce afterwards,' Victor said. 'The devil's in the irrelevant detail.'

'Well, it's just that Bob Gomer spent weeks puzzling about how the theft was done and he thought, at the end, that he was on to something because his vacuum flask went missing.'

'You mean he had it in the van but when the van was examined it wasn't there?'

'I assume that's what he meant.'

'There you are, then. It sounds as though the vans were switched.'

'But that doesn't help us. The painting had already disappeared by then.'

'So, we must be dealing with a double switch.'

Nat shook his head. 'I'm lost.'

Victor looked at him, his mouth arced in a wide grin. 'Clever,' he muttered. 'Classic but clever. Make the audience look in the wrong direction. Everyone goes into the gallery. They're only interested in the painting. Who cares about an empty van, heading out of the yard to get filled up with petrol? Of course,' he mused, 'it would have to be timed to perfection. I guess they only had a couple of minutes. And it would take at least three or four people to pull it off.'

'Yes, but why?'

'That's obvious. Because the painting—'

'Was still in the first van,' Nat burst in with sudden revelation.

'You can bet your life on it. While everyone was frantically searching the replacement van and the petrol station and getting in a high old state of agitation, the first van was miles away, carrying its valuable cargo and an empty vacuum flask. Oh, it's neat.' Victor laughed. 'I like it.'

Nat did not catch his friend's mood. 'But this only makes things worse for Bob Gomer. It suggests that during the journey to Bath he took the painting out of the crate, somehow concealed it in the van and substituted the wooden panel. I can't believe that. And anyhow, that would mean he'd have to break the gallery seal and fix another one to make it seem that the crate had not been tampered with. No,' he shook his head, 'it just doesn't hang together.'

Victor shrugged. 'In that case we've only solved half your mystery. But I assume that's better than nothing.'

'Yes, that's very helpful,' Nat muttered distractedly. 'Sorry, Victor, I didn't mean to sound ungrateful.'

'If you're absolutely convinced your friend was innocent, see if you can't think the first switch through in the same way that we've worked out the second. I'll give it some more thought myself and call you if I come up with anything.' He stood abruptly. 'Right now I'd better get these lazy layabouts back to work.' He shook Nat's hand. 'Good to see you again, Nat. Look, I'll get Penny to send you a couple of tickets for the show. Bring Kathryn and we can make a night of it.'

He turned to remount the stage and the last Nat saw of him he was clapping his hands and calling out, 'OK, people, let's move it. Where's Penny?'

Nat emerged from the theatre and stood briefly to collect his thoughts. Beside him there was a more-than-life-size cut-out of

157

Victor and a blown-up review quote, 'BIG ZEE AMAZES LONDON'. Before him traffic crawled along St Martin's Lane. It was moving so slowly that he decided against taking a taxi, calculating that he could get to King's Cross station by tube in time to catch the 12.15 back to Cambridge. That would enable him to grab a quick lunch in college before setting out for his meeting with Mrs George.

Over the weekend since Kathryn's return they had drawn up a plan of campaign. It was based on Nat's firm insistence that they should make their enquiries with the utmost caution and hand everything over to the police as soon as they had anything positive. Nat was very sceptical about their prospects because, as he insisted, it would be absolute folly to approach anyone who might have been involved in the theft of the Antonello portrait. His main concern was to be able to convince Pearl Gomer and, now, Kathryn that every avenue that could be safely explored had been explored. To that end he had arranged a meeting with the formidable Mrs George. In his experience mediums were highly practised intelligence gatherers. When young Tracy and old Widow Jones were 'amazed' that a fairground clairvoyant or a seance performer told them things about themselves or their departed loved ones that they 'couldn't possibly have known', that was no proof of revelations from the world beyond. Spiritualists were, almost by definition, men and women of considerable human sensitivity. They were adept at reading body language and tuning in to their customers' mental wavelength. If anyone knew what was going on in Bob Gomer's head during his last, intensely troubled weeks, Nat suspected, it would be Athalie George.

*   *   *

Prompt on three o'clock he ascended the three steps to a wide black door honoured with a well-polished, antique brass knocker. The house fronted Parker's Piece, a large area of public lawn close to the city centre. Council workers were busy preparing cricket pitches and the sweet smell of mown grass filled the air. Nat had no need to put a hand to the brazen grotesque mask; there was a discreet button on the door frame. When he pressed it he could hear a bell reverberating somewhere in the cavernous interior. As he waited, Nat recalled the contemptuous words of Rosie Hardwick about the 'big house' the medium lived in. Certainly this was one of the most desirable residences in Cambridge. Most other conveniently situated residential buildings had long since been bought up by one or other of the colleges to boost their property portfolios or to provide additional student accommodation.

The door was opened by Mrs George herself.

'Dr Gye, do come in. I've ordered tea in the drawing room. I hope it's not too early for you.' She led the way to a first-floor room overlooking a garden at the rear of the house.

Nat's first impression was one of faded elegance—faded but expensive. The long salon was decorated throughout with eighteenth-century mahogany furniture. Its classic, unfussy lines were set off by peach-coloured walls and velvet drapes in smouldering red. The numerous pictures in their gilt frames were, he guessed, all original oils and watercolours. Mrs George placed herself in an upright chair with its back to the window and waved her guest to a deep armchair opposite.

Nat smiled inwardly. It was a manoeuvre straight out of a standard interpersonal communication manual: always be on a higher level than your dialogist and place him where you can study his reactions very clearly. 'Do you mind if I sit here?' he asked, moving to one side where the oblique sunlight would miss him.

Mrs George honoured him with an almost-smile that seemed to say, 'Round one to you.' She was an imposing figure, upright, angular, clad today in a brown silk suit with a large cameo brooch on the lapel. 'You have come to quiz me about Bob Gomer,' she announced, getting straight down to business.

'If I may.'

'I am delighted that you are taking his message seriously.'

Nat avoided a direct response. 'I imagine that Bob confided in you a great deal, especially, perhaps, during his last, troubled months.'

'During his last months on this plane,' Mrs George corrected with the slightest inclination of her head.

'Did he give you any indication that he was proposing to take his own life?' Nat asked the question sharply, hoping for an unguarded response.

'Certainly not!' Athalie George snapped. Nat noticed the colour that came suddenly to her cheeks, darker than the skilfully applied rouge. She collected herself quickly. 'That was totally alien to his aura. He was loyal.'

'To his wife, you mean?'

'Yes.' There was a slight hesitation. 'Of course. And to his principles. Bob held all life as sacred. He would never—'

'But he did, didn't he?' Nat urged gently.

Mrs George pursed her lips. 'No, Dr Gye, he did not. That is why his spirit is so troubled now. I thought you understood that.'

'Indeed. It's just that I don't know what I can do that the police haven't already done. When they investigated his death, did they look into the possibility that it might have been anything other than self-inflicted?'

At that moment there was a soft tap at the door followed immediately by the appearance of Kevin George bearing a silver tray of tea things. This he set down on the low table beside his mother.

'Thank you, dear,' Mrs George said, busying herself with teapot and milk jug. 'You remember Dr Gye, don't you?'

Kevin muttered 'Hello' and stood rocking from foot to foot and looking for all the world like a schoolboy who had been told to be on his best behaviour and was eager to make his escape. As soon as his mother gave him a dismissive nod he withdrew.

Mrs George poured tea into fine porcelain cups. 'You must excuse Kevin. He is only really at ease when he's pottering in his shed.'

'Pottering at what?' Nat enquired.

'He was bitten by his father's motor car bug at an early age. Now he spends most of his time taking engines to pieces in order to put them together again.'

Nat took the opportunity to study his surroundings more closely. On a bureau beside the window there was a single photograph in an ivory frame. It showed a well-built man in an open-necked shirt standing beside a rather flashy sports car. 'I presume this is your husband.'

'My late husband. I'm afraid he was a little too fond of fast cars. They were the death of him.'

'I'm sorry. I didn't mean . . .'

She shrugged. 'When one is certain about the spirit world one isn't afraid to speak of these things. Edgar was a loss, not only to me. He was very well thought of in his field.' The explanation seemed cold. Nat had the impression that Mrs George did not recall her wedded life with pleasure.

'What was that?'

'He was an art dealer.'

'Ah, hence this fine collection of yours.' Nat waved a hand towards the wall.

'Edgar was very talented and very knowledgeable. He travelled widely and always bought well.'

'Did you work in the same world, Mrs George?'

For the first time she smiled a genuine smile. 'I come from a family whose female members are not accustomed to having to earn their own living,' she said.

She took a sip of tea then set down the cup carefully. 'We were talking, I believe, about the police investigation into Bob Gomer's death. What I can tell you is that they were totally incompetent. Those of us who were close to the poor man tried to impress upon them that Bob was incapable of suicide. We might as well have saved our breath.'

'They took no notice?'

'As a medium one is quite used to being

dismissed as a batty old hen. They smiled politely and took notes—and did nothing. They already had a nice, convenient theory to explain Bob's death. Here was a man, they said, depressed by his wife's illness, driven to commit a crime of which he was thoroughly ashamed and facing a prison sentence. He couldn't live with that and so he took the easy way out. They simply weren't prepared to listen to anything that might prevent them being able to wrap up the whole case tidily.'

'Did you attend the inquest?'

'I most certainly did. A travesty of justice! It was all over inside an hour. The coroner swallowed the police version hook, line and sinker. He failed to ask the pathologist whether there were any contributory factors to the cause of death.'

'Such as?'

Mrs George gave him an exasperated glance. 'Oh, you know the sort of thing. You must have seen some of these crime dramas on television. I don't watch at all often. Too much taking of loose morals for granted. But in the police dramas I have seen they always seem to be minutely examining dead bodies for anything that might show that the cause of death was something other than the obvious— a blow to the head, an injection, an excessive amount of alcohol in the bloodstream.'

'Do you think—'

But Mrs George was now too much into her

stride to brook interruption. 'But, of course, they had very good reason to keep their minds firmly closed. Bob's death was an absolute godsend. Their case against him was full of holes. I'm sure that if the question had been put to the jury they would have exonerated him. I told Bob so the last time we met and he accepted that the situation was far from hopeless. Any suggestion that he was suicidally depressed throughout the trial is absolute nonsense.'

'When did you see Bob last?'

'Two days before he . . . passed over.' She paused, pulled a lace handkerchief from her sleeve and made a pretence of blowing her nose. She cleared her throat, straightened her shoulders and continued speaking slowly in order to keep the tremor from her voice. 'He came here to supper on the Friday. He was, naturally, subdued but by no means in despair. Do you know what distressed him most? The realization that the robbery was an inside job. That meant that there were people he knew who knew the truth and were prepared to let him shoulder the blame. He was very relieved when he reached the spirit realm and realized that the crime must have had its origin in Italy. That was why he wanted you to go there.'

'But when he came here that Friday, did he say he suspected anyone in particular?'

'If he did he didn't give me any names. He was such a trusting soul. I can see him now, sitting in that very chair and saying, "Attie, I just can't believe anyone would do this to me."' Again the tiny square of lace fluttered to her face.

'Did he suggest that he had worked out how the painting was stolen?'

'Not in as many words. He did say that something odd had occurred to him but that he couldn't work out what it meant. Something to do with a thermos flask, as I recall. "If only I could talk it over with Dr Gye," he said, "he'd be able to get to the bottom of it."'

'He never contacted me.'

'No, he wouldn't.' Mrs George smiled ruefully. 'He had this conviction that he had let all his friends down. He was sure that everyone at Beaufort College must be ashamed of him—even though he had received several messages of support. He was a silly . . . dear man. His sense of honour was—I don't know, almost childlike. And yet, in other ways, he was very mature. The way he coped with poor Pearl. He was spiritually very strong.'

'A valuable member of your congregation?'

'A tower of strength. A man who held to the truth no matter how much the world might mock.'

'Can you think why he should have warned me not to take my wife to Italy?'

The medium's reply was prompt, almost pat. 'The spirits can see things we cannot. They are not subject to the confines of space and time. Have you been to Italy, Dr Gye?'

Nat nodded. 'I spent a few days there over Easter.'

Athalie George's eyes lit up. 'What did you discover?'

Nat considered his answer carefully. 'Not much. The man to whom the missing painting belonged had recently met with a violent death.'

'Aha! That sounds suspicious. Do you think there's a connection?'

'I suppose it's possible.' Nat gave a non-committal shrug. A sudden thought struck him. 'Your husband must have had contacts with art dealers in Rome?'

'Undoubtedly. He went there often enough. He spent more time in Rome, Paris, Vienna, Amsterdam, etc., etc., than he ever did at home.'

'You wouldn't happen to know if he was friendly with a man named Bregnolini?'

'No, but I could look through his papers if it's important. There are boxes of them in the attic. I'm afraid I'm a bit of a hoarder. If I find anything I'll call you.'

'I don't want to put you to any trouble. It's only the wildest long shot.'

'No trouble at all. I'll get Kevin on to it. He needs to be kept occupied. More tea?'

Nat declined and after a few more minutes of polite conversation he took his leave. In the wide hallway he noticed something he had not seen on his way in. A large, faded but impressive heraldic escutcheon hung on the wall facing the stairs. As he descended the front steps and stared out across the vast expanse of Parker's Piece he wondered how it was that a woman of such taste, conscious of her ancient breeding, should have been in love with Bob Gomer.

*   *   *

That evening Nat sat at his desk conversing with his on-screen journal. After adding the latest information gleaned from Victor Zeeman and Athalie George, he typed in some questions.

Victor's theory about the van switch is ingenious but does it work?
Complex. Would take careful planning and involve at least four or five people.
Could not be done without Samson's involvement. Certainly it points the finger at Gomer's colleagues, Hardwick and Randall. Expensive. But perhaps worth it if masterminded by Italian crooks who have something big to hide.
What to make of the George menage?
Mrs George a formidable woman long accustomed to wielding wealth and authority.
Marriage to Edgar not a success. She

168

obviously came from good family who probably thought she had married 'beneath her station'.

If her husband was a strong character, too, there must have been tension.

Has his connection with the international art world any relevance?

Kevin! Very unhealthy mother-son relationship.

What was going on between Mrs George and Bob Gomer?

He must have been a very willing disciple and she would have lapped up his devotion. Could they have been waiting for Pearl to die to become more than good friends? Were they already lovers?

Obviously it was Mrs George who wanted to get me involved. She used her 'spirit voices' to manipulate Pearl into making an appeal for my aid.

Why?

Deeply distressed by Bob's death and doesn't believe he killed himself. Outraged at police 'incompetence'. Cheated out of her future with Bob. Not the sort of woman to sit back and accept life's reverses.

Are her suspicions justified? There's no actual proof that any third party had a hand in Bob's death.

Nat felt the pressure of Kathryn's hands on

his shoulders. 'How's it going?' she asked.

He sat back with a sigh. 'Beware the widows' curse,' he said.

'Stop being enigmatic. I'm not one of your students.'

'I'm quite serious. We've got caught up in this business because of three husbandless ladies and, if we're not careful, the results could be disastrous.'

'You're not suggesting Pearl Gomer had sinister intent when she came to you?'

'No, she was being manipulated. It's the others that we have to watch. Mrs George is determined to use me as the agent of her vengeance and Mrs Talenti is equally determined to stop me at all costs.' Nat swung his chair round with sudden force. 'And I'm damned if I'm going to be used as their tennis ball!'

Wider Still and Wider

> . . . *Begin elsewhere anew!*
> *Boston's a hole, the herring pond is wide . . .*

The beginning of Easter Term brought with it all the usual sights of a Cambridge summer—empty lecture halls, undergraduates spreadeagled on the river banks surrounded by piles of books and notepads (the desiderata of last-minute revision), crowds spilling over on to pavements from town pubs, punts weaving their way along the Backs manoeuvred with varying degrees of skill or incompetence, patchworks of vivid posters everywhere, proclaiming the varieties of entertainment that would be on offer once the tedious business of exams had been got out of the way, and gaggles of tourists clogging every city centre street. For Nat, as for most senior members of the university, this was the start of the year's busiest few weeks. On top of all the usual routine college and faculty meetings, there were examination papers to be checked, invigilation rotas to be drawn up, and personal research to be hurriedly finished or set aside in anticipation of the piles of papers that would all too soon be on his desk waiting to be marked. The Gomer affair had been pushed to the back of his mind and it took a slight interruption of his routine to set him thinking about it again.

He had dined in college and then returned to his rooms to carry on working. It was almost ten o'clock and he had just decided to call it a day when there was knock at the door. It opened to reveal a junior porter clutching an envelope.

'Sorry to disturb you, Dr Gye, but it says "urgent".' The bearer placed the letter on Nat's desk and withdrew on deferential tiptoe.

Nat recognized the writing immediately.

171

Only one man that he knew affected such a flowing copperplate hand. He tore open the envelope and drew out two sheets of college notepaper.

'My dear Nat,' the letter began, 'I hasten to report on the little commission you entrusted to me last Tuesday.'

Was it really that long ago since his telephone conversation with Barny Cox? he mused. It seemed like only yesterday that he had asked a favour of the old lawyer. 'Barny, this business of Bob Gomer. I've been doing a bit of ferreting around.'

'Yes, dear boy, I heard you'd rushed off somewhat precipitately to Italy. Is all well with Kathryn?'

Nat chuckled. Nothing that happened at Beaufort ever escaped the astute eyes and ears of Barny Cox. 'She's fine, thanks.'

'I'm delighted to hear your fears were unfounded.'

'Barny, if you have a spare moment, I wonder if you could dig out the coroner's report on Gomer's death.' There was a slight pause before his friend replied, 'Nothing easier, dear boy, but you do realize it's in the public domain. You can check it for yourself.'

'Yes, I know. The thing is, I'd rather not draw any attention to my interest in the matter.'

'Aha!' Nat envisaged the old man's eyes lighting up. 'And what exactly is your interest

172

in the matter?'

'I'd like to know what you make of the police pathologist's evidence. Did he carry out a thorough investigation? Is he convinced there was no possibility of anyone else being involved?'

'Intriguing. Do you have good grounds for suspicion?'

'None whatsoever, except that everyone who knew Gomer well is convinced that suicide was totally out of character.'

Barny sighed. 'Ah, how often one has heard that from grieving and bewildered relatives.'

'I know. Frankly, I'm inclined to dismiss any thought of foul play. If you can establish that the police got it right, then at least I can try to help his widow come to terms with her husband's death.'

Barny had eagerly accepted the assignment and Nat had mentally ticked checking the post-mortem off his list. Now, as he glanced at the lines of neat script, it seemed that his agent had more to report than a mere confirmation of the coroner's verdict. He read the letter carefully.

I was able to do rather more than you actually asked. In point of fact, there were three stages to my research.

Stage One: I read the coroner's report carefully. This was not difficult, as the document might best be described as minimalist. As to the pathologist, he did not even grace the proceedings with his presence. He sent his assistant to state the cause of death. The deceased, he confirmed, had met his end as a result of asphyxiation due to inhaling carbon monoxide. He was not pressed to elaborate on this and did not choose to do so.

Stage Two: I invited the coroner to lunch. His name is George Beddows and I know him from certain social events organized by the local legal fraternity. One could scarcely imagine a duller companion and I spent a dreary couple of hours with him. I hope you appreciate the sacrifice I have made on your behalf. When I probed on the Gomer inquest, he could scarcely remember it. However, he did eventually recall that a detective inspector from Bath had come to give evidence before him and had presented his information with exemplary clarity. That had, apparently, rendered Beddows' task easy and he was in no doubt whatsoever about the reliability of his verdict.

My enquiries so far having proved less than satisfactory, I proceeded to:

Stage Three: This involved calling in a favour from a certain DS Denzil Howard of the Cambridge CID. I have been giving him some help with the legal aspects of his Inspectors' Exam. Over a pint at the Mill he proved to be gratifyingly garrulous. The Gomer case had, it seems, lodged in his mind for certain unhappy reasons. It came at an appallingly busy time. There had been a string of drug abuse fatalities on the city streets and the police were being pressured to track down the suppliers of badly cut heroin. There had also been a fire in an old people's home. As a result of all this the mortuary was, in Howard's colourful words, 'piled high' with corpses. The pathologists were working overtime and my contact reckons that anything 'routine' was disposed of with the utmost despatch. Added to this was the fact that Howard's chief was an old friend of the officer who came up from Bath to give evidence, DCI Jack Hawkins. Hawkins was the investigating officer on the painting robbery case and he apparently made it crystal clear that he expected co-operation from his Cambridge colleagues. He did not want anything to come out at the inquest that might throw doubt on his prosecution of Gomer. I asked Howard if he had any reason to doubt the coroner's verdict and the question obviously made him uneasy. He refused to say anything on the record but, when I pressed him, he recounted a conversation with a friend who works in the pathology lab. This friend spoke of observing bruises at the base of Gomer's head that could not be easily accounted for. When he remarked on this to his superior he was told not to rock the boat.

So, dear boy, there you have it. I am not sure whether it does anything to lift the fog. Howard's evidence is hearsay and it would be more than his job is worth to repeat on oath what he told me. I can only advise you that, were we discussing a case in the appeal court, his evidence would carry weight and might well persuade their lordships that an earlier conviction was unsafe. My opinion, for what it is worth, is that I am inclined to share your uneasiness about Gomer's tragic end and conclude that, if there is doubt about that, then such doubt might very well extend to the matter of the robbery.

Having roused my curiosity, you will, I hope, keep me fully apprised of your thinking on this sad affair and let me know if I can be of any further assistance.

I remain, Yours sincerely,
Barnaby Cox

Nat slipped the letter into his briefcase along with other papers he was taking home.

As he left his rooms and descended the narrow staircase to Simeon Court he mused on Barny's words. The old lawyer was absolutely right. The closer one got to the events surrounding Bob Gomer's trial and sudden death, the stronger the odour of fish became. Everyone who knew the ex-Beaufort porter was convinced that the official version of events simply did not hang together. Yet, infuriatingly, there were not even the beginnings of an alternative scenario that could be put forward for consideration. 'Damn!' Nat muttered to himself as he crossed the fellows' garden. As the misadventures that had befallen him and Kathryn in Rome receded further into the past his anxieties had weakened, or rather they had been pummelled into silence by his sheer anger at the way the Gomers had been used by others for their own purposes. Colleagues, friends, even their own spiritual adviser had taken advantage of their simple good nature for their own selfish ends.

Nat fumbled in his pocket for the key to the iron gate of the fellows' car park. What kind of a world are we living in? he asked himself. Once, colleges had been bolted and barred at night to keep their younger, more exuberant members from slipping out to the city fleshpots. Now, those same young people had to be protected from nocturnal prowlers, trying to get in. Only a couple of years ago Beaufort had had to pay for arc lights in the car park and now there was talk of security cameras.

He had taken a few paces across the tarmac when a figure detached itself from the shadows of the shrubbery. Someone called his name.

'Dr Gye.'

Nat stopped, fear grabbing his stomach. The burly figure of a man, holding something heavy in a gloved hand (a bottle? a club? a gun?), blocked his path. Nat squinted in an effort to recognize the intruder's features.

He adopted what he hoped sounded like an authoritative tone. 'Who are you? What are you doing here? This is private—'

'I just want a chat, Dr Gye. A *quiet* chat where we shan't be disturbed. Let's go to your car.'

'If you want to talk to me you can make an appointment.' Nat tried to sidestep the human wall but it shifted.

'Here and now will do nicely.' The gloved hand was raised and Nat saw that it held something wrapped in rolled newspaper. With this the man prodded him in the chest. Doing so, he moved forward into a pool of light and Nat instantly recognized him.

'Mr Hardwick! What's the meaning of this?'

'Like I said, just a chat.' The lamplight was reflected in the beads of sweat on Ted Hardwick's brow. 'Now, let's get to your car, shall we?'

Nat glanced around. There were only three

178

vehicles in the car park and no sign of any other owners. With the gates tight shut there was no prospect of escape from his assailant. He led the way across to the Mercedes. As soon as the doors were unlocked Hardwick demanded, 'Keys!'

Reluctantly, Nat handed them over. He lowered himself into the driver's seat and seconds later Hardwick took his place beside him, wiping a hand across his brow. Obviously, he was nervous. That could mean he was potentially dangerous. Nat could now smell alcohol on his assailant's breath and guessed that Hardwick had fortified himself for this encounter. He wondered what the man had wrapped in the newspaper. Nat's own pulse was racing but he knew it was important to appear calm and in control. 'Well. Here we are,' he said. 'Can we keep this short? It's getting late.'

'What have you been saying about me?' Hardwick's voice was thick; his tone truculent.

'I don't know what you mean,' Nat responded.

'You've been talking about me; asking nosy questions,' the man insisted.

Nat's mind raced. Hardwick knew of his interest in the Gomer affair. Hardwick had a guilty conscience about his own involvement in it. Therefore, he had put two and two together and convinced himself that he was under investigation. Nat decided that only a slightly coloured version of the truth would serve to lower the temperature of suspicion. 'I'm afraid you've been misinformed, Mr Hardwick. I've not been prying into your affairs and for a very good reason: your Italian friends went to great lengths to warn me off.'

Hardwick's response was abrupt. 'I don't know what you're talking about!'

Nat let the following silence run. When Hardwick broke it the aggression had gone out of his voice. 'He shouldn't have been there.' The words were a maudlin murmur.

'Are we talking about Bob?' Nat asked quietly.

'Yes, of course. He wasn't down for the Bath trip. We didn't need him. It was that bloody fool, Barry Cheeseman, sticking his oar in at the last minute. If anyone's to blame it's him.' He turned to face Nat, suddenly aggressive again. 'So, just get off my back, will you?'

A figure emerged from the darkness of the fellows' garden and Nat recognized the athletic frame of Peter Chelt, the college bursar. He and Hardwick watched while the ex-banker jumped into his open-topped MG and roared through the automatically opening gates into Silver Street. When quiet had been restored, Nat asked cautiously, 'Don't you think it would be better for everyone, especially Pearl, to explain to the police exactly what did happen on that trip to Bath?'

Hardwick sneered. 'I thought you university

types were supposed to be clever. What good's it going to do Pearl me getting bumped off? The truth didn't do Bob no favours, did it?'

'Did he work out how the robbery was done?'

'It would've taken someone a hell of a lot brighter than him to do that.'

'But you know, don't you?'

Nat realized at once that his response had been too eager. Hardwick raised the newspaper and waved it in front of his face. Nat saw what looked like a large monkey wrench wrapped in its pages.

'There you go, asking your bloody questions! Well, just get this inside your thick skull: whatever we may or may not have done, we never meant any harm to Bob or Pearl. You leave us alone and forget whatever it is you think you know and we'll see Pearl all right. If you spoil everything, she'll suffer even more. Just let things settle down. OK?' He tapped the weapon against Nat's forehead.

Pressed hard back against the headrest, Nat did his best to nod.

Hardwick let himself out of the car and tossed the keys on to the passenger seat. Nat saw him stumble away into the shadows. When he had collected himself, he switched on the engine and eased the Mercedes forward. As he approached them the gates swung inward and an ungainly figure slipped through the widening gap.

'Enjoy yourself in Spain,' Nat muttered bitterly.

When he reached home he found Kathryn sprawled on the sofa watching television. 'Good day?' she asked with a yawn, making room for him beside her.

'Interesting,' he said. 'You?'

'Interesting. I made contact with the Millennium Gallery, Bath.'

'And?'

'Heather Miles has parted company with the gallery. In fact, she left soon after the robbery. She's joined the editorial team of *Beau Monde*.'

'The French art magazine?'

'International. The head office moved from Paris to London a few years back.'

'That should make it easier to contact her.'

'Already done. We're lunching tomorrow. I intend to ply her with wine and see if I can't get her to dish the dirt on friend Theophrast. So what have you been up to?'

Nat told her about Barny Cox's research and his own brush with Hardwick.

'Wow!' Kathryn stared, wide-eyed. 'This thing gets murkier by the day.'

Nat sighed. 'Yes, murky in the sense of unpleasant and also obscure.'

'Surely not. We now know that Ted Hardwick and his friend, Charlie . . . er . . .'

'Randall.'

'Yes. We know that they were the main

agents in the robbery and that they deliberately let Bob Gomer take the blame.'

'No doubt about that. And they must have been paid off very handsomely. The Hardwicks are retiring to sunnier climes.'

'And shoving poor Pearl Gomer into a home she doesn't want to go into. God, how despicable can you get!'

Nat lay back and closed his eyes. 'It's been a long day and maybe I can't think straight but I don't see that we're any further forward. There was always a possibility that Gomer was killed because he knew something and would have brought it out in court. That is still only a possibility. It was obvious that Hardwick and Randall must have had some hand in the robbery. Now, Hardwick has virtually admitted as much but he hasn't told us who was behind it.'

'Probably he doesn't know,' Kathryn mused. 'Remember we're dealing with a criminal organization. Its minions operate on a need to know basis. My guess is Hardwick and Randall were given enough information to do their part of the job and nothing more. Someone promised him a pile of cash to drive the company van to Bath and swap it for a duplicate and he didn't ask any questions.'

'I think you're right. To him it must have seemed like money for old rope. All he has to do when the police question him is say, "I went to fill the van with petrol as soon as the crate had been unloaded, because we didn't want to waste any time getting back to Cambridge." Everything would have gone smoothly from his point of view if Bob Gomer hadn't been assigned to the job at the last minute. That change of plan genuinely upset him.'

'Huh!' Kathryn scowled. 'It didn't upset him enough to make him step in and come to his brother-in-law's rescue.'

'No, when the police decided to pin the crime on Gomer the pressure was really on Hardwick. He'd got himself mixed up with some very dangerous people and you can bet they all told him to keep his mouth shut—or else. And, of course, there was the money. By that time he'd probably promised his wife a life in sunny Spain and the charming Rosie doesn't strike me as a woman who would take kindly to disappointment.'

Kathryn nodded thoughtfully. 'But then Bob Gomer worked out how the robbery was done. Suppose he said something to Hardwick. That would throw Hardwick into a panic, wouldn't it? Do you think he killed Gomer?'

'It's possible. He strikes me as someone terribly guilt-ridden and, from what I saw this evening, he's very adept at handling blunt instruments.'

'There we are, then.'

'Where are we? Floating on a sea of conjecture with some nasty-looking sharks circling around us. Who do you think put

184

Hardwick up to tonight's little demonstration? It was our Italians' way of letting us know that they're still watching us.' He drew Kathryn to him. 'For heaven's sake go carefully. There are more important things in this wicked world than securing justice for the dead.'

Art for Greed's Sake

. . . men love money—that you know—
And what men do to gain it . . .

Kathryn had chosen Lampreys, just off Berkeley Square, because it was currently one of London's most fashionable restaurants, because she knew the patron and his staff and because the food was, quite simply, marvellous. She wanted to overawe Heather Miles and calculated that flatteringly lavish treatment might loosen the tongue of a serious young woman from an academic background just entering the world of high class journalism and not yet inured to its cynical, glossy exploitation. She arrived early and spent a few minutes chatting with the darkly good-looking Giles, who personally escorted her to her table. Giles had made his first fortune from motor racing and its attendant sponsorship deals and was now building a second with the successful and expensive Lampreys. Kathryn had chosen a table in the far corner from where she could watch for her guest's arrival and scrutinize her carefully as she made the long journey from the entrance.

Heather Miles arrived punctually at 12.45 and Kathryn's first impression warned her not to put much faith in the idea that this initiate to the world of sophisticated ballyhoo was a naive intellectual. As Heather approached, conducted by the head waiter, Kathryn did a quick assessment: Age, just the right side of thirty; make-up understated but skilful; hair, done by a top stylist; suit, hand-tailored and severe but softened by the cerise silk shirt that complemented her natural colouring; jewellery, a simple gold chain of antique design around her neck. This young lady, Kathryn decided, knows what she is about.

She devoted pre-lunch drinks and starters to the business of establishing rapport. This was not difficult because Heather was still in the eager networking stage of the ambitious arriviste. She needed to build up contacts, find new ideas and stamp her own personality on her department. Kathryn waited until they were well into their main course before easing the conversation in the direction she wanted it to go.

'It's good that you've settled so quickly. You and *Beau Monde* will suit each other very well. Now, what I wanted to explore with you was the possibility of our magazines working together occasionally. We're not in direct competition but our markets do, obviously, overlap. Our market surveys tell us that fifteen per cent of our regular readers are serious collectors at one level or another and, of course, many more are intelligent gallery and exhibition goers.'

Heather nodded, her bobbed blonde hair gleaming in the subdued lighting. 'Yes, that sounds like an avenue we certainly should explore. We live in a crossover age and my lords and masters are gradually waking up to the fact. *Beau Monde* is a serious, specialist magazine and will remain so but we have to widen our appeal.'

'We all have to keep our eyes on the bottom line, don't we, Heather?' Kathryn smiled—one professional to another. 'Great art is great art but we shouldn't lose sight of /its human context. It's not just the painters and sculptors whose lives are interesting. My readers are fascinated by the mystique of the whole art world. Who are the people who commission new work? Who buy and sell the stuff? Who put exhibitions together? What lies behind the cut and thrust of the saleroom and the discreet frontage of the West End galleries?'

'And you would want us to help you with contacts?' Heather asked cautiously.

Kathryn recognized her guest as someone who thought carefully and assessed shrewdly before verbalizing a response. '*Panache* is fine on contacts,' she said airily. 'What I had in mind was more the possibility of doing some things in parallel. For example, supposing there was a new loan exhibition at the Royal Academy. *Beau Monde* would obviously provide critical coverage but *Panache* would be interested in doing a piece on the locales of individual items—photojournalism on the odd Bavarian schloss or Manhattan penthouse—that sort of thing. That would generate interest in the exhibition but also in your copy.'

'This sounds good, Kathryn. Let me get some notes down.' She pulled a pad and a pen from her handbag.

While Heather was occupied scrawling words on the page, Kathryn judged the moment right to move closer to the centre of the target. 'We're planning a series of bios in the autumn—a sort of "Who's Who of the Art Establishment". How would you feel about giving us a personal interview?'

Heather looked up, surprised. 'Oh, I'm very small fry,' she said, modestly but obviously pleased.

'On the contrary,' Kathryn replied, leaning forward. 'You're the sort of fresh blood the art world needs. You're coming in with new ideas—like crossover culture which you've obviously given a lot of thought to. And you've served your apprenticeship in the tough business of a regional gallery. My readers will be interested to know what your years in Bath were like.'

Kathryn was relieved that Heather did not ask how she knew about her past. Instead she smiled sardonically. 'It certainly had its moments,' she said.

'I gather Dr Theophrast wasn't the easiest of men to work for,' Katherine ventured.

Again Kathryn noted the slight hesitation, the pause for calculation. 'Jo?' Heather said in an emotionally neutral tone. 'He's a human dynamo, a go-getter, drives himself and his staff tremendously hard.'

'In other words, he's a bully?'

'I suppose. But he's worked like a Trojan to build up the reputation of the Millennium Gallery. It's beginning to get international status. He put on some super exhibitions in the five years I was with him. Small, but very high class. We showed the public several works that hadn't been seen outside private collections for decades, centuries even. That was all down to Jo. He's the sort of man owners find it difficult to say no to.' Clearly Ms Miles was determined to be diplomatic.

'He must have a great web of international contacts. I presume he's of Greek origin?'

'Albanian originally, though I think he spent part of his early life in Italy.'

Kathryn did a mental double take. Albania and Italy—staging posts on the notorious 'heroin highway' from Afghanistan. She tucked the thought away for further reflection.

She said, 'Sounds like a colourful character. Perhaps we should include him in our "Who's Who".'

Heather pulled a face. 'You could try but I doubt you'd get much joy. He hates talking about himself. He's intensely private; secretive in fact.'

Kathryn shrugged. 'How's your sole?' she enquired. The conversation drifted on to matters gastronomic and culinary. It was only when they were on to their coffee and she had asked for the bill that she suddenly looked up with a puzzled, frustrated frown. 'There was something . . . What was it? We were talking about the Millennium Gallery and it stirred a memory at the back of mind. What was it?' She tapped her forehead. 'No, it's gone.'

The head waiter arrived with the bill in its discreet leather folder. Kathryn busied herself checking the figures and getting out her credit card. Then, 'Got it!' she announced. 'Wasn't there some trouble about a loan painting that went missing two or three years ago?' She handed the folder back to the waiter, deliberately not catching Heather's eye.

But Heather did not appear to be startled by the question. 'The notorious Antonello da Messina. That was a weird business if ever there was one.'

'Wasn't it supposed to have disappeared into thin air?'

'Yes, it was pretty spooky. I'd love to know

how that trick was managed. There are a few things I'd like to despatch into oblivion, not to mention a few people.' She laughed. 'But that wasn't all that was odd.'

'Oh?'

'They caught one of the gang responsible and put him on trial. Then, just when it seemed we might discover the truth of the matter, he killed himself.'

'That's right. It's coming back to me now. So what happened after that? Did the painting ever show up again?'

'Well, that's the final mystery. I left Bath days after the robbery. Jo had recommended me for a curatorship up north. It didn't work but that's another story. It was the following summer that I went down to the south of France to spend a few days with some cousins of mine—my mother's French. One evening we were all invited out to dinner with some neighbours of theirs in a nearby chateau.'

'Sounds nice.'

'Actually it was a bit depressing. The Montgardes are one of those families that's seen better days and tries to go on living in them. Anyway, to cut a long story short, they had lots of old pictures on the walls. Dreadfully bad conditions—too damp. And there it was, halfway along a corridor, the Antonello. Naturally, I told Monsieur Montgarde how delighted I was that they'd got it back. And he looked puzzled. "But that was

191

years ago," he said. "You were only a little girl when it was stolen."'

'What a coincidence. It was obviously a copy.'

'Yes, of course. I had a good look at it later and that was the answer. I suspect most of their paintings are copies, there for the sake of keeping up appearances. The originals will have gone to the salerooms over the years in order to repair the roof or replace rotten window frames. Sad really.'

Minutes later the two journalists said goodbye, promising to keep in touch, and Kathryn made her way thoughtfully back to her office.

It was late in the evening before she had a chance to report to Nat about her meeting with Heather Miles. They had been to a recital in Queens' and to drinks in the president's lodge afterwards. Kathryn, who had kept religiously to orange juice during the party, drove them home.

As they headed south through Trumpington and Great Shelford she listed the bullet points of her conversation with the ex-assistant director of the Millennium Gallery.

Nat stared gloomily out into the darkness. 'Fakes!' he muttered.

After several seconds' silence Kathryn asked, 'Is that all you've got to say?'

'Sorry, but doesn't it strike you that in this business we're surrounded by fakes and copies and frauds and substitutes? We've got a suicide that might not be a suicide, a medium who might not be genuine, paintings that are probably copies, vans that get swapped around. Nothing is what it seems. It's a nightmare. It's surreal.'

'Well, at least there's nothing odd about the French version of the Antonello portrait. The Montgardes obviously sold the original years ago.'

'And it ended up in Talenti's stolen hoard? What I wouldn't give to be able to check out Don Alberto's exquisite little collection.'

'But we can—assuming you were able to take your eyes off Mrs Talenti long enough to get a good look at some of the paintings. You remember I told you about IFAR, the organization that traces missing artworks? Well, they keep a register of all precious objects that are reported stolen or recovered.'

Nat ignored the barb. 'I can remember some of them but I couldn't put a title or artist's name to any of them.'

'That doesn't matter. These guys are experts. If you can provide some descriptions I'll email them to the IFAR head office in New York. We'll have an answer within hours.'

'It's worth a try. I'll cudgel my brains in the morning when they're a bit less fuzzy. But how about this Theophrast fellow? Weren't you going to prime one of your journalistic admirers to do an interview with him?'

Kathryn swung the car off the main road and on to the narrow lane leading to Great Maddisham. 'Drawn a blank there, I'm afraid. Heather was right about Theophrast. He's tight as a duck's arse. I put Jake Andersen on to him. Jake's a freelance investigative journalist and *very* persistent. He phoned, emailed and even went down to Bath in person but he couldn't get near Theophrast. His secretary is a professional stone wall. All Jake could get out of her was "The director does not give interviews."'

'Not the best way to run a gallery in this publicity-conscious age.'

'Not unless you have a great deal to hide. For my money Theophrast is a class A crook. He knows what happens to members of the brotherhood who open their mouths and let out information that could prove inconvenient. Whatever the beautiful widow says, I'll bet Jonah was one of the brains behind the disappearing picture and picked up a nice slice of the insurance money. Heather Miles reckons he's a miracle worker. At a time when public galleries and museums are really struggling, the Millennium is going from strength to strength. That doesn't happen without cash.'

They had reached journey's end. Kathryn pulled the Mercedes on to the house drive, braked and switched off the engine. But she did not open her door. 'Something's just occurred to me,' she said, with an excited lift to her voice. 'Supposing the gallery is a front.'

'What do you mean?' Nat asked sleepily.

'Well, as guardian of a public collection Theophrast is always buying and borrowing paintings. He must have scores of them stuffed away in the vaults. No one would think of examining them to see if any weren't kosher. What better place to store stolen old masters while his associates are negotiating nefarious deals?'

Nat yawned. 'Let's not let our imaginations get ahead of us, eh? Let's think it all through carefully tomorrow. Right now I'm whacked.' Nat stepped out of the car and fumbled in a pocket for his house key.

*   *   *

In the morning Kathryn's enthusiasm had not abated. Before she took her younger son to school she reminded Nat about writing down all he could remember of the Talenti collection. He scribbled some notes and left them on the kitchen table before setting off for college in their other car. Kathryn, as was her custom on Fridays, was working from home. She had a pile of proofs and layout designs to check but before settling down with them she typed Nat's sketchy reminiscences into her laptop and despatched them to IFAR's distant headquarters on New York's East 70th Street.

195

She did not expect a reply before the weekend but when, around five o'clock, she opened up her email reams of text and attachments scrolled in front of her eyes. Jeremy had brought a couple of friends home for tea so she had no time to give the report more than a glance before Nat returned.

'As far as I can tell, there's good news and bad,' she said, thrusting the printouts into his hand. 'They think they've identified at least three of the paintings and they *have* been stolen but they've also been recovered. Do you want to escape from the chaos?' She nodded towards the three writhing bodies on the living-room floor that their au pair was struggling to separate. 'I'll help Amy sort this lot out then come and see how you're getting on.'

An hour later she entered the study.

'Peace restored?' Nat asked, looking up from the desk.

'Eventually.' Kathryn dropped into a chair beside him. 'We had some tears but nothing that Amy's chocolate chip cookies couldn't cope with. The twins have gone home and Amy's putting Jerry to bed. So, how are you getting on?'

Nat stared back, grim-faced. 'Well, as you said, the news is good and bad. Unfortunately, the bad outweighs the good.'

'In that case give me the good first.'

'OK, at long last I can see pretty clearly

what we're up against and why.'

Kathryn leaned forward. 'The IFAR stuff was useful?'

'They're certainly remarkably thorough. They identified two of the Talenti pictures correctly. I recognize them from these photographs.' He handed her two of the printout sheets.

' "*Temptation of St Anthony* by Francesco del Cossa, c.1470" and "*Right Wing of an Altar Triptych* by Andrea Mantegna, c.1460",' she read out. 'One stolen in 1986, the other in 1990. Both recovered within months.' She looked up. 'But, if these are two of the paintings that you saw, it doesn't make much sense, does it?'

Nat smiled grimly. 'Oh yes it does. It makes perfect sense. I should have worked it out for myself but the answer's right here in black and white.' He indicated a paragraph in the IFAR report and read it aloud.

'Two of the items on your list are of particular interest to us because recovery was not the end of their story. Although we cannot identify them positively from a written description, certain factors do arouse our suspicion. *Madonna with Rose,* School of Titian, c.1530 and *Temptation of St Anthony* by Francesco del Cossa, c.1470 both went missing in Italy in the 1980s and both were recovered by police fine art squads, one in Paris and the other in Los Angeles. However, the returned items were subsequently identified as copies when the original owners died and their collections were valued for probate. Our experts suggested that the forgeries may well have come from the same studio.'

Kathryn stared at him with sudden comprehension. 'So what Talenti was up to was having privately owned paintings stolen, getting them copied and then tipping off the police so that they could "find" the fakes. The owners were delighted because they thought they'd got their property back and the priceless originals went into Talenti's personal bank vault.'

'That's it exactly. According to IFAR, there are several gangs running this kind of scam. Most of them are after a quick profit and some come unstuck when they try to fence the originals through shady dealers or even sell them on the open market.'

'But Talenti's operation was more sophisticated and on a larger scale.'

'Yes, he built up an impressive collection of precious objects—'

'Which he could use for buying drugs and arms,' Kathryn added eagerly.

'They were in the bank ready for any kind of secret deal he wanted to pull off.' Nat swivelled his chair round. 'Of course, "secret" is the key word. Talenti had to be as sure as he could be that items passing through his hands never saw the light of day in case the original owners got to hear about them.'

'So Sylvia Talenti was right when she said that he went bananas over her lending the Antonello for display in a public gallery?'

'Looks like it. That certainly explains why his associates went to such elaborate—and expensive—lengths to recover the portrait. Something that's always worried me about the "disappearance" of the Antonello is the sheer cost of organizing it. At short notice the crooks had to work out a vanishing act so brilliant that no one has yet been able to fathom it. Then, they had to bribe some of Samson's people to carry it off. It was risky and, as I say, expensive. Only people who were really desperate would do something like that. But now it all falls into place. With their entire fine art scam at risk money was no object. They knew that, once that was uncovered, it would lead the police to enquire into a much wider area of their activities.'

'It also explains why they got so twitchy about your visit to the non-grieving widow. They were convinced that you must be working for the police or Interpol or one of the insurance companies.'

'And why they've been leaning on Hardwick.' Nat stopped abruptly. He frowned.

199

'At least, I think they have. There's something not quite right there.'

Kathryn was also pensive. 'I don't see where Theophrast fits into all this. He must have known what Talenti was up to. Do we believe Sylvia's claim that he twisted her arm in order to get his hands on the Antonello or was he mixed up in some devious plan with Talenti?'

Nat shook his head. 'I don't know. That's just another aspect of this business that smells fishier the closer you get to it. What's more important right now is that Don Alberto's heirs and assigns are busy plugging any gaps in the dyke.' Nat searched the printout pages and drew Kathryn's attention to another paragraph.

'We were interested in your reference to Pietro Bregnolini. The Rome police have kept a close watch on his activities for the last three years. He was known to have criminal contacts but was always careful to cover his tracks and no charges were ever brought against him. You have perhaps not heard that Signore Bregnolini is now beyond the law. His body was discovered in the Tiber two weeks ago.'

Kathryn shivered. 'Nasty!' she said. 'Is that the bad news you mentioned?'

'That's only part of it. There's worse to come. This is how the IFAR letter ends up.'

200

Nat read from the final page of the email.

'We are enormously obliged to you for your help in this matter and have passed on the information to the relevant authorities. In your email you did not mention where Dr Gye saw the articles he described. This, of course, will be vital to their recovery and any ensuing prosecution. I hope you will provide this information as soon as possible. We will also need your written permission to give your contact details to any investigating officers who may wish to interview Dr Gye.'

Nat sat back, rubbing a hand wearily over his eyes. 'You do realize what that means, don't you?'

Kathryn stared back blankly.

'It means we're running out of time. If the police don't close the net on the crooks before the crooks close the net on us . . .' He left the sentence hanging in the air.

Kathryn vividly recalled the suffocating black bag, the relentless questions, the threats. 'But IFAR are keeping our identity out of it.'

'Don't be naive!' Nat snapped. 'How long do you think that'll last? Now that the cat's out of the bag they're not going to leave us alone. The police of various countries will be leaning on them and you can bet they will lean on us. I don't think we can stall for more than a few days. Even that could be dangerous. Damn! Damn! Damn!' He thumped the desk with his fist. 'I told you we ought to steer clear of this.'

'Don't take it out on me!' Kathryn threw back. 'Anyway, I'm sure you're exaggerating.'

'Oh, you are, are you? Listen. Once the police start reopening old files and making enquiries, how long do you think it will take the crooks to work out where the information leak came from? And then? We've seen how efficient they are at dealing with people who have become "inconvenient".'

'So, what's to do?'

'We have to drop everything else, go over every aspect of this business from the beginning and hope that we can come up with enough real evidence to enable every police force involved to move swiftly and decisively.'

'Is that all?' Kathryn asked sarcastically.

'No. We also have to watch our backs.'

Never Pure and Rarely Simple

. . . every cheat's inspired, and every lie
Quick with a germ of truth.

34 Endfield Road was in a state of chaos. Boxes and tea chests, some full of newspaper-wrapped items, others waiting to be packed,

202

covered the floor of Pearl Gomer's lounge and flowed over into the hall. Pearl, herself, manoeuvred her electric wheelchair (which Nat noted was new) with difficulty around the obstacles. The only other occupant of the house was Kevin George who seemed to be busy gathering up ornaments, crockery, pictures and framed photographs and sorting them into piles under their owner's direction. Pearl was obviously both pleased and embarrassed to see Nat and Kathryn.

'Dr Gye, what a lovely surprise,' she exclaimed when Kevin showed them in. 'You must forgive the mess. We're having a grand sort-out.'

Nat introduced Kathryn, who said, 'I understand you're moving into St Luke's Hospice. I've heard very good things about it.'

Pearl sighed. 'Yes, I didn't really want to go but my sister's been trying to talk me into it for weeks. Then someone from the hospice came to see me and she was very kind. So, perhaps it won't be so bad, dear.' She checked herself abruptly. 'I shouldn't really call you "dear", should I, your husband being at the college and all that?'

Kathryn smiled. ' "Dear" is fine. I know how you feel; moving is such an upheaval, isn't it—working out what to keep and what to throw away. Is there anything we can do to help?'

Pearl looked shocked. 'Oh, no, I wouldn't dream . . . And my friends are all very good to me. Young Kevin was here all yesterday and he's come back for more this morning. He's a good lad.'

Kevin stood awkwardly in the lounge doorway polishing his glasses. 'We're all here for you, you know that, Pearl.'

Coming to Endfield Road on Saturday morning to talk with Bob Gomer's widow was part of Nat's strategy to go back to the beginning. He was determined to re-examine all the evidence, to make sure he had missed no detail that might be significant. He had not reckoned on bumping into Kevin George but was pleased to have the opportunity to talk with him also. There were several things he wanted to know about the redoubtable Mrs George.

Pearl tut-tutted anxiously. 'Now where are you going to sit?' She glanced around at the cluttered chairs. 'Kevin, could you . . . ?' As he hurried forward to move a scattering of newspapers from the sofa, she added, 'And put the kettle on, could you? I'm sure we could all do with a cuppa.'

With a quick glance at Kathryn, Nat said, 'I'll give him a hand. Must make myself useful.'

In the narrow kitchen at the back of the house he began his probing. 'I enjoyed my chat with your mother the other day. She's a remarkable woman.'

'Yes, she is.' Kevin filled the electric kettle from the tap, avoiding eye contact.

'Has she always had psychic gifts?' Nat saw a frown flash across Kevin's face. He added quickly, 'I don't mean to pry but, as you know, I have a professional interest in these things.'

'We all have psychic abilities, Dr Gye. We're programmed for communication with those who have moved to a higher plane. It's just that most people don't realize this and the gifts lie dormant. My mother didn't know she was particularly sensitive till after my father died.'

'She was eager to make contact with him?'

'I think it was for my sake rather than her own. As you know, the medium is a conduit for other people on both sides of the divide. That's what the word "medium" means, isn't it? Mother doesn't work for her own gratification.'

Nat decided to take the conversation off at a tangent. 'From what I gather, your father was a very accomplished man.'

'Cups are in that cupboard on the end. Would you mind?' Kevin pointed to the row of mounted wall units. 'He died when I was twelve so I never really appreciated just how important he was. What I remember most is how the house was always full of his friends. He seemed to have hundreds. They came from all over the world to stay with us. Even after his death they often called in. That was before we came here, of course.'

'Where did you live then?'

'Milk in the fridge.' Kevin busied himself

proficiently with teapot, crockery and a tin of biscuits. 'Oh, we had a place in London and another in Wiltshire, near Devizes. Right, I think that's it.' He picked up the laden tray. 'If you wouldn't mind holding the door for me ...'

Nat decided on a long-shot question. 'You don't happen to remember any of these visitors, do you? For instance, does the name Talenti ring a bell?'

The cups and saucers rattled with what might have been the result of a sudden muscular spasm but Kevin only gave a quick shake of the head as he passed into the hall.

In the lounge it was obvious that Kathryn and Pearl were getting on well.

'Your wife's been telling me all about her job, Dr Gye. It sounds very exciting—all those celebrities and suchlike. I must get Kevin to find me a copy of the magazine. What was it called, dear?'

'*Panache.* I'll put a copy in the post to you.'

'Oh, will you, dear? That is kind. Not that Kevin would mind. I think he actually enjoys running errands for me, though I can't think why.'

Kevin handed her her cup. 'Because you're a very special person and it's a privilege to be able to keep an eye on you,' he said with an arch smile.

'Well, you certainly do that, dear,' Pearl responded. 'You've no idea how clever he is,' she said, turning to Kathryn. 'Any job that needs doing, he can do it. Turn his hand to anything, he can. You see that van of his outside? Made it himself, he did and put in a special ramp for my wheelchair.'

'Not made, Pearl. Rebuilt, adapted. It's my job-cum-hobby,' he explained to the others. 'I buy up old motors and restore them.'

'Is there much money in that?' Nat asked.

'You'd be surprised. The gap between showroom and second-hand prices gets wider and wider. I reckon by the time I've finished with a car that someone's written off as clapped-out it's as good as new and half the price.'

'Speaking as someone who can't tell one end of an engine from the other, I'm impressed,' Nat said. He turned to Mrs Gomer. 'Pearl, I've been trying to follow up what Bob asked me to do.'

'Oh, it's so good of you to bother, Dr Gye.'

'I wonder if I might ask you one or two questions—just to help me get things clear in my mind. He obviously spent a lot of time going over and over the details of the robbery, trying to work out how it was done. His notes suggest that towards the end he thought he was on to something. Did he give you any indication of what that might have been?'

Pearl's wrinkled face creased still further. 'It's so difficult. I've thought and thought about it but there's really nothing . . . Bob always wanted to keep unpleasant things from me . . . didn't want me to worry. Of course not knowing made me worry all the more. The only person he talked about the robbery with was Ted. He was a great help; always ready to meet Bob and discuss things. Night after night they'd sit in a corner at the pub, racking their brains, trying to figure out how that wretched painting could just vanish. The best thing you can do is ask Ted.'

Nat thought, yes and I'm sure he'll tell me! He said, 'There was no one else Bob confided in? Mrs George, for instance?'

It was Kevin who said quickly, 'My mother and Bob weren't on the level of sharing intimate secrets.'

Pearl laughed. 'That's right. In fact, I think Bob was always a bit scared of Athalie. Well, no, not scared, exactly. What's the word I want?'

'Overawed?' Kathryn suggested.

'Yes, that's it, overawed. He was very impressed by her psychic powers. Well, we all are.'

'So, she wasn't the sort of person Bob might look in on for a chat?'

The thought obviously struck Pearl as very funny. She cackled a laugh that ended in a cough. 'Bob and Athalie? Oh dear me no. Not in a month of Sundays.'

'So we don't know what new ideas Bob may have had about the robbery or who he discussed them with?' Nat asked, wondering as he did so whether this visit was not fruitlessly using up precious time. 'I seem to recall that, when we met in February, you said that something had cropped up, some new "evidence" that he planned to discuss with his barrister.'

'That was the phone call, you see. That was what got him quite excited.'

'Phone call? You didn't say anything about a phone call.'

'Well, there didn't seem much point, Dr Gye, what with me not knowing who it was or what they said.'

'Perhaps you could tell me about it anyway,' Nat urged.

Pearl shrugged. 'Well, I can't see as it'll help any, but all right. It was that Sunday.'

Nat realized she was talking about the day her husband died.

'We'd been to church and had dinner and Bob was doing the washing up when the phone went. It wasn't a long call . . .'

'And you didn't hear anything that was said?'

'No, Bob was in the kitchen using the cordless phone and I was in here. When he came back in he said he had to go and see someone who might be able to help. He went round to get the car out—our lock-up is in Endfield Gardens—and that was the last I saw of him.'

'He didn't say where he was going or who he had to see?'

'No, he was very moody. Well, preoccupied I suppose I'd say. I had no idea. Kevin, here, phoned up later to talk to Bob and I had to say I didn't know where he was, didn't I, dear?'

Kevin nodded in confirmation. 'That's right, Pearl.'

'Did you get the impression that he was going to drive quite a distance?'

'I didn't think much about it then but when he wasn't back by bedtime I got really worried. I phoned Ted and asked what he thought I should do and he said he'd check the garage to see if Bob was back.' Pearl paused and took a deep breath. 'Well, you know what he found.'

'Didn't any of this come out at the inquest?'

'Yes, of course—not that I reckon the coroner took much notice of anything I had to say.'

'Dr Gye.' It was Kevin who broke in. 'Is it really necessary to rake all this up again? Pearl has relived the events of that terrible day a thousand times in the hope of remembering something that might help remove the stain of suicide from Bob's name. I know Pearl appreciates all you're doing, but . . .'

Nat nodded. 'You're right, of course, Kevin. It's just that Pearl wanted me to investigate and I didn't want to leave any stone unturned but now . . .' He shrugged. 'I think we have to accept that the police and the coroner were probably right. Even if they weren't, if there are still unanswered questions remaining, it would take more time and resources than I have to resolve them.' With a wan smile he turned to the woman in the wheelchair. 'I'm sorry, Pearl, but I really think you ought to give all your energy to settling into your new life. As soon as you're comfortable at St Luke's, I'll come and visit you and bring Bob's file back.'

Pearl was painfully understanding. 'That's quite all right, Dr Gye. To tell you the truth, it really doesn't seem that important any longer. There was a time when it mattered to me but now . . . I'll be seeing Bob again soon enough and then I can explain that I did all I could. I know he'll understand. I shouldn't be surprised if we'll have a good laugh about it.' She fumbled for a handkerchief and Nat knew it was time to leave.

*   *   *

'You can't really mean what you said to Mrs Gomer! You're not giving up just like that, are you?' Kathryn rounded on her husband as soon as he had turned the car out of Endfield Road in the direction of the city centre.

'No, I'm not, but right now I want her and her circle to believe exactly that.'

'Isn't that a bit mean?'

'Not if it gets us closer to finding out who

killed her husband.'

'But I thought you said—'

'Can we leave this discussion till we get home?' Nat slowed the Mercedes to a crawl in a convoy of Saturday shopping traffic. 'I've got ideas spinning round in my head like the wheels in a fruit machine and I'm trying to get them to line up and deliver the jackpot. Do you think you could go back over everything you saw and heard back there and make a note of anything that seems to you at all odd or interesting?'

'Such as what?'

'Anything, absolutely anything. I don't want to put ideas into your head.'

Kathryn shrugged and pulled an old envelope from her jacket pocket. For several minutes she stared vacantly out at the crowded pavements but then she started scribbling and Nat noticed that she had almost covered both sides by the time they had escaped from the urban frenzy and reached Great Maddisham.

There was a note from Amy on the kitchen table: 'Taken Jerry swimming. Back about 12.30. Victor Zeeman phoned 10.50. You can call him back on this number before 12.' Nat checked his watch. The time was 11.43. He immediately went to the phone in his study and punched in the mobile number on the au pair's note.

There were several rings before Zee's energetic voice came on the line. 'Nat, hi!

212

Look, I'm a bit pushed right now. Matinee in a couple of hours and the cauldron fire for the finale is playing up. Just wanted you to know that there's only one way your vanishing picture trick could be done. There's something you need to find out first. If that checks, then the switch is a simple matter of engineering. Have you got pen and paper handy? You might want to take this down.'

Zee went, point by point, through his theory while Nat scribbled notes. At the end, the magician muttered a hurried, 'Got that? Hope it helps! Good hunting! Cheers! Oh, and remember it would only take a few seconds.'

Nat put the phone aside and grabbed up Bob Gomer's file. Hurriedly he read again the account of the security van's journey from Heathrow to Bath. He laughed aloud.

At that moment Kathryn came in. 'You sound happy,' she said. 'Good news from Victor?'

'Absolutely. He told me about the Chomsky illusion.'

'Wonderful,' she said, sarcastically. 'That must have made your day. Who's Chomsky?'

'Apparently he's an American magician who specializes in spectacular effects and builds all his own equipment.'

'So, what's he got to do with our disappearing old master?'

'I'll explain later. Right now I'd like to hear your impressions of this morning's episode.'

Kathryn dropped into a chair. 'Well, desperately sad for that poor woman. The only good thing is that she has caring friends.'

'Hm! I wonder why.'

'*Why!* That's a bit cynical, isn't it?'

'Probably. Let it pass. What did you make of Kevin?'

'Beyond the fact that he's gay, you mean?'

'Gay!' Nat laughed. 'What makes you say that?'

'Trust me. And that's not just intuition either. Any man who gives time and, I would guess, genuine affection to old women instead of chasing after young ones is definitely not heterosexual. I get the impression you don't like him.'

'Not much.'

'Repressed macho prejudice!'

'Not at all. I just don't like being lied to.'

'What did he lie about?'

'He wants us to believe that there was nothing in any way special about the relationship between his mother and Bob. That wasn't the impression I got from mama.'

'I expect he was trying to spare Pearl's feelings. She obviously didn't know there was anything going on between her husband and their psychic friend—if there was.'

'No, there was more to it than that, I'm sure of it. And what Victor has just told me strengthens that suspicion.'

'Are you going to tell me, now, what that is?'

214

'Chomsky is reckoned in the magic fraternity as the grand master of spatial illusion, creating empty cabinets that aren't empty, transparent walls that aren't transparent.'

'False bottoms, mirrors, that sort of thing?'

'Yes, only a lot more sophisticated. Many of the tricks, according to Victor, are essentially the same. You know, beautiful assistant gets into box from which there is no possible exit; puff of smoke; assistant disappears. It's just the ways of achieving the illusion that go on developing. But even in the most up-to-date tricks there still has to be what, I gather, is known as the "moment of invisibility". The door is closed or a curtain is drawn or the cabinet is turned round. Just for a few seconds the accomplice is hidden from view and in those seconds she works the contraption that makes her apparently vanish. Now, success depends on the girl being able to do the necessary and that means perfect timing and lots of practice. What Chomsky has done is work the same trick with inanimate objects. No well-trained bimbo able to curl herself into a hidden compartment or swivel a fake wall. The trick has to be performed from elsewhere by mechanical or electronic means.'

'And that's what was done with our wretched painting?'

'I'm sure of it.'

'How?'

'Most security trucks obviously have to be built to very elaborate specifications. Many are encased in two layers of armoured plate, a bit like double glazing. Now supposing you take one of these vehicles and adapt it. You strip out one inner wall and the inner ceiling. You replace the wall with a lighter construction that looks identical and you leave enough space between the inner and outer walls to take a narrow crate, a crate containing a panel of worthless timber. Then you have your accomplice lash the crate containing the real painting to the inner, false wall. Are you with me?'

'So far.'

'OK. That wall is hinged at the top. When you're ready to work the trick, you press a button that activates a simple electric motor which swings the wall up into the ceiling. The outer wall now looks like the inner wall, the fake crate has all the appearance of the real one. At journey's end, as we've already worked out, the wrong crate is taken into the gallery and the van makes a quick getaway, to be replaced by a perfectly standard replica. Only one thing is necessary for the trick to be done.'

'The moment of invisibility?'

'Precisely. There had to be a time when the inside of the van was hidden from view. Victor suggested that I try to find out if there was such time. As he said, it only needed to be a few seconds.'

'And did you find it?'

Nat picked up the file. 'God bless boring, meticulous Bob Gomer. Listen to this:

'Charlie and me strapped it up tight, with Miss Miles watching us like a hawk. When the doors were locked Charlie signed the delivery note to say that Samson's had taken responsibility for the consignment. Ted was in a hurry to get started so I got into the back straight away and we set off.

'It's not exactly deathless prose but it does give a very clear picture, doesn't it? There's Ted Hardwick sitting in the cab, impatient to be away while his associates are dealing with the formalities. In reality he's operating the mechanism that works the switch. When Bob climbs aboard he doesn't notice anything different but then why would he? He doesn't know he's going to spend the next couple of hours guarding a worthless cargo.'

Kathryn gasped her astonishment. 'It sounds so simple when it's explained like that.'

'Victor says all the best tricks are simple.'

'But that would need an awful lot of engineering work to be done on the fake van.'

'And now we know someone capable of doing it, don't we?'

'Kevin George?' Kathryn shook her head emphatically. 'No, I don't buy that. You can't tie his little back street car renovation business in with an international crime syndicate.'

'Ah, but you're forgetting that his father made his money as a top London art dealer. He knew the European and American art markets intimately and I'm betting he had more than a few shady contacts. Mrs George as good as told me she didn't approve of her ex-husband's way of life and I suspect the name Talenti is not unknown to Kevin.'

Kathryn still looked doubtful. 'But how did Kevin get hold of one of Samson's vans to doctor?'

'Money was no object to the people he was working for.'

'Hm, I still think there are problems about that but let it pass for the moment. What about the seal?'

'Seal?'

'Yes, when Theophrast had checked the painting he fixed a gallery seal to the crate. Are you suggesting the crooks faked that, too?'

'That depends on whether Theophrast was in on the scam or not.'

There was the sound of a car drawing up outside the house. Kathryn stood up. 'That'll be Amy and Jerry. I'd better go and do something about lunch.' She sighed. 'I don't know about all this. It seems all we've got is inspired guesswork. We still need hard evidence.'

'Yes, and precious little time to find it. If we can only tie some of the apparently unconnected people together . . . Look, have you got any contacts you can probe about Edgar George? I'll try my luck with Theophrast.'

'How are you going to manage that? According to Heather Miles he's very wise to all the wiles of journalists and would-be interviewers.'

'I guess it'll have to be a frontal assault.'

Winged Chariot

On we sweep with a cataract ahead.
We're midway to the horseshoe, stop who can.

The weekend was frantic. Kathryn made a series of phone calls to older society friends who might have known Edgar George and began to build up an intriguing picture of a life lived in the fast lane often with scant observation of the traffic laws. She set up a Sunday afternoon meeting with a retired auction house director in Sussex who promised some gossipy tales about George's gambling exploits. Nat, meanwhile, sat at his computer long into the small hours of Sunday, redrafting his journal entry on the Gomer case, programming in the latest information and trying to make all the details fit together. He made one phone call and that was to Barny Cox to ask if the old lawyer could obtain a complete transcript of Bob Gomer's trial. Eagerly Barny promised to look up the appropriate volume of the Law Reports and provide a photocopy. He then went on to quiz Nat about the progress of his investigation. Finally he said, 'Well, do go carefully, dear boy. It worries me that these singularly nasty people you've become involved with have extended their reach into our quiet, academic backwater. They must be stopped—but not at any price.' Nat could hear the genuine anxiety in his voice.

Shortly after Kathryn had left, Nat set out to drive to Bath and arrived to find the Georgian city basking in the slanting, crystalline sunlight of a May evening. After checking into a hotel he went in search of the Millennium Gallery. He wanted to acquaint himself with the geography of the area while the building was closed and the streets quiet. As the latest attraction in the cultural life of a city that had been accumulating attractions for nineteen centuries Theophrast's contribution had to be content with modest premises or, at least, with premises whose frontage was modest. The gallery was a couple of streets away from the Regency heart of Bath with its elegant terraces and crescents and expensive antique shops. It presented a double facade, flanked by

Ionic columns. Over the half-glazed doors was a banner announcing the current main attraction: SEA AND SAIL—DUTCH AND ENGLISH MARINE PAINTING, 1650-1850. Peering in, Nat saw a surprisingly large vestibule and realized that the building must have considerable depth.

In order to locate the rear entrance he walked down the nearest side street. It fed into a main thoroughfare, part of the city's inner circuit. Less than a hundred yards away on the opposite side of the road there was an Esso service station. Nat approached it, watching on his left for an opening between the shop fronts lining the pavement. He found it almost directly opposite the petrol station. An arched entrance originally designed to accommodate a horse and cart was just wide enough to admit a medium-sized van. The passageway was deep in shadow as Nat made his way along it. Where it emerged from the premises on either side into an open space beyond, his way was barred by a padlocked iron gate. Nat peered through the grille. The paved area was large enough for half a dozen cars but was empty. The rear wall of the buildings opposite was studded with doors and windows from which no lights shone. He pictured a security van parked beside one of those doors while a delivery was in progress, then turning to make its way back into the street.

He retraced his steps. If Big Zee's switch

theory worked, the second van must have been waiting within about fifty yards of the entrance. Double yellow lines on both sides of the road indicated that the council were determined to keep the thoroughfare clear of congestion. Any vehicle parked on the street would draw attention to itself and that was the last thing people planning a crime would want to do. There had to be somewhere that a medium-sized van could be concealed but able to change places with its counterpart without arousing curiosity. Nat spent several minutes trawling along the pavement in both directions. There was no alley corresponding to the one he had just left. No garage, no warehouse, no cul-de-sac. The road was an unbroken terrace of small shops. He looked across the road. The property development on that side was more varied but there was nowhere that a van could be parked. To the left of the service station old housing stretched as far as the next crossroads. To the right there was a new office block, an ancient warehouse with FOR SALE notices glued to the first-floor windows, and three shops—a chemist's, a newsagent's and a general store on the corner. Nat sighed. The theory did not work.

He turned and began to walk back towards the hotel. Suddenly he stopped. He stared again at the buildings opposite. Spotting a gap in the traffic flow, he ran across the road and into the petrol station. There were two women in charge, engaged in bored, desultory conversation. Nat picked up a packet of wrapped sandwiches and a bar of chocolate from the displays.

'Good evening,' he said with a pleasant smile, laying his purchases on the counter. 'Not very busy?'

'It comes and goes of a Sunday evening,' one of the assistants, a middle-aged woman with somewhat startling magenta hair, replied. 'It's either empty out there or queuing up as far as the road.' She rang up the prices on her till.

'I was curious about the building next door; the office block,' Nat said nonchalantly. 'How long has it been there?'

The woman wrinkled her brow in concentration. 'Warburton's? I don't know. What do you reckon, Jem?' She consulted her colleague, younger by about twenty years and skimming through a magazine. 'About a year?'

'Mmm, I suppose,' the younger assistant mumbled uninterestedly.

'Can't have been much more because it took Warburton's ages to get planning permission after the old building was pulled down.'

'When was that?' Nat asked eagerly.

'Ooh ages. Years. Probably three years, wouldn't you say, Jem?'

'Mmm, probably.' The girl's gaze scarcely flickered up from the magazine.

'It was a real eyesore for ages.'

'An empty building site?'

'Yes, the council put a solid wooden fence around it, which, of course, was an open invitation to the local yobs to cover it in graffiti. Anyway, it didn't stop winos and druggies getting in there. They'd break the padlock on one of the gates and doss down inside. The police got tired of moving them on.'

'It can't have been very pleasant for you,' Nat suggested sympathetically.

'You can say that again. It got so as we had to have extra male staff to deal with possible attacks. Head office was going to close the station down. Then Warburton's actually started building. That would be around the Christmas before last. So, it must have been soon after Easter that they opened.'

'How do they get on for parking?'

'It's round the back. All these properties have access from Charlecombe Road, which, of course, is very convenient for the A4 and the motorway.' She handed Nat his change and wished him a good evening.

Nat did not exactly have a spring in his step as he went in search of dinner but he had that light-headed feeling that comes to every researcher who knows he has accumulated enough facts to make up a convincing case and that all he has to do is assemble them in the right order. He found a quiet Chinese restaurant and, over a remarkably good

Szechwan duck with watercress, he vigorously attacked the mystery of the vanishing masterpiece.

Ted Hardwick had been the paid agent and, in all likelihood, Charlie Randall had also been involved. They had been hired to make the Antonello portrait disappear in such a way that no one could prove that they had any complicity in the theft. With Theophrast and his assistant watching every stage of the transfer of the picture from airport to gallery, whatever the police might suspect, they would be able to prove nothing. The only complication was that, at the last minute, the incorruptible Bob Gomer had been added to the security team. That must have panicked Hardwick and Randall but, if so, they had recovered well. All they had to do was make sure Bob travelled in the back of the van so that he could not see the driver operate the mechanism which switched the crates and secure a 'moment of invisibility' to work that switch. Arrived in Bath, Hardwick, insisting that he was in a hurry to get home, took the van to fill the tank with petrol while his colleagues escorted the crate into the gallery. He knew he had only a few minutes for the next vital stage of the operation. But everything had gone with oily smoothness. Confederates had the gates to the waste lot open ready for him to drive in. The duplicate van was already waiting with its engine running. Hardwick transferred to the other vehicle and drove straight on to the service station forecourt, ready for the alarmed gallery staff to come and find him. Meanwhile, the other van had made its exit via the rear gates of the waste ground, heading for the motorway and all points east, carrying a priceless old master—and an empty vacuum flask.

So much for the 'how', Nat reflected. What about the 'who'? Theophrast? Surely he had to be involved. Only he would have known about the empty building site on the gallery's back doorstep. The police, Nat reflected, might have suspected him of involvement in the fraud but with Heather Miles backing up his story in every detail they would have no case against him. No wonder Theophrast had insisted on being accompanied by his assistant. The gallery owner's motive was not entirely clear but Nat hoped he might be able to shock him into some kind of revelation on the morrow.

That left the organization of the vans. How had Kevin George managed to lay his hands on one of Samson's vehicles? What was his connection with Talenti? Nat had to admit that Kathryn's difficulty about tying Kevin in with syndicated crime had substance but, with any luck, this would be resolved when she had delved into George senior's murky career.

*　　　*　　　*

Kathryn was, in fact, feeling very pleased with herself. While Nat was finishing his meal she was winding the Mercedes through a Sussex landscape of clipped hedges, shaven lawns and impeccable thatched desirable residences on her way back to Cambridge. The cosmetic rurality of the stockbroker belt, which would normally have depressed her, could not dampen her spirit this evening. She, too, was piecing together the various snippets of information she had gleaned over the past couple of hours.

Somerset Spens, who had agreed to meet her, turned out to be a garrulous and delightfully indiscreet little man with flowing white hair and a ruddy complexion. His large, red-brick and timber house commanded a wide, impressive, uninterrupted view of woods and meadows stretching as far as the distant South Downs.

'Bloody local bureaucrats wanted to put a relief road through there,' he explained, waving a proprietorial hand towards the landscape, 'but we soon put a stop to that.'

They were sitting on a terrace enjoying a late afternoon gin and tonic and they were alone, except for two large but genial Great Danes sprawled on the warm flagstones. Spens, one-time senior executive of Baron's, the Bond Street auctioneers, had welcomed Kathryn enthusiastically and with a frankly appraising eye. 'You must call me SS,' he said. 'Everyone does. My staff used to say it was highly appropriate and they weren't always joking. I ran a pretty tight ship. One had to. International fine art selling is a dog-eat-dog business.'

For some minutes Kathryn listened to the auctioneer's reminiscences, concluding that he must, indeed, have been a hard taskmaster. He was the sort of man who was incapable of being neutral on any subject. His opinions on everyone from contemporary politicians to erstwhile colleagues were uncompromising and, in some cases, potentially slanderous. She was wondering how to bring the conversation round to Edgar George when her host saved her the trouble.

'You wanted to talk to me about Georgie Porgie,' he announced. 'I always thought what someone said about Byron applied very well to him—"Mad, bad and dangerous to know". Eddie was a charmer and a chancer. In fact, I'd call him the king of chancers.'

'I gather he was good at his job; that he had an eye for art.'

SS gave a snort of a laugh. 'Eddie had an eye for many things but art wasn't one of them. Cars, horses, women . . .' He stopped abruptly and treated Kathryn to a hard stare. 'He wasn't your father, by any chance, was he?'

Kathryn laughed. 'No, I come from boringly respectable New England stock.'

'No offence intended. It's just that Eddie George put himself about very generously, so one never knows. Now, was he a good judge of art? No, but he was a good judge of people who were good judges of art. He hired the best brains in the business either as employees or agents. He made the contacts and paid others to follow them up. That was how he was able to beat rival dealers—and auctioneers—to some of the best items hidden away in private collections all over the world. He'd meet Lord X at the race track or Senator Y at a White House reception and the next thing one heard he was offering one of their Van Dycks or Van Goghs on the network.'

'He must have made a lot of money then.'

'Made, yes, and spent. What came in the front door very quickly went out the back. He married money. Some chit of a girl from among the chinless aristocracy who fell for his smooth chatline and devil-may-care style. He used her fortune to shoulder his way into the West End art scene—'

'Sorry to interrupt but I do want to get as clear a picture as possible. Where did he come from? What did he do before?'

'Ah, now that's probably the sixty-four thousand dollar question. He was always very chary about his origins, which means, of course, that he came from nowhere. His enemies—of whom there were plenty—put it about that he started life as a shady second-hand car dealer. The less charitable suggested that he had done at least one spell as a guest of Her Majesty. All I know for sure is that he loved fast cars. He was into the formula one racing scene long before I knew him and he was a dedicated rally driver.'

'I gather people also say that he mixed in very dubious company.'

'There's no doubt about that. Fine art is a rich man's hobby or business and not all rich men come by their fortunes in ways that are scrupulously open and above board. If you want to keep your hands clean as an auctioneer or dealer you have to be eternally vigilant about who you associate with. Some of us are more vigilant than others and Eddie George sailed closer to the wind than any supposedly reputable dealer I've ever come across.'

'Do you know if he was ever involved with a man called . . .'

Spens stood suddenly. 'It's getting chilly out here. Shall we adjourn? Dante, Beatrice, come on!'

Obediently the two dogs struggled to their feet and lolloped towards the french windows.

Kathryn had been too absorbed to notice the passing of time but now she saw that a stiffening breeze was fidgeting the topmost branches of a magnificent cedar and that its shadow had reached the terrace. She followed Spens into the house. It was the sort of interior which often featured in the lifestyle pages of *Panache*. They passed through a succession of rooms whose colour schemes had been expertly chosen and then filled with a mix of antique and modern hand-crafted furniture and fittings. What it lacked, Kathryn realized, was a woman's touch. Was there a Mrs SS? she wondered.

As if reading her thoughts, Spens said, 'Bloody rambling old place, isn't it? Too big for me since I sent my baggage of a wife packing. I don't know why I don't move. Yes I do: I'm too lazy. Let's go in here. It's where I spend most of the time.'

'Study', 'atelier', 'den'—none of these words described the room Kathryn now entered. Or perhaps they all did, since it obviously contained everything that was important in the life of its occupant. Two walls were full of books, another was mostly view-capturing window and the remaining wall was stuccoed with original pictures. At a glance, they seemed to be a jumble of early watercolours and old master drawings. The painterly theme was taken up by a large easel in a corner by the window on which was propped a canvas with a design hurriedly splashed in in blues and greens. A large mahogany desk, its furniture neatly arranged, stood like a rock in the centre of the room, seeming to resist the encroachment of paper, books and journals which flowed across the floor and every other flat surface.

Spens cleared the Sunday newspapers from a leather armchair for Kathryn and said, 'Another drink?'

'Thanks, but better not. Driving,' Kathryn explained.

'Sure? I can give you a coffee before you go. Pump you full of caffeine.'

Kathryn shook her head.

Muttering about hating to drink alone, SS poured himself another generous measure of gin, then seated himself in the large swivel chair behind the desk. He waved a hand at the neat pile of box files on his left. 'Don't let a publisher ever talk you into writing your memoirs,' he advised. 'It's the very devil of a job and they only do it because they think you're not going to be around much longer so they'd better cash in before the old fool's gone completely gaga and can still string a couple of sentences together.'

Dante and Beatrice took their places either end of the desk like supine bookends.

'Now, where were we?' Spens asked.

'I was about to ask if you'd ever come across a certain Alberto Talenti, who might have been an associate of George's. He was,' Kathryn chose her words carefully, 'a big Italian businessman and connoisseur. He died a couple of years ago.'

Spens frowned. 'Talenti, Talenti. Talenti. Now why does that name ring a bell?' He clenched his eyes shut with the effort of memory. Then shook his head. 'No, it's gone. Ask me another.'

Kathryn swallowed her disappointment. 'You mentioned on the phone that George was a compulsive gambler.'

'Eddie would place a bet on anything that moved. If he was sitting where you are now he'd probably say, "I'll lay you a pony that Beatrice gets up before Dante."'

'Really?'

'Oh, yes. But then his whole life was one long gamble, a game. I don't think he took anything seriously—certainly not money. When he had it he'd flash it around in a way that was just short of vulgar. When he hadn't he'd run up debts or try to gamble his way out of trouble or sell whatever was left of the family silver. He was a fascinating phenomenon to watch. One tended to get mesmerized by his antics. We all followed his hectic career in the gossip columns. You'd see his photograph taken with jockeys and owners at Ascot, Longchamp, Dubai or playing the tables with the cream of society. Casino owners from Monte to LA rubbed their hands when they saw Eddie George coming. Then there was his passion for motorsport. He poured millions into developing his own racing car. Thought he could compete with the Ferraris and BMWs of this world. That scheme collapsed, as did others he turned his hand to. There were at least two occasions when everyone thought he was finished. Then, up he bobbed, like a jack-in-a-box, brandishing some fabulous old master one of his agents had tracked down in an old schloss in the middle of God-knows-where. The next one knew, collectors and gallery directors the world over were running after him brandishing their chequebooks.'

'A darling of the gods.'

'Yes, but even they couldn't protect him for ever. Still, at least his death was as spectacular as his life. He took one chance too many and drove his car off the Corniche near Nice.'

'When was that?'

'I don't have much of a head for dates. Must have been mid-seventies. You'd be too young to know anything about it but it made quite a splash at the time. No one saw the accident and no other vehicle was involved, so, inevitably it gave rise to all sorts of conspiracy theories—murder by a swindled associate or cuckolded husband or contract killer; that sort of thing.'

'How intriguing. I—'

'Got it!' Spens interrupted. 'Talenti! I knew there was some reason why the name had lodged itself in the subconscious. I read about his death at the time and I remember thinking, "That's what happened to Georgie Porgie."'

'Talenti was killed in a car crash?'

'Yes. You didn't know that? It happened in

almost identical circumstances. This Talenti fellow was driving alone along the Grande Corniche and ran out of road for no obvious reason.'

Kathryn's mind was racing to make all sorts of connections but she said, 'There must be lots of accidents on that tortuous cliff road.'

'Undoubtedly. It was just the coincidence of his death being so similar and giving rise to the same kind of suspicions. As I recall this Italian was something big in the world of syndicated crime and the paper headline ran along the lines of "Suspected gangland killing".'

Kathryn stuffed her notebook back into her handbag. 'SS, thank you so much for your time. It's been absolutely fascinating.'

Before she could get up Spens jumped to his feet. 'I don't like to think of you driving all that way back to Cambridge on an empty stomach. Why don't we adjourn to the village pub? They do a very passable line in bar snacks.'

Kathryn pleaded the need to get home quickly and, with some difficulty, managed to fend off Spens' importunate hospitality. As she headed north through the Sussex lanes she had much to think about. She contemplated stopping en route to phone Nat but decided against it. Better to digest everything she had learned, decide what was important and what was not before comparing notes with him. Nat expected to be back by Monday afternoon.

That would be time enough to work at fitting their pieces of the jigsaw together.

*   *   *

At nine the following morning Nat stationed himself close to the rear entrance of the gallery to watch for Theophrast's arrival. He intended to confront the director without warning and the only way to achieve that was to make sure he was in his office before calling there. Nat thought it was a fairly good guess that Theophrast would drive or be driven to work and that was why a grey morning of intermittent drizzle found him skulking in a bus shelter from which he could see the passage leading to the Millennium Gallery premises. He felt foolish and conspicuous pretending to read a newspaper and remaining detached from the queues of genuine travellers which formed around him, then surged forward to embark when their transport arrived. What made him appear even more suspicious was the fact that every time a bus stopped he had to walk along the pavement so that his view would not be obscured. He reflected that if this was how private investigators operated they earned every penny of their fees.

After an hour he had seen two modest saloon cars arrive, both driven by women, and watched one Royal Mail and one delivery van come and go. Now, with every minute his doubts grew more clamorous. Suppose Theophrast lived within walking distance of the gallery and went in by the front door? Suppose he was one of those bosses who liked to get to his desk early in order to check the punctuality of his staff? Worst of all, suppose he was away and not coming into work at all today?

At seven minutes past ten a gleaming black BMW approached from the out-of-town direction, slowed to walking pace and cautiously turned into the alleyway opposite. It was driven by a chauffeur and Nat caught a glimpse of the other occupant, a middle-aged man with black hair. Minutes later the car reappeared without its passenger.

Nat walked around to the front of the gallery. He ascended the three shallow steps and pushed open the door. There were few visitors at this early hour and Nat joined a queue of three people waiting to buy tickets for the current exhibition. When his turn came he smiled at the young female assistant. 'I'm here to see Dr Theophrast,' he announced.

'Is he expecting you?' she asked pleasantly.

'No.'

'Dr Theophrast doesn't see anyone without an appointment.'

'He'll see me.' Nat stood his ground and stared fixedly back.

The girl looked at him, then at the party of

half a dozen Japanese tourists who had just arrived and were now lined up behind him. 'We have strict orders . . .' She faltered. 'Well, I'll have a word with his secretary but I'm sure it won't be any use. Can I have your name, please?'

'Just say it's Antonello—from Messina.' He watched as she picked up the internal phone and relayed the information. Having done so, she turned her attention to her customers.

Nat withdrew into a corner of the foyer near the door. From this vantage point he could watch the receptionist and the broad, carpeted staircase which curled round from beside her desk to the upper floors. If, as was probable, the offices were housed in rooms above, it was likely that the director would despatch his secretary to screen the unwelcome arrival. Nat steeled himself to deal with this next obstacle.

But it was not a formidable, business-suited lady with an *'ils ne passeront pas'* air who appeared round the bend in the stair a few minutes later. The stocky figure leaning slightly on a cane could only be Theophrast himself. He paused on the half-landing and peered down into the foyer through thick-rimmed spectacles. Nat turned to face the door, determined to keep his quarry guessing as long as possible. In the glass he could see a dim reflection of the lit area around the desk. Into this area Theophrast walked and leaned across to speak with the receptionist. She pointed in Nat's direction and the director slowly crossed the intervening space. At the last moment Nat turned, with a slight smile but saying nothing.

Theophrast looked him up and down and Nat sensed his nervousness. 'We have not met, have we?' He spoke with the precise accent of a man who has learned a language not his own.

'No, but we have much to discuss.'

Theophrast nodded. 'Then we had better go to my office.' He turned and led the way. Nat summed him up: fifties, slightly overweight, expensive Italian suit, white rose buttonhole providing a dash of flamboyance, stout ebony cane with a silver handle. His office was a large first-floor room at the front of the building and, looking round, Nat reflected that the squat little immigre had done very well for himself. The serpentine-fronted, Louis XV library table serving as Theophrast's desk was either genuine or an excellent nineteenth-century copy. Nat guessed that there was no question about the originality of the four paintings that graced the walls. Even he could tell that they were fine examples of portraiture dating from the sixteenth and seventeenth centuries.

Theophrast took his seat behind the desk and waved his guest to a trio of elegant fauteuils in front of it. Nat elected to remain standing. He noticed the slight tremor in the hand resting on the tooled leather.

'So, am I to know your name?' Theophrast opened.

'It's of no importance. We both know why I am here.'

'Antonello da Messina?'

Nat nodded. *'Portrait of a Doge.'*

Theophrast sighed. 'A truly amazing masterpiece by the greatest innovative genius of the Quattrocento.'

'And extremely valuable.'

'So the Philistines say!' Theophrast snorted. 'How can you put a monetary value on the work of a master who changed the whole course of Venetian art? What we owe to this mysterious genius is way beyond price. He arrives like a *deus ex machina* from Sicily, of all places, which has no strong tradition, and yet he has mastered the technique of van Eyck and the great Netherlanders. He actually *teaches* the Venetians to paint in oils, with precision of detail and miraculous luminosity. Without Antonello you have no Bellini, no Carpaccio, perhaps even no Titian.' There was no doubting the genuineness of the man's passion.

'An enthusiast might go to great lengths to possess the work of such a master,' Nat suggested, 'even theft.' He saw vividly in his mind's eye Alberto Talenti's very private salon.

Theophrast opened his mouth to say something, then closed it and sat with lips firmly pursed. Nat saw a shimmer of sweat begin to form on his forehead. He was about to challenge the director with what he knew or guessed about the vanishing picture trick when something in the other man's demeanour checked him. Theophrast seemed to be shrinking in his chair and he was staring up with dilated pupils. He was, obviously, terrified. Nat realized, to his surprise, that Theophrast thought his visitor had been sent from Italy to wreak vengeance. Well, if the gallery owner suspected that he was a hit man, Nat was not going to disabuse him, not if it meant getting the picture back.

'There are, of course, men from whom it is unwise to steal,' he said. 'Men with ruthless associates and international connections.'

Theophrast cleared his throat. He was thinking fast. 'The painting you mentioned . . .'

'Portrait of a Doge, believed to be Pietro Mocenigo.'

'Yes. There was, indeed, an attempt to steal it. A very clever attempt. The thieves got away with the portrait. But I was determined to recover it, knowing, as you say, how important it is to those who own it. I left no stone unturned. You must believe me.' Theophrast dabbed his brow with a silk pocket handkerchief. 'The police were useless but I persevered. I have contacts they lack. Just a week ago my efforts were successful.'

'You found it?' Nat tried to conceal his astonishment.

'Yes, yes,' Theophrast babbled eagerly, desperate to be believed. 'I would have contacted the owners sooner but, of course, I had to check the painting minutely for any possible damage. Mercifully it has been quite unharmed by its adventure.'

'The owners will be delighted to hear it. Where is the painting now?'

'In the basement storeroom downstairs. Would you like to see it?'

'Of course.'

'Then shall we?' Theophrast waved towards the door. He opened a drawer in the desk and Nat heard the rattle of keys as the director transferred the contents to his trouser pocket.

As he descended the grand staircase beside the limping director Nat's mind went into overdrive. What was he about to be shown? Antonello's fifteenth-century original? Yet another copy? Whether masterpiece or fake it was extremely unlikely that he would be able to tell the difference. Would he be any closer to the truth or just left struggling with yet one more enigma in an already Byzantine course of events? From the ground floor they descended by a narrow flight of stone steps and were confronted by a heavy steel door. Theophrast opened it with a key and preceded Nat into a corridor that was no more than three paces in length. They came to a halt before another barrier, an openwork iron gate that was obviously integral to the building and controlled access to what had once been a wine cellar. Again Theophrast plied his bunch of keys.

When a light had been switched on Nat saw that they were in a long cavern that stretched the full depth of the building. The old stone compartments that had once held bottles now contained a medley of items—empty frames, bundles of catalogues and rolls of what were probably exhibition posters. The opposite wall had been furnished with a long wooden rack and in this the paintings stood, each in its own stall and wrapped in hessian or canvas.

Theophrast hurried ahead. He laid aside his stick and, extracting a bundle from the row, placed it reverentially on a table in the middle of the room. Carefully he unfolded the painting and stood back for Nat to inspect it. In the dim light he looked once more on the florid features of a long-dead merchant prince. The face was mesmerizing. The doge met his gaze with a sardonic, questioning smile, as if to say, 'Well, am I genuine?'

Nat was aware of stentorious, agitated breathing behind him. 'It is . . . It is . . . There are no words,' Theophrast muttered. 'And that monstrous Philistine kept it locked away to gloat over in private.'

Nat heard Theophrast take a couple of steps backwards but was still admiring the freshness of Antonello's flesh tones and the jewel-like quality of the embroidered cap. The

sudden snapped command, therefore, took
him completely by surprise.

'Wrap it again!'

Nat turned to see Theophrast standing in
the middle of the cellar. In his shaking hand he
held a small pocket pistol. 'Wrap it!'
Theophrast repeated. 'And then hand it to
me.'

Nat stood very still, his eyes fixed on the
excitable man's trigger finger. The slightest
involuntary twitch might cause the thing to go
off. 'Dr Theophrast,' he said as quietly as he
could, 'there is no need—'

'Hold your tongue! Do as you're told! Wrap
it! Now!' Nat moved cautiously to take hold of
the cloth and begin folding it over the panel.
'You're making a terrible mistake. I'm—'

'No, it's your masters who are making the
mistake. This painting is not going back to
their hoard. It's mine. I had a deal with
Alberto, years ago. He cheated me. Do you
know what he did? He fobbed me off with a
copy, a sacrilegious imitation! He thought it a
great joke. Well, I'm the one who's laughing
now. I have recovered what rightfully belongs
to me. Tell your bosses I defy them. They can
do their worst. They'll have to kill me before I
give it up. Now, bring it here!'

Nat advanced, holding the wrapped panel
like a shield before him, his eyes fixed on the
other man's. 'Look, let me explain . . .'

Theophrast waved the gun with a jerky,

uncontrolled movement. Nat stopped in his tracks, heart beating. Somehow he would have to get the weapon away from the other man before there was a terrible accident. His only implement was the painting. Slowly he held it out. Then, as Theophrast reached for it with his left hand, Nat made a sudden lunge at the pistol.

Everything happened in an explosive fraction of a second. There was a cry, a sharp crack. Nat was thrown back by something that thudded into his chest. He sprawled on the stone floor, hitting the table with his shoulder as he fell. This clattered to the ground. As he looked up confused sounds were still echoing round the walls. Theophrast was staring down, mouth open. Screaming, 'No! No!'

The moment seemed frozen. It was shattered by Theophrast's sudden movement. He made a halting, crab-like shuffle to the door. As Nat struggled to his feet the director clanged the barrier to behind him and turned the key. Seconds later he had disappeared beyond the farther door, fastening it also.

A Dish Served Cold

*You're satisfied at last? You've found out
    Sludge?
We'll see that presently: my turn, sir, next!
I, too, can tell my story.*

Nat staggered across to the gate. Rattled it.
Shouted. There was no response. No sound
could penetrate the outer door and reach the
inhabited floors above. Yet other people must
have seen him come down with Theophrast.
Surely, Nat reasoned, someone would want to
know what had happened to the stranger who
had turned up unexpectedly and, even more
unexpectedly, been received by the director.

It was as he propped himself against one of
the empty stone embrasures that he became
aware of the pain in his chest. He looked down
at the front of his jacket. There was nothing to
see. No tear. No bloodstain. Yet as he rubbed
his breastbone he knew that it was bruised.
The force of the shot must have rammed the
painted panel against his rib cage. The
wrapped painting lay where it had fallen. Nat
picked it up. There was a circular powder burn
mark on the straw-coloured hessian and, in the
middle of it, a tiny hole. Carefully Nat folded
back the layers of cloth. In the middle of
Pietro Mocenigo's cheek there was a grey-

246

black splodge surrounded by an area of chipped and discoloured paint. He held the panel under a light bulb to examine the damage more closely. The bullet seemed to have struck at a slightly oblique angle and flattened itself against the close-grained, ancient oak. He turned the picture over. A tiny bulge in the wood showed where the missile had almost penetrated. Had it done so . . .

Nat stared at the wounded doge. 'My thanks, *padrone*,' he muttered. Then he set the painting down carefully and turned his attention to the problem of escaping from his prison.

He took out his mobile phone and switched it on. There was no signal. He walked around the cellar holding the receiver before him but to no effect. Even when he stood beneath the small barred window high up in the wall at the far end of the room the tiny screen remained stubbornly blank. Nat looked up at the grimy, arched fanlight which had once surmounted a door, long-since bricked in. He guessed that it looked out on the rear courtyard. If he could break the glass perhaps he would be able to see when anyone passed and call for help. He collected the fallen table and placed it directly beneath the window. It was a flimsy affair but with any luck it would stand his weight. The next thing he needed was a suitable weapon. One lay to hand, neatly propped against the picture rack. Nat grabbed Theophrast's ebony cane with its heavy, silver handle in the shape of a swan's head and neck.

He climbed gingerly on to the creaking table. His head was now level with the glass which had been rendered virtually opaque by years of grime. He had nothing to hold on to to steady himself and when he swung the stick the table swayed ominously. There was only about six inches between each pair of bars. Striking at this small target area while at the same time maintaining his balance took all the concentration he could muster. His first blows produced no result. Either the glass was too thick or the force he could bring to bear upon it in the cramped conditions was inadequate. He paused and took stock of the situation. There was only one answer. Grasping the cane in both hands and taking careful aim, he brought the swan's head down with all his strength upon the window. With a protesting creak the table legs bent away from the wall. One splintered and Nat half fell, half jumped to the floor. But his efforts were rewarded with the tinkling sound of breaking glass.

Daylight now streamed in. Staring through the jagged hole, Nat was greeted with the close-up view of a car number plate.

He cursed his luck. He had hoped that beyond the wall of his prison there would be an old flight of external steps. The gap would have afforded him a reasonably wide field of vision, allowing him to watch for any movement. As it was, the old entrance had obviously been filled in when the doorway had been blocked, probably to provide maximum parking space. That might mean that he would have to wait until the owner of the car finished work for the day, unless, of course, the said owner went out for lunch. And the longer Nat remained incarcerated the more time Theophrast had to get clean away.

He examined the broken table to see if anything could be done with it. He found that it could be made to lean against the wall and might be rendered stable if he could do something about the broken leg. He searched among the empty frames until he found one more or less the right size. With a dusty coil of old picture cord recovered from the back of a shelf he lashed this to the table in a very Heath Robinson fashion. When he mounted the makeshift platform he discovered that it would support him as long as he kept very still. He looked out. Between the car wheels he could see a narrow slit of back yard. It was enough to give him a view of any feet that wandered across his narrow arc of vision. It would have to do.

It was while he was wondering whether a shout might produce any result that another thought struck him. He took out his mobile phone again and switched it on, holding it up to the window. This time 'SOS ONLY' flashed in the little luminous rectangle. Thanking heaven for modern technology, Nat made a 999 call.

When he had persuaded the operator that his was not a hoax message and received the assurance that his problem would be dealt with immediately, Nat found, to his surprise, that he could relax. Perhaps it was reaction after the trauma of narrowly escaping assassination. Perhaps it was the restful atmosphere, for the temperature and humidity in the gallery storeroom were very strictly controlled. Perhaps it was the entertainment on offer, for Nat passed several idle minutes taking paintings from their racks and enjoying a private view. Whatever it was, he experienced a remarkable mental calm. It was as though the mystery that had danced, now in a frenzy, now with tantalizing languor, through his life ever since Pearl Gomer's February visit to Beaufort, was casting aside the last few of its seven veils. Nat found, to his intense relief, that he could *think*.

He sat down on the floor in an angle of the wall close by the door and reassembled all the salient facts as he now understood them. Frauds. Fakes. Counterfeits. Copies. That was what this business, or, rather, as he now realized, these businesses were about. Deception and the anger of the deceived. He pictured Browning's Mr Sludge, the unmasked false medium, grovelling before his fuming, humiliated patron, begging for mercy. Then his thought went to the poet, penning that vitriolic denunciation of spiritualism because his own dear Elizabeth had been so cruelly deceived by Sophie Eckley. Congreve was wrong: hell *did* have a fury greater than that of a woman scorned; the fury of a woman or man who has been made a fool of. He had seen that fury in Theophrast this morning, a long-maturing rage that had coldly and carefully planned its revenge. He imagined the anguished wrath that must have consumed Bob Gomer when he worked out for himself, or with the aid of the mysterious caller, that Ted Hardwick, his friend and confidant, was, in reality, the agent of all his woes. Then there was the dangerous resentment of all those owners who might discover that they had been palmed off with modern copies of their masterpieces by Talenti and his gang. Deceit, secrecy, exposure, anger, fear—most of the pieces now fitted together. Most, but not all. And even if he could assemble every last one, would it ever persuade the authorities of the need for urgent action? If not, Bob Gomer's killer would go unpunished. And he and Kathryn would be forever looking over their shoulders.

It was cramp in his legs that brought Nat out of his reverie. He paced his prison, took a look through the broken window at the still-deserted yard, then picked up the Antonello and laid it on the table, carefully pulling back

251

all the wrappings. The jagged crater fringed by flakes of paint and gesso underlay had taken away the corner of the subject's mouth and quite changed his expression. Instead of an ironical smile the doge now stared back with what seemed grim bewilderment. 'Well may you look puzzled, my friend,' Nat said. 'It seems you're not as important as you may have thought. No, don't turn that scandalized look on me. You're not the cause of all this mayhem. Catalyst, certainly, but not the *primum mobile*.'

'Anyone down there?' A woman's voice came from above.

'Yes!' Nat carefully removed the painting and climbed on to the swaying table. 'Yes, I'm here,' he called through the window. Squinting to the left, he saw the crouching figure of a young WPC beside the parked car.

'And you're definitely locked in?'

'Definitely. Look, you need to find the gallery director, Jonah Theophrast. I'm pretty sure he's done a bunk. It's vital you track him down.'

'Very good, sir.' The officer put on her best 'calming the victim' voice. 'My colleague has gone into the gallery to find out what's what. We'll soon have you out of there.'

That proved to be an empty promise. When the constable's male companion rejoined her it was to report that the gallery director had, indeed, vanished and that he had taken with him the only keys to the storeroom. This information was relayed to Nat by the WPC. He could now see other pairs of feet through the gap beneath the car's chassis. Minutes later he heard a door slam and an engine rev up. Slowly the vehicle withdrew from Nat's field of vision. Now he could see the policewoman and her colleague squatting in front of the window.

'Sorry about the delay, sir. Everything's at sixes and sevens in there,' a moustached PC explained. 'Seems the boss has left in a hurry and no one knows what's going on. We've closed the gallery and moved the visitors out. Looks like we'll have to get a locksmith to come and open up. I'm afraid I don't have the authority to organize that. But don't worry, sir, someone from CID will be here shortly to take over.'

'Look, officer, the man who needs to be told about this is DCI Jack Hawkins.' Nat did his best to stress the urgency of the situation without giving the impression of just being a hysterical victim who'd been attacked and shut up in a cellar.

'Will that be Superintendent Hawkins, sir?'

'Yes, yes, very probably. Could you please get a message to him? I must speak to him. If you can't get me out quickly, please ask him to come here.'

'Ah, well, sir, the Super's a very busy man . . .'

Nat jumped down and picked up the

damaged painting. He held it to the window. 'Look, constable. You see that? It's a bullet. It was meant for me. It was fired by Theophrast. I don't want to be alarmist but you have a potential murderer running around out there.'

There was a brief silence, followed by a whispered conversation between the police officers. The man said he would report and Nat saw him walk across to his patrol car. When he returned it was to say that a message had been relayed to Hawkins but that he could not say how the Superintendent would react.

It was mid-afternoon before Nat found himself sitting across the desk from a bald, square-jawed, gaunt man in his mid-fifties. Apart from a cursory greeting Superintendent Hawkins paid no attention to his visitor for several minutes while he read the statement Nat had made on his arrival at police HQ. The Detective Sergeant appointed to take charge at the Millennium Gallery had deployed his limited staff efficiently but it was a couple of hours before a locksmith had been found and Nat had been released from his prison. This had been followed by the journey to the station, the dictation of a statement and a long discussion with the officer in charge of the case which had developed into an argument thanks to Nat's insistence on speaking to Hawkins. Now, having obtained that objective, he found himself staring with mounting frustration at the man who had precipitately 'solved' the original Gomer case and was, evidently, in no hurry to reopen it.

Hawkins read through to the end of the text and then reread some passages, the whole leisurely process being punctuated by a succession of grunts, sniffs and sighs. When, at last, he dropped the papers on his desk and looked up Nat grabbed the initiative.

'Have you found Theophrast?' he demanded.

Hawkins rubbed his eyes wearily. 'Dr Theophrast is not at home and his car is missing. We've spoken to his chauffeur, who says that his boss came back to the flat unexpectedly and in a state of some excitement and went out immediately without saying where he was going. I've had his description and the car details circulated to all our patrols. It won't take us long to find him and then, of course, we'll question him.' He looked levelly at Nat as if to say, 'I do know my job.' He tapped the pages before him. 'You've made a very serious allegation here and one that, I must say, is not easy to credit. You may not be aware that Dr Theophrast is something of a local celebrity, a wealthy and generous philanthropist. That gallery of his was a gift to the people of Bath. It belongs to the council but it was funded entirely with Theophrast's money.'

'Has anyone enquired where the good doctor's fortune came from?' Nat asked. 'I happen to know that he was once and perhaps still is up to his armpits in organized crime.'

Hawkins ignored the intervention. 'You see, what this statement of yours doesn't make clear to me is just why you were in the Millennium Gallery in the first place. Did you go with the express intention of having a violent row with Dr Theophrast?'

'My statement does explain that I went to discuss with him the disappearance of a valuable painting over eighteen months ago.'

Hawkins either did not listen to Nat's reply or chose to ignore it. 'You see, at the moment I only have your version of what passed between you and Dr Theophrast.'

Nat scowled. 'So, what are you suggesting—that I came here to threaten him with a gun?'

Hawkins shrugged.

'In that case where is the pistol that fired the bullet which your forensic experts will find lodged in the painted panel and why has Theophrast performed a vanishing trick?'

The policeman's face remained a mask of impassivity. 'Oh, I didn't say I didn't believe you, Dr Gye. If I thought you were spinning us a yarn you wouldn't be sitting there now. What I'm trying to get my head round is who you are and why you're involved in what are strictly police matters.'

Nat was on the point of blurting out, 'If you're more concerned with protecting your reputation than catching criminals, you're in the wrong job.' He said as calmly as he could, 'When the portrait went missing, all the evidence pointed to a clever theft managed with the aid of members of the security firm which was transporting it. It is only recently that, by chance, information came my way that suggested that the real mastermind was Jonah Theophrast.'

'Information which, like a conscientious citizen, you passed on to the police?'

With difficulty Nat ignored the taunt. 'I wanted to check my facts first. Far be it from me to be guilty of wasting police time, Superintendent.'

'You're a clever man, Dr Gye. Otherwise you wouldn't be able to hold down your job at Cambridge. So, you must see my problem. A complete stranger turns up in our fair city and within hours he is involved in a nasty fight over a stolen picture with a highly respectable member of our society. Now, if you were me, would you take the word of this stranger at face value?'

Nat opened his mouth to reply but Hawkins went on. 'This department has one of the best clear-up rates in the country. We're very proud of our record. *I'm* very proud of our record. And it's all down to thorough policing, Dr Gye—checking, probing, leaving nothing to chance. Much of it's pretty dull work, if the truth be told, but it gets results. Far better results—if you'll forgive my saying so—than

257

any amateur dashing about the country following a hunch is likely to come up with.'

That was the point at which Nat's patience snapped. 'A good man is dead and his killer is still at large thanks to your "thorough policing". I never wanted to get involved. I've quite enough to do as you say "holding down" my university job. But when I got pitchforked into this business I knew it was no use coming to you with a "hunch", so I tried to produce some solid evidence. Now, in my book, getting shot at is pretty convincing as evidence goes.'

Hawkins refused to react. 'If I understand you correctly, you reckon we were wrong in bringing charges against this security guard . . . er . . . Robert Gopher.'

'Gomer. I think you were deceived by what was a very intricate and ingenious crime.'

'Yes, I was intrigued by your explanation of how the crooks carried out the theft. Very clever. Not that we could ever prove it now. If the van was kitted out the way you suggest it will have been trashed a long time ago.'

'Theophrast confessed to me that he planned the robbery. I'll be happy to testify.'

'And if he denies it?'

'He'd still have to explain away having the painting in his possession and not reporting its recovery. But this is not the real point.'

'Oh, I'm so sorry. Dull Mr Plod missing the obvious again?'

'No, that isn't what I meant.' Nat searched

for words which would not fracture Hawkins' eggshell-thin ego. 'What I was thinking was that Theophrast is on the edge, the outer rim, of something much bigger and more important. When you have him under lock and key I'm sure you can get him to talk about his association with the Talenti group. If that information was shared with other professional bodies—the Italian police, Interpol, IFAR—well, I just thought that you could be instrumental in closing down a major international crime syndicate.'

Hawkins' thin features contracted into a mirthless smile. 'Oh, look!' he said, pointing to the window.

'What?' Nat turned his head.

'A squadron of pigs doing a fly-past.'

Nat stood abruptly. 'Good afternoon, Superintendent.' He strode out of the office.

On the steps outside the station he bumped into the woman constable who had come to the gallery.

'How'd you get on with the Super?' she asked.

'Let's just say I'm profoundly sorry for all those who have to work with him.'

The WPC laughed. 'Don't mind "Hurry" Hawkins. He's just demob happy. Counting the days to his retirement to a nice villa in Spain. He doesn't want anything to complicate his life.'

'Spain, Spain, Spain,' Nat mused as he

opened up the car on the M4. Why did that country keep cropping up? The Hardwicks had chosen it for their early retirement, financed, no doubt, by their share of the robbery loot. What was it they had said about that? 'A villa overlooking the sea'. Costa del Crime, perhaps? He tried to recall in detail the brief conversation he had had with the loathsome Ted and Rosie in the supermarket. She had explained that a 'good friend' had pressed them to follow him to the land of sun and sangria. Could that friend, by any chance, have been Charlie Randall? Ted had certainly been quick to shut her up when she started boasting about their emigration plans. Randall was an ex-policeman. And now, here was the senior investigating officer of the Bath robbery also heading for the same destination. Could it be . . . ? Or was that just conspiracy theory run riot?

He raised the suspicion with Kathryn later that evening as they sat at home comparing notes.

'Well, it would certainly explain why Hawkins was in a hurry to wrap up the case and why he persuaded his local friends here not to probe Bob Gomer's death too closely.'

'Apparently such slipshod policing is totally out of character.' Nat smiled. 'He's known as "Hurry" Hawkins to his underlings and that's a kind of reverse nickname. He prides himself on being slow and thorough. It's hard to conceive of anyone more fastidiously unimaginative than our Jack.'

Kathryn lay full length on the sofa, eyes closed in concentration. 'So, we were barking up the wrong tree when we assumed that the Talenti crowd were behind the robbery, it was Theophrast all the time?'

'Yes, I'd worked that out before my dramatic tête-à-tête with our chubby friend. I realized we'd got it wrong because our minds were unavoidably clouded by our experiences in Italy. We assumed that the inheritors of Talenti's empire were trying to get the painting back to avoid it going on public display. But that theory presented enormous problems: how could they have organized so intricate a crime at long range and comparatively short notice? But clear away that idea and you're left asking the question, "Who was really best placed to organize the robbery?" There's only one answer. Theophrast arranged for the painting to be borrowed in the first place. He fixed its transport. He knew the geography of the area around the gallery. He had the resources and the time to plan the crime in minute detail. When I confronted Theophrast all I didn't have was a motive and he very kindly provided that.'

'And he also had the police in his pocket— as a back-up, just in case anything went wrong?'

'It's a tempting thought. Theophrast has

261

been brooding on the recovery of the Antonello portrait for years. It was a passion, an obsession. He had much more than money invested in the robbery. He wasn't going to leave anything to chance. It would certainly make sense to imagine him having a top member of the local constabulary in his pay. But it may be that I'm just prejudiced against Hawkins' damned arrogance.'

'I suppose we'll only know when we see how energetically he goes about tracking Theophrast down.'

'Yes, if he is involved he has a real problem on his hands and one that can only be solved by Theophrast doing as impressive a vanishing trick as the picture.' Nat sighed. 'Perhaps it would be better for all concerned if that happened.'

'Why do you say that?'

'I've been worrying about the fallout from this all the way back from Bath. My attempt to put a bomb under Hawkins was a miserable failure. There's no way that the international forces of law and order are going to swoop down on the Talenti operation in days—if ever. So that doesn't solve our problem.'

'But it's Theophrast who's in the frame for the robbery now. If he's charged with it . . .' Kathryn stopped, hand to mouth. 'Oh my God, I see!'

'Yes, as soon as the latest instalment of the *Portrait of a Doge* saga gets into the media our

Italian chums are going to get very twitchy.'

'Perhaps Hawkins will keep the newshounds at bay. He won't want the embarrassment of having his handling of the original case called in question, not to mention his possible stifling of the enquiry into Bob Gomer's death.'

There was a long, gloomy silence. Then Kathryn sat up. 'Oh, what a mess! We're only going to be safe as long as that oily Albanian bastard gets away with robbery and murder.'

'Well, probably not murder.'

Kathryn looked up sharply. 'But surely it must have been him who ordered Bob Gomer's death. He had to stop him telling the court what he knew about the robbery.'

'I don't see how he can have. Even if Theophrast is the sort of man to order a contract killing—and I'm not altogether sure about that—he wouldn't have had time to get an assassin on the job.'

'But he could have phoned Ted Hardwick.'

'Ted hasn't the bottle to murder his own brother-in-law in cold blood. Bob's death was . . .'

The telephone rang. Kathryn walked across the room and picked up the receiver. Nat watched as his wife asked, 'Who's calling?' He saw her eyes widen in alarm. He heard her say in her well-practised, polite and neutral telephone voice, 'I'm afraid not at the moment . . . Tomorrow sometime, I think . . . May I ask what this is in connection with? . . . What! Oh no, that's impossible. You must have mixed him up with someone else . . . Yes, of course. I'll pass that on . . . Yes . . . Yes . . . Goodbye.' She plumped herself down on the sofa. 'That was the *Bristol Times* wondering if they could have a few words.'

'Damn! Let's hope your quick thinking throws them off the scent.'

'If they're any good at all at their job they won't be fooled for long.'

'No, and what's in the regional press tomorrow or Wednesday will be in the nationals the day after. I can see the headlines now: "TV don in Bristol shooting". We've just run out of time.'

Gathering

The miraculous proved the commonplace . . .

It was only minutes later that another call came through. This time it was the news desk at BBC Radio Bristol that wanted to talk to Nat about an incident in the Millennium Gallery at Bath. When Kathryn had put the receiver down she disconnected the phone.

'Right, that's it!' Nat said, jumping up. 'We'll have the press camped all over the front lawn within hours. We obviously can't stay here.'

'Agreed.' Kathryn frowned. 'Where shall we go and for how long? We can't have our lives turned upside down indefinitely.'

'I think the best plan will be for you to take Jerry and Ed to Wanchester and stay put. Can you cope with email businesswise?'

Kathryn brushed her hair from her forehead with an impatient gesture. 'For a couple of days, perhaps. No longer. The group auditor is coming over from New York at the end of the week. He'll expect me to be there and I, sure as hell, intend to keep a beady eye on him. Anyway, where are you going to be all this time?'

'I'll hole up in college and get the porters to tell any unwelcome visitors that I'm out of town. It'll take a very canny journalist to get past Bramley and his praetorian guard.'

'But we can't just stay in hiding and hope the problem goes away.'

'And we can't sit around waiting for the slow wheels of Superintendent Hawkins to grind exceeding small.'

'So?'

'So, I'll have to try and bring things to a head; find some way of getting the right people behind bars without starting up international shock waves.'

She stared back at him. 'But, how on earth . . . ?'

'I wish to God I knew.' Nat came over and held her very close.

'It's all so surreal,' Kathryn murmured. 'Like a nightmare in reverse. Everything seems so calm and ordinary here but when we wake up in the real world we might find all sorts of horrors waiting.'

'We'll get through it,' Nat said. 'Trust me, I'm a doctor.'

It was almost midnight by the time Nat had packed Kathryn, the au pair and a sleepily protesting Jerry into the Mercedes and seen them on their way. It took him little extra time to gather together all he needed and drive into Cambridge. Once ensconced in his rooms at Beaufort he brewed up a large cafetiere of coffee and settled at his desk with all the relevant Gomer documents, his own scribbled notes and his computer journal. He was determined to keep a clear head and to get every scrap of information into chronological order. First he took a printout of everything on screen. Then he opened a new file.

BOB GOMER AND A VANISHING PAINTING 2

Past Events:

Years ago Alberto Talenti set up art theft and fraud organization.

Jonah Theophrast one of his lieutenants.

At some point they parted company.

Dispute over ownership of Antonello's *Portrait of a Doge.*

Talenti tries to trick his partner with a copy.

Jonah becomes highly respected citizen of Bath (perhaps following the Talenti pattern in Ferrara?).
But determined to get his hands on the portrait.
Grabs chance while Alberto is away to talk his wife into loaning the Antonello to Millennium Gallery.
Plans elaborate robbery. Painting must 'disappear'.
Talenti not able to make a fuss because doesn't want the robbery to get media coverage which would draw attention to his activities.

Nat sat back, surveying the screen. So far, so good, he thought. Theophrast's scheme was little short of brilliant. Talenti would know exactly what had happened. He would, undoubtedly, be extremely angry at having his old colleague turn the tables on him but he would do nothing about it as long as the incident did not attract publicity. Anyway, in due course he would be able to collect the insurance money.

Question: Was Edgar George involved with Talenti and Theophrast?
Inconceivable that he did not know them. They were all in the business of tracking down masterpieces secreted away in private collections.

267

Can't be a coincidence that his 'accidental' death was identical to Talenti's years later. George must have been killed because he was in some way a threat or a nuisance to the Talenti organization.

Nat drank a whole mug of coffee while he looked at the Talenti-George-Theophrast connection from every angle. Eventually he set the problem aside and went on to consider,

The Robbery:
Meticulously planned by Theophrast, even down to moving Heather Miles on to a better job. But careful to have her with him to collect the painting from the airport so that she could verify all the details about its 'disappearance'.
Theophrast on good terms with local police. Even if nothing irregular about his relationship with Hawkins he was well placed to throw him off the scent if he got too close.
So, who else did he involve in the robbery?

Nat now spent some time studying the trial transcript that Barny Cox had obtained for him and had delivered to his room. Something immediately leaped out from Gomer's evidence. A trivial point until one realized that the crime depended on there being two, outwardly identical, security vans. Gomer had told the court, 'Ted and Charlie collected the van and picked me up from home. They'd already done one job that day.' Of course. No doubt that job involved a trip somewhere to the west of London. Probably set up by Theophrast, a man who never left anything to chance. The problem of others at Samson's being involved now disappeared.

Hardwick and Randall took the genuine Samson's van to Bath on the morning of the robbery. They left it on the building site and collected the adapted vehicle. Randall the real connection with Theophrast? It would be interesting to know where he served in the police and why he left.

Hardwick easily corruptible. Status-conscious wife constantly nagging him to better himself.

Hardwick easily persuaded that they weren't really stealing—just doing something a bit unusual for the client they were already working for.

So, these men involved in robbery:

(a) Theophrast
(b) Hardwick
(c) Randall
(d) Someone to do the van conversion
(e) A second driver (probably the

same as (d))
Why did Theophrast choose a Cambridge-based security firm?
Because he was in touch with Kevin George and knew about his skill in van conversion!
If that connection can be proved, everything about the robbery falls into place.
Theophrast could well have kept in touch with Edgar George's widow and son.
But can we credit mummy's boy Kevin with a creative criminal brain? Like father, like son?

Nat stood up and took a few turns round the room to ease his stiff limbs. The next part of the story, the part that had once seemed the most puzzling, was now the most transparent, thanks to Big Zee's expertise. Nat now knew how a valuable painting could be made to vanish from a locked van constantly under supervision. Yet the trick had very nearly gone wrong because, at the last moment, Bob Gomer had been assigned to the job. That must have been a devastating blow. Nat imagined the two other guards, now completely keyed up, nervously discussing what to do about their painfully honest colleague as they drove around on the morning of the robbery. 'They probably considered cutting him in on the crime, only to realize that, even if he agreed, he would be a weak link when it came to police investigation. The safe thing to do would be to abort the whole operation but that was equally unacceptable. They had no intention of facing Theophrast's wrath nor of forgoing his money. Simply 'forgetting' to pick up Gomer also had to be rejected; that would be to attract suspicion. Only one alternative was left. Somehow their unwanted companion had to be kept completely in the dark. It was risky but, the more they thought about it, the more they realized that Gomer might actually be an asset. Let him travel in the back with the crate. He would then be able to swear that no one had tampered with it during the journey. It would make the vanishing trick even more convincing. And it would require only slight modification to the original plan. Instead of having all the time in the world to operate the mechanism which switched the crates they would have to time it very carefully in the few minutes after the painting had been loaded and before Gomer climbed aboard. What they failed to work out was that they were making Bob Gomer the prime suspect.

OK, so what happened next? Nat resumed his seat.

After the Robbery:
Theophrast made a great song and dance about the painting being stolen, the

271

reputation of his gallery, etc., etc.

Hawkins interviewed everyone involved in the transportation of the painting. Hardwick and Randall stuck to their pre-arranged story. The other witnesses—primarily Gomer and Miles—were quite genuinely puzzled.

The crooks had got away with the perfect crime.

Only they have reckoned without the tenacity of 'Hurry' Hawkins, paranoid about his clear-up rate and with zero tolerance of unsolved crimes.

Convinced that he could break Gomer, he had him charged and brought to trial.

If that's right we must abandon any suggestion of Hawkins being criminally involved with Theophrast. Pity!

And so it was, Nat reflected, that Bob Gomer was brought before the assize court, indicted with a major felony. Hawkins may have had to lean on the Crown Prosecution Service to get them to sanction the case but he would have had the support of the painting's insurers, hopeful of forcing Gomer to reveal its whereabouts. Nat returned to the transcript. There was no doubt that Barny's criticisms of the incompetence of the defence team were justified. Without any evidence to lay before the jury to explain how the painting had been stolen, the prosecution's case was paper thin. They had relied to an almost scandalous extent on browbeating the accused once they had him in the witness box. And so, we come to . . . Nat typed in the next sub-heading:

Bob Gomer's Last Weekend:
Athalie George says Bob had supper with her on the Friday.
Their relationship? She reckons they were very close. Pearl and Kevin are emphatic that no such intimacy existed.
Pearl knows nothing of what went on between the medium and her devotee.
Kevin is almost certainly in denial.
Mrs George says the Friday was the last time she saw Bob. Odd. What about their church meeting on Sunday?
She says he was still struggling to work out how the robbery was done.
In fact, at my meeting with her all she told me about Bob Gomer was how spiritually sensitive he was.
The one person he did confide in was Ted Hardwick. Ted, of course, would make sure that Bob got nowhere near the truth.
Ted was caught between fear of discovery and guilt about what he's done to the Gomers.
Guilt about killing Bob?
At some point in his last few days Bob

realized the significance of his missing vacuum flask.

He checked with the depot manager and noted it in his file.

He must have discussed it with Ted.

Therefore Ted knew it would come out at the trial.

That must have thrown him into a panic and forced him to discuss the new problem with his accomplices.

And that brings us, Nat thought, to the mystery phone call. It must have come from one of Theophrast's gang. Presumably Bob was lured out by the offer of information that could help him at his trial. It was presumably Ted who made the call. So what would have happened at such a meeting? Nat enumerated the possibilities on screen:

Did they offer him money for his silence? Not difficult to imagine Bob's response. Anger. Outrage at being betrayed. Ted, his friend, the man who had got him the well-paid job at Samson's. The man who had attended the trial to give him moral support. All the time he'd been using Bob, shielding behind him, making sure he didn't stumble on the truth. Oh yes, beyond doubt Bob must have been beside himself with rage. What then? A refusal to co-operate with criminals. A fight?

Whatever, the consequences were fatal.

Nat yawned and stretched. The caffeine was wearing off. He stared at the screen and the lines of print began to merge and blur before his tired eyes. Had he got it right? he wondered. Was there still something missing? He wandered over to the window and looked out on the fellows' garden. The first rays of sun were tinting the tops of the cedars. This was where his involvement in the business had begun, he recalled. Standing here on a wet February morning and being summoned to meet Pearl Gomer. Pearl with her conviction that her husband's spirit was crying for vengeance from beyond the grave. Yet, given the opportunity, that same spirit had proved remarkably reticent about denouncing the guilty party. There had been no dramatic *J'accuse* about the Endfield Road seance. In fact there had been no revelation at all that Mrs George could not have gleaned from Bob Gomer when he was still in the land of the living.

As mediums went, Nat decided, she was not very impressive. Deliberate fake? More likely a woman who desperately needed to be needed, a common trait among those who suffered from delusions or psychosis. Such people sometimes posed as doctors, nurses or priests, anything to obligate others to them. In extreme cases they saw themselves as the Holy

Spirit or the angel of death. Nat thought of Sophie Eckley, lavishing her expensive gifts on the Brownings, trying to organize their holidays for them, captivating Elizabeth with spirit writing and thought transference. Creating dependence, not out of a conscious desire to manipulate, but feeding her own deep need to be loved.

He walked back to the desk and gazed down at the screen, depressed. He had answered some important questions to his own satisfaction but what had he got but a bundle of unproven hypotheses? The answers were there. In the notes. No doubt about that. But his mind was too tired to wrench them from the gelatinous matrix of implausibility and wilful deception. He needed a rest. Just a few minutes. Fifteen or, perhaps, twenty. He stretched out on the sofa and closed his eyes. Browning. Eckley. Sludge. Instantly he was asleep. And, in the blackness of the unconscious, impulses flickered along neural pathways to make unforeseen connections.

Nat did not wake until the chapel bell struck ten but the moment he opened his eyes he knew.

*   *   *

'The artist does not draw what he sees but what he must make others see.' So Edgar Degas observed and he was well qualified to pontificate on the subject. Nat now found himself in the painter's creative dilemma. He grasped with visionary clarity the competing ambitions and clashing passions which had led to Bob Gomer's death. He could not provide every clamouring question with its own neat, rational answer but he could see the pattern which alone made sense of all the clashing and apparently incompatible elements. The problem was how to make others understand and relate to the underlying truth of events, and how to do that in the shortest possible time.

The first and fundamental task was to check one point in Bob's file that he had passed over as insignificant but which he now realized was crucial. He telephoned Samson's Cambridge depot and had a brief conversation. It proved highly satisfactory. Now he faced the much more difficult job of eliciting the co-operation of Superintendent Jack Hawkins. This involved another and much longer phone call, during which Nat had to consume a sizeable portion of humble pie and offer the assurance (repeated several times) that he wanted his name kept out of the business and wished to take no share of the credit for a successful outcome. Eventually he persuaded the Superintendent to travel to Cambridge the following day. When Nat asked tentatively how the investigation of the gallery business was going, Hawkins did unbend sufficiently to reveal that Theophrast had been located and detained and that he was currently helping the police with their enquiries. Nat now braced himself to put his final request.

'Could you possibly bring Dr Theophrast with you?'

'That's quite out of the question. Cambridge is well outside my jurisdiction.'

'I fully appreciate that, Superintendent. I'm sure you will want to square everything with the local CID. In fact, I think it would be an excellent idea if they were well represented tomorrow.'

'Why would I want to bring Dr Theophrast all the way over there?'

'In order to wrap the case up as quickly as possible. If you were to confront him with certain people here, well, I think the result would be very revealing.'

The best that Nat could get out of 'Hurry' Hawkins was a grudging promise to 'think it over' and with that he had to be content.

The remaining invitees all had a vested interest in being present at Nat's soirée and required little persuasion to agree to attend. All he told them was that Bob Gomer's widow had asked him to make enquiries about her husband's death and that he had arranged this meeting so that they could all pool their knowledge and lay the matter to rest once and for all. The innocent had no reason not to come. As for the guilty, Nat reasoned, correctly, that they would not want to absent themselves for fear of attracting suspicion from what was, after all, only a private gathering.

The first group to arrive in the ground-floor fellows' parlour that Nat had booked for the evening were Hawkins, Theophrast and a pair of plain clothes officers from the local CID. The gallery owner scowled at Nat and, beyond demanding to know 'what the hell all this is about', made no attempt at conversation. Hawkins lodged his charge in a corner chair and stationed one of his detectives close by him. Nat busied himself offering drinks and nibbles to his guests as they arrived. They were a nervous and ill-assorted group and it could scarcely be said that the party got off to a swinging start. Barny Cox dutifully circulated and Nat noticed with interest that Kevin George seemed relaxed and gregarious. The Hardwicks stayed close together, talking to no one else until Pearl Gomer propelled herself in their direction. Nat noticed that the couple did not even have much to say to the small, dark-suited man from Samson's. Athalie George selected an upright chair in a prominent position from which she surveyed the company with an air of condescending minor royalty.

Without making it too obvious, Nat placed himself where he could watch the various body language negotiations in progress. Mrs George studiously avoided looking at Theophrast. He, by contrast, seemed fascinated by her. Ted unconsciously kept a barrier between himself and the local policemen, whom, perhaps, he recognized. Kevin was his usual solicitous self as far as Pearl Gomer was concerned, making sure that she had a drink and offering her bowls of nuts. He did, however, make the effort to talk to others and had quite a long conversation with Hawkins.

Nat chose the moment when all the guests had settled as much as they were going to and were surveying their fellows with varying degrees of curiosity and distaste, to take a deep breath and address the company.

'Ladies and gentlemen, thank you all for coming. I know you are wondering what you've come for and I'll explain that in just a moment. First, may I ask you if you would be good enough to take your seats around the table.' He indicated the large piece of Jacobean furniture which impressively dominated the centre of the room and, with a certain amount of muttering, the guests placed themselves around the gleaming oak oval. He sat at one end where he could watch the others.

'All of you share a concern about the death of poor Bob Gomer and the events leading up to it.'

'Not me!' Theophrast blurted out. 'I never knew the man. He is no more than a name to me.'

Nat ignored the interruption. 'When someone dies in tragic and somewhat mysterious circumstances, as Bob did, it can be very difficult for those left behind to come to terms with it. It was for this reason that Pearl came to see me in February and asked if I could clear up some of the unresolved issues surrounding Bob's death. Through the good offices of Mrs George, who is an accomplished spiritualist medium, she had made contact with her late husband and knew that he was restless on two counts.'

'Bloody ridiculous!' Ted Hardwick glared across the table at Athalie George. 'That woman's an interfering phoney! She preys on other people's misery. You ought to have more sense than to listen to her!'

Nat proceeded with an outward calm not representative of the nervousness which was making his blood race. The people around him were a volatile mix and if he did not retain control there was no telling what might happen. If the evening ended in disorganized disaster his only chance of drawing a line under the Gomer affair would be gone for ever. 'I can't agree with you there, Mr Hardwick. Whatever you or I might think about spiritualism, Mrs George has been of great assistance in helping me get to the bottom of this business. I very much hope we may call upon her to aid us again this evening.' Nat hurried on before there could be any reaction to that statement. 'As I was saying, Bob Gomer's spirit was grieved by two things. He felt that he had died unjustly with a serious stain upon his character and he was distressed that his death was officially attributed to suicide, whereas the truth was that he was murdered.'

That provoked gasps and *sotto voce* protest. Nat saw Hawkins open his mouth to challenge the assertion and he hurried on to avoid interruption. 'We may or may not believe in spirit voices but Pearl and some of Bob's closest friends were convinced that someone had made him a scapegoat for a crime he did not commit and that that someone had silenced him permanently to protect himself from discovery. I agreed to make a few simple enquiries. In retrospect, I realize that I let myself get too deeply involved and that I should have gone to the police sooner than I did.' Nat hoped that the Superintendent would be satisfied with the sop and not intervene as he approached the crucial part of his discourse.

'I thought at that stage that the likely outcome would be confirmation of the official verdicts on these matters which would enable me to allay the suspicions of those who were understandably distressed at the manner of Bob's passing. However, there was one aspect of the whole business that intrigued me, as it has intrigued and puzzled the police and everyone else who has thought about it: how did a valuable painting disappear from a locked van while it was being watched by a security guard? I now know the answer to that riddle. Would you like to hear it?'

Nat looked round the table. He now had the undivided attention of everyone present and studied their facial reactions as he went, point by point, through the details of the robbery. 'Clever, wasn't it? Brilliant, really, and worked out in great detail by someone highly intelligent and thoroughly painstaking.' He glanced in Theophrast's direction but the eyes behind the thick-framed spectacles stared unblinkingly back.

'Of course, the mastermind could not carry out the crime all by himself. That required a team and he set about assembling one. Not dyed-in-the-wool criminals like himself. The robbery depended totally on having people on the inside.' Nat saw Hardwick glance towards the door and the plain clothes man stationed firmly in front of it. 'Security guards do a laborious and sometimes dangerous job and the pay isn't exactly princely, is it, Ted?'

'What are you suggesting?' Hardwick demanded, staring aggressively along the table. 'Any more of this nonsense and I'll have you for slander.' He half stood. 'Come on, Rosie. We're going.'

But his wife remained in her seat beside him. 'Sit down!' It was an order. 'If he's got

283

something to say, he can say it in front of all these witnesses. That'll make our claim for damages even stronger.'

'That's good advice, Ted,' Nat said. 'If I'm wrong you can take me for every penny I've got. Talking about pennies, I understand you've bought yourself a very impressive villa in Spain and are taking early retirement. More than that, you're contributing handsomely to hospice care for your sister-in-law. I can't help wondering how you can afford all that on a security guard's pay.'

'No mystery there, Mister Smart Alec!' It was Rosie who offered the explanation. 'We've got the money from selling our house and Ted's had some luck on the horses. Tell 'em, Ted.'

But Ted remained mute.

Nat said, 'Thank you, Mrs Hardwick. That's set my mind at rest. I presume you'd have no objection to the police doing a financial check. There's no chance of them discovering large payments made to a foreign account—in Spain, perhaps.'

'You bloody stupid cow!' Ted turned on his wife, eyes glaring out of a face moist with sweat. 'It was all your sodding fault in the first place! Never satisfied! Always wanting more! Now see what you've done—you and Charlie between you!'

Pearl stared at her brother-in-law, open-mouthed with shock and dismay. 'Oh, Ted, no!

It couldn't have been you! My Bob trusted you. Surely you didn't let him take the blame and worry himself silly. Ted, Ted, tell me Dr Gye's got it wrong.'

Ted hung his head. 'Sorry, Pearl,' he muttered almost inaudibly. 'It wasn't meant to be like that. Bob shouldn't have been there at all. If anyone's to blame, it's him.' He pointed to the little man in the dark suit. 'Right at the last minute he insisted we took Bob with us.'

Several people started talking at once and making angry gestures and it was with some difficulty that Nat regained control. 'I ought to introduce Mr Barry Cheeseman to those of you who don't know him,' he said, indicating the man beside him. 'Mr Cheeseman is the depot manager of Samson's Cambridge branch. Without knowing it, he's the key to this whole business. I imagine, Mr Cheeseman, that you have a number of ex-policemen working for you.'

'Yes, that's right. We find that they're almost always tough, well trained and reliable.' Cheeseman's delivery was clear and succinct.

'You had no hesitation about taking on ex-Sergeant Charlie Randall a couple of years back?'

'We were aware that he had left his previous employ under a slight cloud of suspicion but his qualifications were excellent and the firm was undergoing rapid expansion at the time so we needed more staff. We couldn't afford to be ultra-choosy.'

'Of course not. Now, there's someone here who knew Randall in his earlier incarnation. Isn't that so, Dr Theophrast?'

The dapper Theophrast shook his head. 'I'm saying nothing without my lawyer.'

'Quite right, too.' Nat smiled. 'We'll just have to take it as read that Randall was known in certain criminal quarters where you also have contacts. And that's important because it suggests an answer to a problem that struck me early on in this affair: why hire a security firm in Cambridge to carry a consignment from London Airport to Bath? Am I right in thinking that that's rather unusual, Mr Cheeseman?'

The little man nodded. 'We have certain established clients who like to know who they're working with and use our depot to do jobs anywhere in the UK but we hadn't handled Dr Theophrast's business before, so it was a bit out of the ordinary, especially as our head office is in West London.'

'The reason, of course, was Charlie Randall. If you had known about his earlier connection with Dr Theophrast I imagine you would have smelled a rat.'

'Certainly.'

'How did Randall and Hardwick come to be put on the Bath job?'

'I gather a certain amount of gentle arm-twisting went on. The job list is organized by our assignments officer. His task is to balance the work out fairly but it's not unknown for the lads to try to influence him if they have a particular reason for wanting to be on a certain job. Ted and Charlie said they both needed the overtime and wanted to fit in two runs that day.'

'Where was the earlier run to?'

'Just outside Cheltenham. Except that it didn't happen. The client changed his mind in the middle of the day and I had to call the van back.'

'And Cheltenham, of course, is not a million miles away from Bath. What a coincidence! It was you who decided to assign an extra man to the afternoon job. Why was that?'

'The consignment was small but of enormous value. Also it was the first job Samson's had done for the Millennium Gallery. I felt we should take extra precautions and I hoped to impress a new client with our efficiency.'

'Thank you, Mr Cheeseman.' Nat looked round the table. 'That's given us all a very clear picture. Now, we've already seen from Ted's reaction that Bob's unexpected assignment to the job was an unwelcome complication. However, he and his accomplice carried out the original plan without a hitch. Everything was fine until the police decided to prosecute Bob Gomer.'

'Pearl, I swear, we had no idea they'd do

that.' Ted looked imploringly at his sister-in-law.

'But you could have gone to the police at any time and told them Bob had nothing to do with the robbery.'

'No! He wouldn't let us!' Ted pointed at Theophrast.

'Ridiculous! I don't know this man.' Theophrast tried to remain calm and dignified but the pose of outraged innocence carried no conviction.

'Oh, we've never met but I know all about you, mate. Charlie told me who we were working for. Said you were a pretty cool customer. Pearl, that's the man you should be angry with. He told us to keep our mouths shut. He promised that when all the dust had settled he would see you and Bob all right. If I'd known he was planning to send his hit man to get rid of Bob I'd have gone straight to the police and to hell with the consequences.'

'What! You stupid man!' Snarling, Theophrast started out of his chair and had to be restrained by his escort. 'Don't you dare accuse me of murder. You were the one who was running scared because of what your precious Mr Gomer suspected. Charlie told me you were panicking. He said he was afraid you might do something silly. And, by God, you did.'

The taunt brought Hardwick to his feet. With a manic yell he rushed towards

Theophrast. Hawkins was too quick for him. He stood in front of his prisoner's chair, placed an open palm firmly in Ted's chest and stopped his bull-like charge. While one of the other policemen forced him back to his chair, the Superintendent turned to Nat. 'Right, sir, you've made your point. We can take it from here.'

'May I detain you and the others just a little longer. There's one more witness we ought to hear.'

'Oh, who's that?'

'Bob Gomer.'

A Dish Served Hot

Aie!-Aie!-Aie!
Please, sir, your thumbs are through my
windpipe, sir!

In an evening of shocks and surprises the company took Nat's comment remarkably calmly. He went on to explain.

'A couple of tantalizing questions remain and Bob is best placed to answer them. I thought that we might prevail upon Mrs George to put us all in contact with him.' All eyes turned to the medium but Hawkins frowned and was about to protest when Nat made a slight gesture which, fortunately, he picked up. Now for it, Nat thought. He smiled encouragingly at Athalie George.

She coloured. She stared back. It was the first time Nat had seen her lost for words. After several seconds it was Kevin who came to her aid. 'Mother needs to prepare. She can't perform to order. Contacting the spirits drains her of psychic energy.'

'Oh, what a shame,' Nat said. 'I feel we're so close to tidying up the last few details.' He watched Mrs George closely and gauged the calculation that was going on behind the pale eyes. He knew she was trying to read him, to work out what he was planning, to decide how best she might take control of the situation. To co-operate might lead her into unfamiliar territory. To refuse might cast doubt upon her powers.

It was Pearl Gomer who tipped the balance. 'Oh, yes, please, Athalie. This is all so awful. I really do want to know what Bob thinks. He so much wanted Dr Gye to look into things. We must let him know what's been discovered.'

Mrs George nodded graciously. 'I will try, Pearl, but I cannot make any promises. This evening has been so very disturbing for all of us. I'm not sure how much strength I have.'

Kevin was fussing. 'Mother, are you sure?' he asked. 'You know how dangerous . . .'

Athalie reached across the table and clasped his hand. 'I am the servant of the spirits, dear. I can only do as they command. Now,' she

290

looked around at her totally captive audience, 'if you will all be very quiet, please, I'll see if anyone wants to come through.'

She went into the closed-eyes, deep-breathing routine. It lasted for a full two minutes and Nat wondered whether she was going to risk opening up a spirit dialogue. But, after one or two deep groans, words came from the medium's mouth in the ponderous, considered style of Bob Gomer. Nat was interested to observe that the precocious Sammy Tuck was not putting in an appearance this time. 'Pearl, are you there?' the voice demanded.

'Oh, yes, Bob dear, it's me. Listen, you know you wanted Dr Gye to look into that business of the picture? Well, he has, and he's proved you didn't have anything to do with it. '

'Oh, good, I am glad. Has he told the police?'

'Yes, dear, the police know. They'll deal with it now.'

The others round the table listened in embarrassed silence to this exchange. No one made a move to leave or seemed to want to disturb the atmosphere.

'Dr Gye's here, Bob,' Pearl said. 'He wants to ask you some questions.'

'Thank you for coming, Dr Gye. That is good of you. And thank you for what you've done to clear my name. You don't know how much that means to me.' The voice seemed to be getting fainter. 'I'll try to answer your questions but I don't know . . .' Mrs George swayed in her seat and made more moaning noises.

Kevin stood up to go round to his mother's side of the table and Nat spoke quickly to forestall his interruption. 'Bob, I need you to help me understand what happened in your last minutes on this side. I think you drove to your garage to put the car away. What happened then?'

'There was a man.' The 'spirit voice' was now little more than a whisper.

'What man, Bob? Did you recognize him?'

'Never seen him before. He came into the garage after me. Then . . . Oh, my neck, my head . . . pain in my head . . . Everything went black . . .' The voice faded away completely.

'Bob! Bob!' Nat called urgently. 'Can you give us a description of this man?'

But the shade of Bob Gomer seemed to have retreated into the ether and, moments later, Mrs George sat up and opened her eyes.

'Well, that was all very interesting,' Hawkins said, 'but it doesn't exactly get us very far, does it? Now, some of us have got a long drive back. So . . .' He pushed his chair away from the table.

'I'm sorry, Superintendent, I'd hoped we might have been able to be a bit more help to you.' Nat turned to the medium with a smile. 'Thank you for all your help, Mrs George. It's a pity Bob couldn't tell us more from the other side than he did when he was in our world. It was you he told about his brainwave, wasn't it? He realized that the disappearance of his thermos flask was significant.'

'Yes, he seemed to have been on the way to working out how the painting was stolen, though I doubt whether he would ever have been able to piece everything together as you have, Dr Gye.'

'And this was on the Friday evening, a couple of days before his death? Supper time, I think you said.'

'That's quite correct.'

'So, we're talking about what . . . seven or eight o'clock?'

'Yes, we always take our meal at seven.'

'Interesting. There was someone else Bob discussed the puzzle of the vanishing painting with. He says so in his notes.' Nat turned to the man sitting next to him. 'He came to see you, didn't he, Mr Cheeseman?'

The man from Samson's nodded. 'Yes, he came to my house in a terrible state. He thought the court case was going badly and he was desperate to find some scrap of evidence that might reveal the truth.'

'And were you able to help him?'

Cheeseman shrugged. 'I offered a sympathetic ear. There wasn't much more I could do. We went over the timetable of the collection and delivery of the picture in minute detail. I was almost as anxious as he was to get to the truth of it. Losing a valuable consignment is very bad for business.'

'And that was when the matter of the missing vacuum flask came up?'

'Yes, Bob was puzzled by the police insistence that the van was totally empty. He wanted to know if anyone at the depot had come across his thermos. I said—and I can remember my words exactly—"No, it definitely wasn't in the van used for the Bath job or in any other van." Suddenly something seemed to click with him. "Another van," he said and he repeated it several times. He asked if there were any of our vehicles unaccounted for on the afternoon of the crime. Well, of course I didn't have that sort of information at my fingertips but I said I'd check the records of all our depots first thing Monday morning. Sadly, by then it was too late. Poor Bob was dead.'

'So this conversation took place just a couple of days before his death?'

'Yes, Friday evening.'

'You're quite sure about that?'

'Quite sure. Bob phoned from Bristol after the court had adjourned for the weekend. He said he was coming home and could he have a chat with me. He arrived just as my wife and I were finishing our evening meal and I took him round the corner to the Templeton Arms.'

'Where you stayed how long?'

'It must have been getting on for ten by the time we left.'

'So he couldn't have had supper with the Georges that evening?' Nat turned to Athalie. 'Are you sure the conversation you told us about actually took place?'

Mrs George jutted her chin defiantly. 'I am not in the habit of lying, Dr Gye. I must have got the date muddled up.'

Nat smiled disarmingly. 'Yes, of course. I wonder when that meeting really happened. It couldn't have been before Friday, because Bob was staying in Bristol for the trial. Saturday, perhaps?'

'No,' Pearl intervened. 'Bob was at home all Saturday. He spent most of the time working at his computer. It was our last day together. I'm not likely to forget it.'

'Ah.' Nat looked thoughtful. 'That seems to leave Sunday, doesn't it?' His tone sharpened abruptly. 'In fact it was you, Mrs George, who telephoned that afternoon and arranged a meeting.'

'Don't be absurd.' Athalie George clung frantically to her last vestiges of dignity.

'I'm afraid it's you who are absurd, Mrs George, in believing that you could lie to us and get away with it. Either the meeting never took place at all or it did not take place when you said it did.'

'Well, I . . . Perhaps . . . This is monstrous . . . A petty mistake . . .' She was flustered to the point of completely losing control.

'Stop bullying her, do you hear!' Kevin shouted the words and positioned himself behind his mother's chair.

Nat watched his reactions: the dilated pupils, the high colour, the twitching around one corner of the mouth. He saw Athalie reach up to take his hand as she spoke soothingly. 'It's all right, dear. Everything's all right.'

'Yes, Kevin,' Nat said quietly. 'We just need you and your mother to help us understand why you wanted to see Bob Gomer that Sunday afternoon and why you don't want anyone to know that you saw him.'

Neither of the Georges was forthcoming. Nat continued. 'Was it, for example, that Bob had come to suspect you of involvement in the robbery? If he had worked out that someone had carried out a clever modification to the van might he not have thought, "I know someone who makes a speciality of that sort of thing"?'

Kevin gave a high-pitched nervous laugh. 'Oh, so now you want to tie me in with the robbery, do you? Well, I can scotch that one right away. I have no connection whatsoever with Dr Theophrast. Ask him.'

All eyes turned to the dapper gallery director. He nodded. 'For what it's worth, what the young man says is perfectly true. I knew his father many years ago but I never met him or his mother.'

'There!' Kevin blurted out triumphantly. 'Leave us alone, can't you!'

'Enough!' Athalie George made a bid to wrest back control of the situation. 'Bob did come to see us that afternoon and I see that it was wrong of me to try to conceal the fact. But, surely, it is not difficult to understand why I was tempted to do so. My son and I are regarded by many people as oddballs. Such has always been the fate of those who are different from their neighbours. In times past they were branded as witches, necromancers, heretics. They were always at the top of the list of suspects when any crime was committed in the neighbourhood. I fear that society has not changed much over the centuries. Can't you imagine what people would say about Bob's death? "He went to see those weird George people and then he went and took his own life." Simple cause and effect.'

'But he didn't take his own life, did he?' Nat persisted. 'Someone took it from him.'

'As to that, all I can tell you is that he was alive and well when he left my house.'

For several silent moments Nat held her gaze until, at last, she looked away. 'That may be all you feel you can tell us, Mrs George, but it isn't all you know, is it?'

She made no reply.

'Is it?' Nat raised his voice.

Kevin let out a roar. 'Don't you shout at

my mother!'

Nat ignored him. 'You've already told us what you know and what only an eyewitness could have known. Your spirit voice described exactly how Bob Gomer died. He was knocked unconscious by a blow to the base of the skull. After that he was bundled into the car. A hose was attached to the exhaust to bring fumes into it and slowly, painlessly, he died.'

'Stop it!' Mrs George screamed. 'It's horrible.'

But Nat went on. 'The exact nature of his injuries didn't come out at the inquest. Because the blow to the head wasn't the cause of death an overworked pathologist didn't think to include the bruising in his report. You couldn't have known what marks were found on the body—unless you'd actually seen them inflicted.'

'It was the spirit voice,' Athalie George blurted out, more in fear than defiance.

Nat did not let her continue. He had to force a reaction. He did not like what he was doing but as he looked from Mrs George's outraged dignity to Pearl Gomer's pained bewilderment he knew he had no choice. If the truth could not be squeezed out in the next few seconds it never would be. His tone became deliberately taunting. 'I'm sure you were right when you said that Bob was alive and well when he left your house but he wasn't when you left him in his lock-up garage, was he?'

With a howl like that of a wounded beast, Kevin leaped on to the table. Papers and smashed glasses flew in all directions as he lunged at Nat. The chair went over backwards with the force of the charge. Nat felt the younger man's hands round his throat. His blotched, twisted face was inches away. 'How dare you say such terrible things to her. You're as bad as him. He said wicked, wicked things.'

It was several moments before others dragged the demented attacker off him. Nat got shakily to his feet and took deep breaths. He looked across at Athalie George. She was bent double in her chair, her body racked by sobs. And Pearl Gomer was beside her, hand on the other woman's arm, offering comfort.

With an effort the medium regained some of her dignity. 'Very well,' she said. 'You are right, Dr Gye, and I hope that affords you some satisfaction. Yes, I struck down Bob Gomer, and I organized—'

'No! No! Don't listen to her!' Kevin, still in the grip of two plain-clothes policemen, shouted the words. 'It's not true! It's not true! It's not true!' He stamped the floor to emphasize his point, for all the world like a child throwing a tantrum.

It was the Superintendent who took charge. 'Then, sir, perhaps you'd be good enough to tell us what *is* true.'

299

*   *   *

On a warm and moist spring afternoon two days later Nat and Kathryn sat with Barny Cox at a terrace table of the Lamb at Frettlingham having lunch. Kathryn had returned from Norfolk that morning and Barny had just given her his version of the drama in the fellows' parlour.

'Then it's really all over?' she asked.

'It is for us,' Nat said. 'Hawkins is ending his career in a blaze of international glory, having recovered an important stolen work of art, and he's more than happy to attribute his success to "an anonymous tip-off". As for our local police, they've taken statements from the Georges and have Kevin under lock and key pending psychiatric report.'

Barny added, 'Your husband has missed his vocation, you know, Kathryn. If you could have seen him the other evening you'd have realized that the bar has lost an impressive courtroom performer.'

Kathryn looked across the table at her husband. 'For someone who has just solved two crimes, he doesn't exactly look elated. Why so glum, darling?'

Nat sighed. 'I suppose because I can't see who wins. The real owner of Antonello's portrait will presumably get it back—with a very nasty bullet hole. Our Italian friends will doubtless have spirited away any incriminating

300

evidence from the Talenti villa long before the police investigators arrive.'

'Pearl can complete the grieving process for her husband,' Kathryn insisted.

'Only at the cost of having her faith in spiritualism shattered. What does she have to look forward to now, if she can't be certain of being reunited with Bob?'

'You mustn't reproach yourself for that, dear boy,' Barny objected. 'It was Mrs George, for her own selfish reasons, who hoodwinked people into believing in contact with the dead. You can't doubt that you've done the world a service in ridding it of one more fraudster. And as for Master Kevin, he'll now receive the treatment he should have had long ago.'

Nat shrugged. 'I can't help feeling that he was more sinned against than sinning.'

'Oh, come on!' Kathryn protested. 'He was a creepy, cold-blooded killer!'

'Any psychoanalyst would tell you that he was the product of a highly unsuitable marriage between an irresponsible playboy on the fringes of international crime and a pampered, sheltered girl from a very respectable family, and that he was almost certain to develop signs of Oedipus complex, hating his father and fixated on his mother.'

'When did you work all that out?' Kathryn asked.

'It was always obvious that the situation in the George household was pretty unhealthy.

301

Kevin had no girlfriends or, for that matter, boyfriends. I'm afraid you were wrong about him being homosexual, Kathryn. His natural drives were sublimated into looking after his mother and fiddling around with cars. You saw how he reacted to any suggestion that his mother might have had a close relationship with Bob Gomer. Any other man in her life provoked jealousy that was ultimately sexual.'

Barny laid down his knife and fork. 'Are you suggesting that he would have lashed out against anyone he saw as a rival for his mother's affections?'

'Potentially, yes. Stupidly, I didn't realize how important that was till very late on. Like everyone else in this business, I was convinced Gomer's death had to be tied up with the robbery. Even when the penny dropped I didn't have a shred of proof to connect him with the murder. The only thing I could do was try to make him flip, to reveal all that anger and violence lying beneath the meek and mild surface.'

'And your success in that was remarkable,' Barny said. 'Kevin went berserk and his mother, realizing what you were doing, made a desperate attempt to take responsibility on her own shoulders.'

Nat shook his head. 'She's a very clever woman. I think she must have realized the game was up when she knew that her story about Bob Gomer's visit on Friday evening

302

had been exposed as a lie.'

'Yes,' Barny agreed, 'after that whatever she said was bound to be viewed with suspicion.'

'Hey, just a minute, you two!' Kathryn glared at the men opposite. 'This is going way over my head. Just what *did* happen on that Sunday afternoon and what screwed Kevin to breaking point?'

Nat took a long draught of his Greene King bitter. 'Can't we just leave it? The last few weeks have been hellish and I'd rather put them behind me.'

Kathryn pouted. 'Don't forget it's been pretty nasty for me, too. You can lay it to rest because you've sorted it all out. It's all there for you, neatly laid out in your journal, and you can draw a line under it. I've still got some blank pages to be filled. Just humour me for the next few minutes, will you? Tell me what really happened on that fatal day.'

'Fair enough,' Nat conceded. 'I owe you that. The final details have only just been filled in by Hawkins. He's been positively generous with information about the Georges' statements. Let me start by giving you my reconstruction of Bob Gomer's last weekend, then add what I've learned since from the Superintendent.

'First of all, we need to get on Bob's emotional wave-length. He's desperate for some last-minute miracle that'll keep him from a possible prison sentence. He spends a couple of hours with Cheeseman on the Friday evening, going over every detail of the robbery. And he sees a glimmer of enlightenment. Of course, someone must have switched the van. He still can't figure out how the robbery worked but it's obvious to him that the vehicle he and the painting travelled in was not the same as the one the police searched. What logically follows is almost unbearable for such a trusting soul as Bob Gomer: he has been betrayed by his mates. Men he thought of as friends were prepared to see him go to jail to cover their own crime. That puts him in a black mood. No wonder he spends all Saturday with his computer, trying to sort out just what his colleagues had done.'

'Why didn't he confront Ted Hardwick with his suspicions?' Kathryn asked.

'I suppose because he wanted to be sure of his ground before he said anything. His one hope was to get his brother-in-law to own up and that wouldn't happen unless Bob could show that he'd something more than vague suspicions to offer the police. Perhaps he would have bearded Ted on Sunday if the Georges hadn't intervened.'

'Yes, why did they?'

'Good intentions—and we all know what road is paved with them. Athalie genuinely wanted to help Bob but she also wanted to have him deeply obligated to her. Kevin, clever as he is in things mechanical, worked out how the switching of the painting could have been done and his mama wanted to pass this on to her disciple. Only she would make out that the information had come from her spirit voices. Thus, she would be Bob's saviour, he would be deeply indebted to her and he would be more than ever convinced of her powers. So she phoned him that afternoon, told him she had some good news and asked him to come round.'

'Without telling Pearl?'

'There was already a clandestine element to their relationship. Whatever Bob may have felt for Mrs George, and however innocent their meetings may or may not have been, he was the sort of man who would have had twinges of guilt and wanted to keep things from his wife. Anyway, that was as far as I had got in my thinking. If I was right, then the Georges became the last people to see Bob alive, except his killer—unless, of course, one of them *was* his killer. If mother and son were implicated in Bob's death, then something must have gone terribly wrong at their meeting. My suspicion was confirmed when Mrs George denied that the meeting had taken place and, then, tried to gild the lily by conjuring up the mysterious stranger lurking around Endfield Gardens. My contribution was all vague conjecture. It was Hawkins who persuaded the Georges to confess to the details.'

Kathryn and Barny were listening

attentively. A flurry of light rain rattled on the gaudy sunshade over their table but they did not notice. It was Barny who asked, 'So what was it that soured the atmosphere in the sedate house on Parkside that autumn sabbath?'

Nat drained his glass. 'I suppose it was the same sort of thing that turned Elizabeth Browning against Sophie Eckley. Suddenly, the devoted acolyte becomes a sceptic; doubt replaces faith; scales fall from the eyes. It may be something seemingly trivial that provokes the transformation but, almost always, the inner tension has built up over a long period. Uncertainties haven't been confronted. Awkward questions have been repressed for fear of unwelcome answers. Then a chance word, an unguarded statement or out-of-character act pricks the bubble of belief. The erstwhile devotee turns on his guru. He feels deceived, betrayed, angry. Reverence becomes contempt, respect becomes loathing. Robert Browning understood this perfectly. In his poem "Mr Sludge, the 'Medium'", into which he channelled all his contempt for the whole mediumistic tribe, he represents Sludge as trying a trick too far. His patron, in a fit of rage, attacks him physically, and actually tries to throttle him.'

'The price of deception,' Kathryn muttered.

Nat gave a slight shake of the head. 'Don't let's be too hard on Athalie George. My impression is that she was a genuine medium who let her feelings lure her into duplicity.'

'*A genuine medium?*'

'Well, darling, perhaps I should say "honest". She really believed in her spirit voices. It's a psychological state called "unconscious fraud"—the mind produces messages which don't pass through the medium's conscious state. When, on that Sunday, Mrs George decided to pass on something she *knew* to be fraudulent there was obviously something different, less convincing about her performance.'

'And Bob spotted it?'

'I believe so. Remember the mood he was already in when he arrived at the Georges'. He had been deceived, lied to, abused by his friends. He must have wondered if there was anyone he could trust. Then Athalie George produced her "revelation" but this time Bob wasn't impressed by her spirit messages. Kevin says Bob reasoned that Mrs George knew about the switch because Kevin had told her, not because she had received information from the other side.'

Kathryn said, 'Yes, now I can picture the scene. What an unholy trinity. There's Athalie George trying to buy Bob's affection. There's Kevin resenting like hell this intruder into their lives. And there's Bob, at his wits' end, looking for further evidence of betrayal. The atmosphere must have been explosive.'

307

Nat nodded mournfully. 'Kevin says Bob went into a frenzy and virtually accused him of being a member of the gang who stole the picture and when his mother protested Bob rounded on her as a fake medium and a manipulative woman. At that Kevin flipped. We saw the other evening what that could mean. He flew at Bob who fell over and banged his head on the brass fender. That threw the Georges into a panic. They spent several minutes trying to bring him round but he was obviously heavily concussed.'

'They should have sent for an ambulance,' Barny commented.

'Of course, but they were both in a state of shock. Hawkins says their statements about what happened next don't agree. Mrs George claims she wanted to get Bob to hospital. Kevin insists that they both agreed to take the injured man home. Anyway, they got Bob into his car and Kevin set off to drive to Endfield Road. It was while he was negotiating the quiet Sunday afternoon back streets that he worked out an alternative scenario. All the time he was brooding on Bob's accusations. If he persisted, and especially if the press picked up his exposé, his mother's life would be destroyed. That had to be prevented at all costs.'

Kathryn sighed. 'One can almost feel sorry for him. He must have realized that without her disciples and acolytes his mother would have no status. She would have been reduced to the level of ordinary mortals. It had happened once before when her husband had stripped her of most of her wealth and social position. After that she'd come to Cambridge and built up her own tiny empire. Within it she was supreme. I wonder whether she'll survive being knocked from her pedestal a second time.'

Nat continued. 'Kevin phoned Pearl Gomer on his mobile—you remember, Kathryn, she told us about the call. He says he was simply going to warn her that Bob had had an accident. It was when Pearl commented that her husband had gone out and she didn't know where he was that Kevin suddenly saw his opportunity. One simple act and he could push the cuckoo out of the Georges' comfortable nest.' Nat shrugged. 'The rest you know.'

There was a long pause, the silence filled only by the twittering of nest-building birds in the pub's eaves. It was broken by Kathryn.

'Hang on a minute.' She frowned across the top of her glass of white wine. 'Something here doesn't add up. If Kevin was the murderer, why did his mother want the case reopened?'

'That's the supreme irony of this whole business. She didn't know, not then. She assumed, as we all did, that Bob's death had something to do with the robbery. She knew Kevin had his problems but it never entered her head that he could be capable of anything so brutal—and vulgar—as murder. The story he told her was that Bob had come round during the journey and they'd had a long chat. Bob had apologized for his bad behaviour and Kevin had left him at his garage putting the car away. He'd waved away Kevin's offer to walk him home, saying he felt a bit groggy but he was sure the fresh air would do him good. In hindsight, of course, it looks a pretty thin story, but bear in mind that Athalie George was desperate to believe it.'

'But, surely,' Kathryn objected, 'when she heard about Bob's death . . .'

'She was utterly distraught. She questioned Kevin closely and he embellished his version of events by inventing the stranger supposedly lurking around Endfield Gardens. Mrs George was indignant. If someone had murdered her close friend she was determined to find out who.'

'So, why didn't she tell the police about Bob's visit?' Kathryn asked.

'Presumably,' Barny suggested, 'because Kevin persuaded her to keep her silence.'

'That's right,' Nat agreed. 'You can imagine his line of argument: "Best to keep out of it, Mother dear. Think of all the publicity. We don't want another spate of press persecution." So, when the police were happy to assume that Bob committed suicide, she set me on the trail. It was Athalie George, not Pearl Gomer, who wanted Bob's death re-examined. I remember Pearl saying that she had quite enough problems coping with her disability without opening up old emotional wounds.'

'So when did Mrs George come to terms with the reality of her son's homicidal act?' Kathryn asked.

'Difficult to say. Love is blind—and maternal love blinder than most. Probably the suspicion grew and grew until she could no longer ignore it. Under pressure from Kevin she was being driven to increasing subterfuge and lies. When I went to see her at her home she'd already reached the point of spinning an elaborate and false version of her last meeting with Bob. She moved it to the preceding Friday and made it all sound very amicable. She was also very keen to steer my attention towards the Italian connection and seemed relieved that I had no progress to report.'

'Did you suspect her then?' Barfly wanted to know.

'I was aware that her words and her body language didn't square up. That may have been because I'd been steeped in all kinds of fakery. By then I knew, instinctively I suppose, that fraud was at the bottom of the whole sordid business.' He paused, staring out across the lawn, sparkling where raindrops caught the sunlight. 'But then is that so terrible? Life would be intolerable if we were one hundred per cent honest with each other all the time.

So we're all frauds, one way or another, whether conscious or unconscious. That's certainly something I've learned about myself over the past weeks.'

For a while they sat sharing the warm silence of the spring afternoon. It was Kathryn who attempted to change the mood.

'Oh, look, swallows!' She pointed to a pair of darting birds flitting in and out of the eaves, then took a deep appreciative breath of the mild air. 'What was it Robert Browning wrote?

'Oh, to be in England
Now that April's there . . .
And after April, when May follows,
And the whitethroat builds, and all the
    swallows.'

Nat stared across the freshly mown lawn to the murky shade of a still-wintry copse beyond.

'I've been catching up on Browning, as you suggested,' he said thoughtfully. 'The couplet that comes to my mind is:

' 'Tis an awkward thing to play with souls,
And matter enough to save one's own.'